I0784674

Frank L. Packard

THE FOUR STRAGGLERS

OK Publishing 2021

Frank L. Packard
THE FOUR STRAGGLERS

A Thriller

Published by
MUSAICUM
Books

- Advanced Digital Solutions & High-Quality book Formatting -

musaicumbooks@okpublishing.info

2021 OK Publishing

ISBN 978-80-272-7596-0

Contents

Prologue:
The Four of Them

The crash of guns. A flare across the heavens. Battle. Dismay. Death. A night of chaos.

And four men in a thicket.

One of them spoke:

"A bloody Hun prison, that's us! My Gawd! Where are we?"

Another answered caustically:

"Monsieur, we are lost-and very tired."

A third man laughed. The laugh was short.

"A Frenchman! Where in hell did you come from?"

"Where you and the rest of us came from." The Frenchman's voice was polished; his English faultless. "We come from the tickling of the German bayonets."

The first man elaborated the statement gratuitously:

"I don't know about you 'uns; but our crowd was done in good and proper two days ago. Gawd! ain't there no end to 'em? Millions! And us running! What I says is let 'em have the blinking channel ports, and lets us clear out. I wasn't noways in favour of mussing up in this when the bleeding parliament says up and at 'em in the beginning, leastways nothing except the navy."

"Drafted, I take it?" observed the third man coolly.

There was no answer.

The fourth man said nothing.

There was a whir in the air ... closer ... *closer*; a roar that surged at the ear drums; a terrific crash near at hand; a tremble of the earth like a shuddering sob.

The first man echoed the sob:

"Carry on! Carry on! I *can't* carry on. Not for hours. I've been running for two days. I can't even sleep. My Gawd!"

"No good of carrying on for a bit," snapped the third man. "There's no place to carry on *to*. They seem to be all around us."

"That's the first one that's come near us," said the Frenchman. "Maybe it's only-what do you call it? —a straggler."

"Like us," said the third man.

A flare, afar off, hung and dropped. Nebulous, ghostlike, a faint shimmer lay upon the thicket. It endured for but a moment. Three men, huddled against the tree trunks, torn, ragged and dishevelled men, stared into each others' faces. A fourth man lay outstretched, motionless, at full length upon the ground, as though he were asleep or dead; his face was hidden because it was pillowed on the earth.

"Well, I'm damned!" said the third man, and whistled softly under his breath.

"Monsieur means by that?" inquired the Frenchman politely.

"Means?" repeated the third man. "Oh, yes! I mean it's queer. Half an hour ago we were each a separate bit of driftwood tossed about out there, and now here we are blown together from the four winds and linked up as close to each other by a common stake-our lives-as ever men could be. I say it's queer."

He lifted his rifle, and, feeling out, prodded once or twice with the butt. It made a dull, thudding sound.

"What are you doing?" asked the Frenchman.

"Giving first aid to Number Four," said the third man grimly. "He's done in, I fancy. I'm not sure but he's the luckiest one of the lot."

"You're bloody well right, he is!" gulped the first man. "I wouldn't mind being dead, if it was all over, and I was dead. It's the dying and the thinking about it I can't stick."

"I can't see anything queer about it." The Frenchman was judicial; he reverted to the third man's remark as though no interruption had occurred in his train of thought. "We all knew it was coming, this last big-what do you call it? —push of the Boche. It has come. It is gigantic. It is tremendous. A tidal wave. Everything has gone down before it; units all broken up, mingled one with another, a mêlée. It has been *sauve qui peut* for thousands like us who never saw each other before, who did not even know each other existed. I see nothing queer in it that some of us, though knowing nothing of each other, yet having the same single purpose, rest if only for a moment, shelter if only for a moment, should have come together here. To me it is not queer."

"Well, perhaps, you're right," said the third man. "Perhaps adventitious would have been better than queer."

"Nor adventitious," dissented the Frenchman. "Since we have been nothing to each other in the past, and since our meeting now offers us collectively no better chance of safety or escape than we individually had before, there is nothing adventitious about it."

"Perhaps again I am wrong." There was a curious drawl in the third man's voice now. "In fact, I will admit it. It is neither queer nor adventitious. It is quite-oh, quite! —beyond that. It can only be due to the considered machinations of the devil on his throne in the pit of hell having his bit of a fling at us-and a laugh!"

"You're bloody well right!" mumbled the first man.

"Damn!" said the Frenchman with asperity. "I don't understand you at all."

The third man laughed softly.

"Well, I don't know how else to explain it, then," he said. "The last time we —"

"The *last* time!" interrupted the Frenchman. "I did not get a very good look at you when that flare went up, I'll admit; but enough so that I would swear I had never seen you before."

"Quite so!" acknowledged the third man.

"Gawd!" whimpered the first man. "Look at that! Listen to that!"

A light, lurid, intense for miles around opened the darkness-and died out. An explosion rocked the earth.

"Ammunition dump!" said the Frenchman. "I'm sure of it now. I've never seen any of you before."

The third man now sat with his rifle across his knees.

The fourth man had not moved from his original position.

"I thought you were officers, blimy if I didn't, from the way you talked," said the first man. "Just a blinking Tommy and a blinking *Poilu!*"

"Monsieur," said the Frenchman, and there was a challenge in his voice, "I never forget a face."

"Nor I," said the third man quietly. "Nor other things; things that happened a bit back-after they put the draft into England, but before they called up the older classes. I don't know just how they worked it over here-that is, how some of them kept out of it as long as they did."

"Godam!" snarled the Frenchman. "Monsieur, you go too far! And-monsieur appears to have a sense of humour peculiarly his own-perhaps monsieur will be good enough to explain what he is laughing at?"

"With pleasure," said the third man calmly. "I was laughing at the recollection of a night, not like this one, though there's a certain analogy to it for all that, when an attack was made on —a strong box in a West End residence in London. Lord Seeton's, to be precise."

The first man stirred. He seemed to be groping around him where he sat.

"Foolish days! Perverted patriotism!" said the third man. "The family jewels, the hereditary treasures, gathered together to be offered on the altar of England's need! Fancy! But it was being done, you know. Rather! Only in this case the papers got hold of it and played it up a bit as a wonderful example, and that's how three men, none of whom had anything to do with the others, got hold of it too-no, I'm wrong there. Lord Seeton's valet naturally had inside information."

"Blimy!" rasped the first man suddenly. "A copper in khaki! That's what! A bloody, sneaking swine!"

It was inky black in the thicket. The third man's voice cut through the blackness like a knife.

"You put that gun down! I'll do all the gun handling there's going to be done. Drop it!"

A snarl answered him —a snarl, and the rattle of an object falling to the ground.

"There were three of them," said the third man composedly. "The valet, who hadn't reached his class in the draft; a Frenchman, who spoke marvellous English, which is perhaps after all the reason why he had not yet, at that time, served in France; and-and some one else."

"Monsieur," said the Frenchman silkily, "you become interesting."

"The curious part of it is," said the third man, "that each of them in turn got the swag, and each of them could have got away with it with hardly any doing at all, if it hadn't been that in turn each one chivied the other. The Frenchman took it from the valet, as the valet, stuffed like a pouter pigeon with diamonds and brooches and pendants and little odds and ends like that, was on his way to a certain pinch-faced fence named Konitsky in a slimy bit of neighbourhood in the East End; the Frenchman, who was an *Englishman* in France, took the swag to a strange little place in a strange little street, not far from the bank of the Seine, the place of one Père Mouche, a place that in times of great stress also became the shelter and home of this same Frenchman, who-shall I say? —I believe is outstandingly entitled to the honour of having raised his profession to a degree of art unapproached by any of his confreres in France to-day."

"*Sacré nom!*" said the Frenchman with a gasp. "There is only one Englishman who knew that, and I thought he was dead. An Englishman beside whom the Frenchman you speak of is not to be compared. You are —"

"*I* haven't mentioned any names," said the third man smoothly. "Why should you?"

"You are right," said the Frenchman. "Perhaps we have already said too much. There is a fourth here."

"No," said the third man. "I had not forgotten him." He toyed with the rifle on his knee. "But I had thought perhaps you would have recognised the valet's face."

"Strike me pink!" muttered the first man. "So Frenchy's the blighter that did me in, was he!"

"It is the uniform, and the dirt perhaps, and the very poor light," said the Frenchman apologetically.

"But you-pardon, monsieur, I mean the other of the three —I did not see him; and monsieur will perhaps understand that I am deeply interested in the rest of the story."

The third man did not answer. A sort of momentary, weird and breathless silence had settled on the thicket, on all around, on the night, save only for the whining of some oncoming thing through the air. Whine ...whine ...*whine.* The nerves, tautened, loosened, were jangling things. The third man raised his rifle. And somewhere the whining shell burst. And in the thicket a minor crash; a flash, gone on the instant, eye-blinding.

The first man screamed out:

"Christ! What have you done?"

"I think he was done in anyway," said the third man calmly. "It was as well to make sure."

"Gawd!" whimpered the first man.

"Monsieur," said the Frenchman, "I have always heard that you were incomparable. I salute you! As you said, you had not forgotten. We can speak at ease now. The rest of the story —"

The third man laughed.

"Come to me in London-after the war," he said, "and I will tell it to you. And perhaps there will be-other things to talk about."

"I shall be honoured," said the Frenchman. "We three! I begin to understand now. A house should not be divided against itself. Is it not so? We should go far! It is fate to-night that —"

"Or the devil," said the third man.

"My Gawd!" The first man began to laugh —a cracked, jarring laugh. "After the war, the blinking war-after *hell!* There ain't no end, there ain't no —"

And then a flare hung again in the heavens, and in the thicket three men sat huddled against the tree trunks, torn, ragged and dishevelled men, but they were not staring into each others' faces now; they were staring, their eyes magnetically attracted, at a spot on the ground where a man, a man murdered, should be lying.

But the man was not there.
The fourth man was gone.

Book I:
Shadow Varne

I

Three Years Later

The East End being, as it were, more akin to the technique and the mechanics of the thing, applauded the craftsmanship; the West End, a little grimly on the part of the men, and with a loquacity not wholly free from nervousness on the part of the women, wondered who would be next.

"The cove as is runnin' that show," said the East End, with its tongue delightedly in its cheek, "knows 'is wye abaht. Wish I was 'im!"

"The police are nincompoops!" said the outraged masculine West End. "Absolutely!"

"Yes, of course! It's quite too impossible for words!" said the female of the West End. "One never knows when one's own—*do* let me give you some tea, dear Lady Wintern..."

From something that had merely been of faint and passing interest, a subject of casual remark, it had grown steadily, insidiously, had become conversationally epidemic. All London talked; the papers talked-virulently. Alone in that great metropolis, New Scotland Yard was silent, due, if the journals were to be believed, to the fact that that world-famous institution was come upon a state of hopeless and atrophied senility.

With foreknowledge obtained in some amazing manner, with ingenuity, with boldness, and invariably with success, a series of crimes, stretching back several years, had been, were being, perpetrated with insistent regularity. These crimes had been confined to the West End of London, save on a few occasions when the perpetrators had gone slightly afield-because certain wealthy West-Enders had for the moment changed their accustomed habitat. The journals at spasmodic intervals printed a summary of the transactions. In jewels, and plate, and cash, the figures had reached an astounding total, not one penny of which had ever been recovered or traced. Secret wall safes, hidden depositories of valuables opened with obliging celerity and disgorged their contents to some apparition which immediately vanished. There was no clue. It simply happened again and again. Traps had been set with patience and considerable artifice. The traps had never been violated. London was accustomed to crimes, just as any great city was; there were hundreds of crimes committed in London; but these were of a *genre* all their own, these were distinctive, these were not to be confused with other crimes, nor their authors with other criminals.

And so London talked-and waited.

It was raining—a thin drizzle. The night was uninviting without; cosy within the precincts of a certain well-known West End club, the Claremont, to be exact. Two men sat in the lounge, in a little recess by the window. One, a man of perhaps thirty-three, of athletic build, with short-cropped black hair and clean-shaven face, a one-time captain of territorials in the late war, and though once known on the club membership roll as Captain Francis Newcombe was to be found there now as Francis Newcombe, Esquire; the other, a very much older man, with a thin, grey little face and thin, grey hair, would, on recourse to the club roll, have been found to be Sir Harris Greaves, Bart.

The baronet made a gesture with his cigar, indicative of profound disgust.

"Democracy!" he ejaculated. "The world safe for democracy! I am nauseated with that phrase. What does it mean? What did it ever mean? We have had three years now since the war which was to work that marvel, and I have seen no signs of it yet. So far as I —"

Captain Francis Newcombe laughed.

"And yet," he said, "I embody in my person one of those signs. You can hardly deny that, Sir Harris. Certainly I would never have had, shall I call it the distinction, of being admitted to this club had it not been for the democratic leaven working through the war. You remember, of course? An officer and a gentleman! We of England were certainly consistent in that respect. While one was an officer one was a gentleman. The clubs were all pretty generally thrown open to officers during the war. Some of them came from the Lord knows where. T.G.'s they were called, you remember-Temporary Gentlemen. Afterward-but of course that's another story so far as most of them were concerned. Take my own case. I enlisted in the ranks, and toward the latter end of the war I obtained my commission —I became a T.G. And as such I enjoyed the privileges of this club. I was eventually, however, one of the fortunate ones. At the close of the war the club took me on its permanent strength and, ergo, I became a — Permanent Gentleman. Democracy! Private Francis Newcombe-Captain Francis Newcombe-Francis Newcombe, Esquire."

"A rather thin case!" smiled the baronet. "What I was about to say when you interrupted me was that, so far as I can see, all that the world has been made safe for by the war is the active expression of the predatory instinct in man. I refer to the big interests, the trusts; to the radical outcroppings of certain labour elements; to-yes!" —he tapped the newspaper that lay on the table beside him —"the Simon-pure criminal such as this mysterious gang of desperadoes that has London at its wits' ends, and those of us who have anything to lose in a state of constant apoplexy."

Captain Francis Newcombe shook his head.

"I think you're wrong, sir," he said judicially. "It isn't the aftermath of the war, or the result of the war. It is *the* war, of which the recent struggle was only a phase. It's been going on since the days of the cave man. You've only to reduce the nation to the terms of the individual, and you have it. A nation lusts after something which does not belong to it. It proceeds to take it by force. If it fails it is punished. That is war. The criminal lusts after something. He flings down his challenge. If he is caught he is punished. That is war. What is the difference?"

The baronet sipped at his Scotch and soda.

"H'm! Which brings us?" he suggested.

"Nowhere!" said Captain Francis Newcombe promptly. "It's been going on for ages; it'll go on for all time. Always the individual predatory; inevitably in cycles, the cumulative individual running amuck as a nation. Why, you, sir, yourself, a little while ago when somebody here in the room made a remark to the effect that he believed this particular series of crimes was directly attributable to the war because it would seem that some one of ourselves, some one who has the entrée everywhere, who, through being contaminated by the filth out there, had lost poise and was probably the guilty one, meaning, I take it, that the chap finding himself in a hole wasn't so nice or particular in his choice of the way out of it as he would have been but for the war-you, Sir Harris, denied this quite emphatically. It-er-wouldn't you say, rather bears me out?"

The old baronet smiled grimly.

"Quite possibly!" he said. "But if so, I must confess that my conclusion was based on a very different premise from yours. In fact, for the moment, I was denying the theory that the criminal in question was one of ourselves, quite apart from any bearing the war might have had upon the matter."

The ex-captain of territorials selected a cigarette with care from his case.

"Yes?" he inquired politely.

The old baronet cleared his throat. He glanced a little whimsically at his companion.

"It's been a hobby, of course, purely a hobby; but in an amateurish sort of way as a crimi-nologist I have spent a great deal of time and money in —"

"By Jove! Really!" exclaimed Captain Newcombe. "I didn't know, Sir Harris, that you —" He paused suddenly in confusion. "That's anything but a compliment to your reputation though, I'm afraid, isn't it? A bit raw of me! I —I'm sorry, sir."

"Not at all!" said the old baronet pleasantly; and then, with a wry smile: "You need not feel badly. In certain quarters much more intimate with the subject than you could be supposed to be, I am equally unrecognised."

"It's very good of you to let me down so easily," said the ex-captain of territorials contritely. "Will you go on, sir? You were saying that you did not believe these crimes were being perpe-trated by one in the same sphere of life as those who were being victimised. Why is that, sir? The theory seemed rather logical."

"Because," said the old baronet quietly, "I believe I know the man who is guilty."

The ex-captain of territorials stared.

"Good Lord, sir!" he gasped out. "You-you can't mean that?"

"Just that!" A grim brusqueness had crept into the old baronet's voice. "And one of these days I propose to prove it!"

"But, sir" —the ex-captain of territorials in his amazement was still apparently groping out for his bearings —"in that case, the authorities-surely you —"

"They were very polite at Scotland Yard —*very*!" The old baronet smiled drily again. "That was the quarter to which I referred. Socially and criminologically-if I may be permitted the word —I fear that the Yard regards me from widely divergent angles. But damme, sir" —he became suddenly irascible —"they're too self-sufficient! I am a doddering and interfering old idiot! But nevertheless I am firmly convinced that I am right, and they haven't heard the end of the matter-if I have to devote every penny I've got to substantiating my theory and bringing the guilty man to justice!"

Captain Francis Newcombe coughed in an embarrassed way.

The old baronet reached for his tumbler, and drank generously. It appeared to soothe his feelings.

"Tut, tut!" he said self-chidingly. "I mean every word of that-that is, as to my determination to pursue my own investigations to the end; but perhaps I have not been wholly fair to the Yard. So far, I lack proof; I have only theory. And the Yard too has its theory. It is a very common disease. The theory of the Yard is that the man I believe to be guilty of these crimes of to-day died somewhere around the middle stages of the war."

"By Jove!" Captain Francis Newcombe leaned sharply forward on the arms of his chair. "You don't say!"

The old baronet wrinkled his brows, and was silent for a moment.

"It's quite extraordinary!" he said at last, with a puzzled smile. "I can't for the life of me understand how I got on this subject, for I think we were discussing democracy-but you appear to be interested."

"That is expressing it mildly," said the ex-captain of territorials earnestly. "You can't in common decency refuse me the rest of the story now, Sir Harris."

"There is no reason that I know of why I should," said the old baronet. "Did you ever hear of a man called Shadow Varne?"

Captain Francis Newcombe shook his head.

"No," he said.

"Possibly, then," said the old baronet, "you may remember the robbery at Lord Seeton's place? It was during the war."

"No," said the other thoughtfully. "I can't say I do. I don't think I ever heard of it."

"Well, perhaps you wouldn't," nodded the old baronet. "It happened at a time when, from what you've said, I would imagine you were in the ranks, and-however, it doesn't matter. The point is that the robbery at Lord Seeton's is amazingly like, I could almost say, each and every one of this series of robberies that is taking place to-day. The same exact foreknowledge, the hidden wall safe, or hiding place, or repository, or whatever it might be, that was supposedly known only to the family; the utter absence of any clue; the complete disappearance of-shall we call it? —the loot itself. There is only one difference. In the case of Lord Seeton, the jewels-it was principally a jewel robbery-were eventually recovered. They were found in Paris in the possession of Shadow Varne. But" —the old baronet smiled a little grimly again —"the police were not to blame for that."

Sir Harris Greaves, amateur criminologist, reverted to his tumbler of Scotch and soda.

Captain Francis Newcombe knocked the ash from his cigarette with little taps of his forefinger.

"Yes?" he said.

"It's a bit of a story," resumed the old baronet slowly. "Yes, quite a bit of a story. I do not know how Shadow Varne got to Paris; I simply know that, had he not taken sick, neither he nor the jewels would ever have been found. But perhaps I am getting a little too far ahead. I think I ought to say that Shadow Varne, though he had never actually up to this time been known in a *physical* sense to the police, had established for himself a widespread and international reputation. His name here, for instance, amongst the criminal element of our own East End was a sort of talisman, something to conjure with, as it were, though no one could ever be found who had seen or could describe the man. I suppose that is how he got the name of Shadow. Some must have known him, of course, but they were tight-lipped; and even these, I am inclined to believe, would never have been able to lay fingers on him, even had they dared. He was at once an inscrutable and diabolical character. I would say, and in this at least Scotland Yard will agree with me, he seemed like some evil, unembodied spirit upon whom one could never come in a tangible sense, but that hovered always in the background, dominating, permeating with his personality the criminal world."

"But if this is so, if no one knew him, or had ever seen him," said the ex-captain of territorials in a puzzled way, "how was he recognised as Shadow Varne in Paris?"

"I am coming to that," said the old baronet quietly. "As you know very well, in those days they were always poking into every rat hole in Paris for draft evaders. That is how they stumbled on Shadow Varne. They dug him out of one of those holes, a very filthy hole, like a rat-like a very sick rat. The man was raving in delirium. That is how they knew they had caught Shadow Varne-because in his delirium he disclosed his identity. And that is how they recovered Lord Seeton's jewels."

"My word!" ejaculated Captain Francis Newcombe. "A bit tough, I call that! My sympathies are almost with the accused!"

"I am afraid I have failed to make you understand the inhuman qualities of the man," said the old baronet tersely. "However, Shadow Varne was even then too much for them-at least temporarily. A few nights later he escaped from the hospital; but he was still too sick a man to stand the pace, and they were too close on his heels. He had possibly, all told, a couple of hours of liberty, running, dodging through the streets of Paris. The chase ended somewhere on the bank of the Seine. He was fired at here as he ran, and though quite a few yards in the lead, he appeared to have been hit, for he was seen to stagger, fall, then recover himself and go on. He refused to halt. They fired and hit him again-or so they believed. He fell to the ground-and rolled over the edge into the water. And that was the last that was ever seen of him."

"My word!" ejaculated the ex-captain of territorials again. "That's a nice end! And I must say, with all due deference to you, Sir Harris, that I can't see anything wrong with Scotland Yard's deduction. I fancy he's dead, fast enough."

"Yes," said the old baronet deliberately, "I imagined you would say so; and I, too, would agree were it not for two reasons. First, had it been any other man than Shadow Varne; and, second, that the body was never recovered."

"But," objected Captain Francis Newcombe, "if, as you believe, the man is still carrying on, having been identified once, he would, wouldn't you say, be recognised again?"

"Not at all!" said the old baronet decidedly. "You must take into account the man's sick and emaciated condition when he was caught, and the subsequent hospital surroundings. Let those who saw him then see the same man to-day, robust, in health, and in an entirely different atmosphere, locality and environment! Recognised? I would lay long odds against it, even leaving out of account the man's known ingenuity for evading recognition."

The ex-captain of territorials nodded thoughtfully.

"Yes," he said, "that is quite possible; but, even granting that he is still alive, I can't see —"

"Why I should believe he is at the bottom of what is going on to-day here in London?" supplied the old baronet quickly. "Perhaps intuition, perhaps the mystery about the man that has interested me from the time I first heard of him in the early years of the war, and which has ever since been a fascinating study with me, has something to do with it. I told you to begin with that my *proof* was theory. But I believe it. I do not say he is alone in this, or was alone in the Lord Seeton affair; but he is certainly the head and front and brains of whatever he was, or is, engaged in. As for the similarity of the cases, I will admit that might be pure coincidence, but we *know* that Shadow Varne did have the Seeton jewels in his possession. The strongest point, however, that I have to offer in a tangible sense, bearing in mind the man himself and his hideously elusive propensities, is the fact there is no absolute proof of his death. Why wasn't his body recovered? You will answer me probably along the same lines that the Paris police argued and that were accepted by Scotland Yard. You will say that it was dark, that the body might not have come to the surface immediately, and under the existing conditions, by the time they procured a boat and began their search, it might easily be missed. Very good! That is quite possible. But why, then, was not the body eventually recovered in two or three days, say —a week, if you like? You will say that this would probably be very far indeed from being the first instance in which a body was never recovered from the Seine. And here, too, you would be quite right. But I do not believe it. I do not believe it was a dead man, or a man mortally wounded, or a man wounded so badly that he must inevitably drown, who pitched helplessly into the water that night. I believe he did it voluntarily, and with considered cunning, as the only chance he had. Go into the East End. Listen to the stories you will hear about him. The world does not get rid of such as he so easily! The man is not human. The crimes he has committed would turn your blood cold. He is the most despicable, the most wanton thing that I ever heard of. He would kill with no more compunction than you would break in two that match you are holding in your hand. Where he came from God alone knows, and —"

A club attendant had stopped beside the old baronet's chair.

"Yes?" said the old baronet.

"I beg pardon, Sir Harris, but your car is here," announced the man.

"Very good! Thank you!" The old baronet drained his glass and stood up. "Well, you have heard the story, captain," he said with a dry smile. "I shall not embarrass you by asking you to decide between Scotland Yard and myself, but I shall at least expect you to admit that there is some slight justification for my theory."

The ex-captain of territorials, as he rose in courtesy, shook his head quietly.

"If I felt only that way about it," he said slowly, "I should simply thank you for a very interesting story and your confidence. As it is, there is so much justification I feel impelled to say to you that, if this man is what you describe him to be, is as dangerous as you say he is, I would advise you, Sir Harris, in all seriousness to leave him-to Scotland Yard."

"What!" exclaimed the old baronet sharply. "And let him go free! No, sir! Not if every effort I can put forth will prevent it! Never, sir-under any circumstances!"

Captain Francis Newcombe smiled gravely, and shrugged his shoulders.

"Well, at least, I felt I ought to say it," he said. "Good-night, Sir Harris-and thank you so much!"

"Good-night, captain!" replied the old baronet cordially, as he turned away. "Good-night to you, sir!"

Captain Francis Newcombe watched the other leave the room, then he walked over to the window. The drizzle had developed into a downpour with gusts of wind that now pelted the rain viciously at the window panes. He frowned at the streaming glass.

A moment later, as he moved away from the window, he consulted his watch. It was a quarter past eleven. Downstairs he secured his hat and stick, and spoke to the doorman.

"Get a taxi, please, Martin," he requested, "and tell the chap to drive me home."

He lighted a cigarette as he waited, and then under the shelter of the doorman's umbrella entered the taxi.

It was not far. The taxi stopped before a flat in a fashionable neighbourhood that was quite in keeping with the fashionable club Captain Francis Newcombe had just left. His man admitted him.

"It's a filthy night, Runnells," said the ex-captain of territorials.

Runnells slammed the door against a gust of wind.
"You're bloody well right!" said Runnells.

II

An Iron in the Fire

It was a neighbourhood of alleyways and lanes of ferocious darkness; of ill-lighted, baleful streets, of shadows; and of doorways where no doors existed, black, cavernous and sinister openings to inner chambers of misery, of squalid want, of God-knows-what.

It was the following evening, and still early-barely eight o'clock. Captain Francis Newcombe turned the corner of one of these gloomily lighted streets, and drew instantly back to crouch, as an animal crouches before it springs, in the deep shadows of a wretched tenement building. Light footfalls sounded; came nearer. Two forms, skulking, yet moving swiftly, came into sight around the corner.

Captain Francis Newcombe sprang. His fist crashed with terrific force to the point of an opposing jaw. A queer grunt-and one of the two men sprawled his length on the pavement and lay quite still. Captain Francis Newcombe's movements were incredibly swift. His left hand was at the second man's throat now, and a revolver was shoved into the other's face.

The tableau held for a second.

"A bit of a 'cushing' expedition, was it?" said the ex-captain of territorials calmly. "I looked a likely victim, didn't I? Just the usual bash on the head with a neddy, and then the usual stripping even down to the boots if they were good enough-and mine were good enough, eh? And I might get over that bash on the head, or my skull might be cracked; I might wake up in one of your filthy passageways here, or I might never wake up! What would it matter? It's done every night. You make your living that way. And who's to know who did it?" His grip tightened suddenly on the other's throat. "Your kind are better dead," said Captain Francis Newcombe, and there was something of horrible callousness in his conversational tones. "You lack art; you have no single redeeming feature." It was as though now he were debating in cold precision with himself. "Yes, you are much better dead!"

"Gor' blimy, guv'nor, let me go," half choked, half whined the other. "We wasn't goin' to touch you. No fear! Me an' me mate was just goin' round to the pub for an 'arf-pint —"

"It would make a noise," said Captain Francis Newcombe unemotionally. "That is the trouble. I should have to clear out of here, and be put to the annoyance of waiting a half hour or so before I could come back and attend to my own affairs. That's the only reason I haven't fired this thing off in your face, and I'm not sure that reason's good enough. But it's a bit of a fag to argue it out, so-don't move, you swine, or that'll settle it quicker still!" His fingers, from the other's throat, searched his own waistcoat pocket, and produced a silver coin. "Heads or tails?" he inquired casually. "You call it."

"My Gawd, guv'nor," whimpered the man, "yer don't mean that! Yer wouldn't shoot a cove down like that, would yer? My Gawd, yer wouldn't do that!"

"Heads or tails?" The ex-captain of territorial's voice was bored. "I shan't ask you again."

The light was poor. The man's features, save that they were dirty and unshaven, were almost indistinguishable; but the eyes roved everywhere in hunted fear, and he lumped the fingers of one hand together and plucked with them in an unhinged way at his lips.

"I—no!" gurgled the man. "My Gawd!" His words were thick. His fingers, plucking, clogged his lips. "I carn't —I —" The mechanism of the revolver intruded itself-as unemotional as its owner-an unemotional click. The man screamed out. "No, no-wait, guv'nor! Wait!" he screamed. "'Eads! Gawd! 'Eads!"

Captain Francis Newcombe examined the coin; the sense of touch, as he rubbed his fingers over it, helping out the bad light.

"Right, you are!" he said indifferently. "Heads it is! You're in luck!" He tossed the coin on the pavement. "I'd keep that, if I were you." His voice was still level, still bored. "You haven't got anything, of course, to do any sniping with, for anything as valuable as that would never remain in the possession of your kind for more than five minutes before you would have pawned it." He glanced at the prostrate form of the thug's companion, who was now beginning to show signs of returning consciousness. "I fancy you'll find his jaw's broken. Better give him a leg up," he said, and, turning on his heel, walked on down the street.

Captain Francis Newcombe did not look back. He traversed the murky block, turned a corner, turned still another, and presently made his way through an entrance, long since doorless, into the hallway of a tenement house. It was little better than a pit of blackness here, but his movements were without hesitation, as one long and intimately familiar with his surroundings. He mounted a rickety flight of stairs, and, without ceremony, opened the door of a room on the first landing, entered, and closed the door behind him. The room had no light in it.

"Who's there?" demanded a weak, querulous, female voice.

The visitor made no immediate reply. The place reeked with the odour of salt fish; the air was stale, and an offence that assaulted the nostrils. Captain Francis Newcombe crossed to the window, wrenched at it, and flung it viciously open.

A protracted fit of coughing came from a corner behind him.

"Didn't I tell you never to *send* for me?" he snapped out in abrupt menace.

"Ow, it's you, is it?" said the woman's voice. "Well, I ain't never done it afore, 'ave I? Not in three years I ain't."

"You've done it now; you've done it to-night —and that's once too often!" returned Captain Francis Newcombe savagely. "And before I'm through with you, I'll promise you you'll never do it again!"

"No," she answered out of the darkness, "I won't never do it again, an' that's why I done it to-night —'cause I won't never 'ave another chance. The doctor 'e says I ain't goin' to be 'ere in the mornin'."

Captain Francis Newcombe lit a match. It disclosed a tallow dip and a piece of salt fish on a battered chair-and, beyond, the shadowy outline of a bed. He swept the piece of fish to the floor out of his way, lighted the candle, and, leaning forward, held it over the bed.

A woman's face stared back at him in the flickering light; a curiously blotched face, and one that was emaciated until the cheek bones seemed the dominant feature. Her dull, almost glazed, grey eyes blinked painfully in even the candle rays; a dirty woollen wrap was fastened loosely around a scrawny neck, and over this there straggled strands of tangled and unkempt grey hair.

"Well, I fancy the diagnosis isn't far wrong," said the ex-captain of territorials critically. "I've been too good to you-and prosperity's let you down. For three years you haven't lifted a finger except to carry a glass of gin to your lips. And now this is the end, is it?"

The woman did not answer. She breathed heavily. The hectic spots on her cheeks burned a little wider.

Captain Francis Newcombe set the candle back on the chair, and, with his hands in his pockets, stood looking at her. His face exhibited no emotion.

"I haven't heard yet *why* you sent for me," he said sharply.

"Polly," she said thickly. "I wanter know wot abaht Polly?"

Captain Francis Newcombe smiled without mirth.

"My dear Mrs. Wickes," he said evenly, "you know all about Polly. I distinctly remember bringing you the letter she enclosed for you in mine ten days ago, because I distinctly remember that after you had read it I watched you tear it up. And as your education is such that you cannot write in return, I also distinctly remember that you gave me messages for her which I was to incorporate in my own reply. Since then I have not heard from Polly."

The woman raised herself suddenly on her elbow, and, her face contorted, shook her fist.

"My dear Mrs. Wickes!" she mimicked furiously through a burst of coughing. "Yer a cool 'un, yer are. That's wot yer says, yer stands there an' smiles like a bloomin' hangel, an' yer says, my dear Mrs. Wickes! Curse yer, I knows more abaht yer than yer thinks for. Three years I've watched yer, an' hif I've kept my tongue to meself that don't say I don't know wot I knows."

"Indeed!" Captain Francis Newcombe shrugged his shoulders. He smiled slightly. "Then I should say, if it were true, that it is sometimes *dangerous*, Mrs. Wickes-to know even a little about some things."

The woman rocked in the bed, and hugged her thin bosom against a spasm of coughing that came near to strangulation.

"Bah!" she shouted, when she could get her breath. "I ain't afraid of yer any more. Damn yer, I'm dyin' anyhow! It's nothin' to you wiv yer smug smile, except yer glad I'll be out of the wye-an'—an', Gawd, it ain't nothin' to me either. I'm sick, of it all, an' I'm glad, I am; but afore I goes I wanter know wot abaht Polly. Wot'd yer tyke her awye for three years ago?"

"For the price of two quid paid weekly to a certain Mrs. Wickes, who is Polly's mother," said Captain Francis Newcombe composedly; "and with which the said Mrs. Wickes has swum in gin ever since."

Mrs. Wickes fell back exhausted on her pillow.

"Wot for?" she whispered in fierce insistence. "I wanter know wot for?"

"Well," said Captain Francis Newcombe, "even at fifteen Polly was an amazingly pretty little girl-and she showed amazing promise. I'm wondering how she has developed. Extremely clever youngster! Don't see, in fact, Mrs. Wickes, where she got it from! Not even the local desecration of the king's English-in spite of the board schools! Amazing! We couldn't let a flower like that bloom uncultivated, could we?"

The woman was up in the bed again.

"A gutter brat!" she cried out. "An' you says send 'er to school wiv the toffs in America, 'cause there wouldn't be no chance of doin' that 'ere at 'ome; an' I says the toffs don't tyke 'er kind there neither. An' you says she goes as yer ward, an' yer can get 'er in, only she 'as to forget abaht these 'ere London slums. An' she ain't to write no letters to me except through you, 'cause hif any was found down 'ere they'd turn their noses up over there an' give Polly the bounce."

"Quite right, Mrs. Wickes!" said Captain Francis Newcombe imperturbably. "And for three years Polly has been in one of the most exclusive girls' seminaries in America-and incidentally I might say I am arranging to go over there shortly for a little visit. If her photographs are to be relied upon, she has more than fulfilled her early promise. A very beautiful young woman, educated, and now, Mrs. Wickes—a lady. She has made a circle of friends among the best and the wealthiest. Why, even now, with the summer holidays coming on, you know, I understand she is to be the guest of a school friend in a millionaire's home. Think of that, Mrs. Wickes! What more could any woman ask for her daughter? And why should you, for instance, ask more to-night? Why this eleventh hour curiosity? You agreed to it all three years ago, Mrs. Wickes-for two quid a week."

"Yes," said the woman passionately, "an' I'm probably goin' to 'ell for it now! I knowed then yer wasn't doin' this for Polly's sake, an' in the three years I kept on knowin' yer more an' more for the devil you are. But I says to meself that I'm 'ere to see Polly don't come to no harm, but-but I ain't goin' to be 'ere no more, an' that's wot I wants to know to-night. An' I asks yer, wot's yer game?"

"Really!" Captain Francis Newcombe shrugged his shoulders again. "This isn't very interesting, Mrs. Wickes. And in any case, I fail to see what you are going to do about it, or what lever you could possibly bring to bear to make me divulge what you are pleased to imagine is some base and ulterior motive in what I have done. It is quite well known among Captain Newcombe's circle that he is educating a ward in America. It is-er-rather to his credit, is it not?"

"Gawd curse yer wiv yer smooth tongue!" said Mrs. Wickes wildly. "I knows! I knows yer got a game-some dirty game wiv Polly in it. Yer clever, yer are-an' yer ain't human. But yer won't win, an' all along 'o Polly. She won't do nothin' that ain't straight, she won't. Polly ain't that kind."

"Oh, as to that, and granting my wickedness," said Captain Francis Newcombe indifferently, "I shouldn't worry. Having you in mind, Mrs. Wickes, I fancy even that would be quite all right-blood always tells, you know."

"Blood! Blood'll tell, will it?" The woman was rocking in the bed again. She burst into harsh laughter. It brought on another, and even more severe, strangling fit of coughing. "Blood'll tell, will it?" she choked, as she gasped for breath. "Well, so it will! So it will!"

Captain Francis Newcombe stared at her from narrowed eyes. "What do you mean by that?" he demanded sharply.

But Mrs. Wickes had fallen back upon her pillow in utter exhaustion. She lay fighting painfully, pitifully now for every breath.

"What do you mean by that?" repeated Captain Francis Newcombe still more sharply.

And then suddenly, as though some strange premonition were at work, all fight gone from her, the woman threw out her arms in a broken gesture of supplication.

"I'm a wicked woman, a bloody wicked 'un I've been. Gawd forgive me for it!" she whispered. "Polly ain't no blood of mine."

Captain Francis Newcombe rested his elbows on the back of the chair, and smiled coolly.

"I think," he said evenly, "it's my turn now to ask what the game is? That's a bit thick, isn't it-after three years?"

The hectic spots had faded from the woman's face, and an ominous greyness was taking their place. She was crying now.

"It's Gawd's truth," she said. "I was afraid yer wouldn't 'ave give me the two quid a week hif yer'd known I 'adn't no 'old on 'er. Polly don't know. No one knows but me, an'—" Her voice trailed off through weakness.

Captain Francis Newcombe, save that his eyes had narrowed a little more, made no movement. He watched her without comment as she struggled for her breath again.

"I didn't mean to 'ave no fight wiv yer, Gawd knows I didn't. Gawd knows I didn't send for yer for that. I only wanted to ask yer wot abaht Polly, an' to ask yer to be good to 'er, an'—an' tell yer wot I'm tellin' yer now afore it's too late. An'—an'—" She raised herself with a sudden convulsive effort to her elbow. "Gawd, I—I'm goin' *now*."

With a swift movement Captain Francis Newcombe whipped a flask from his pocket, and held it to the woman's lips.

She swallowed a few drops with difficulty, and lay still.

Presently Mrs. Wickes' lips moved.

Captain Francis Newcombe, close beside the bed now, leaned over her.

"A lydy 'er mother was, an' 'er father 'e was a gentleman born 'e was. I—I don't know nothin' abaht 'em except she was a guverness an' 'e 'adn't much money. Neither of 'em 'adn't no family accordin' to 'er, an' countin' wot 'appened she told the truth, poor soul."

Again Mrs. Wickes lay silent. Her lips continued to move, but they were soundless. She seemed suddenly to become conscious of this, and motioned weakly for the flask. And again with difficulty she swallowed a few drops.

"Years ago this was." Mrs. Wickes forced the words with long pauses between. "'Ard times came on 'em. 'E got killed in a haccident. An' she took sick after Polly came, an' the money went, an' she wouldn't 'ave charity, an' she got down to this, like us 'uns 'ere, tryin' to keep body an' soul together on the bit she 'ad left. An' she died, an' I took Polly. Two years old Polly was then. There wasn't no good of tellin' Polly an' 'ave 'er give 'erself airs when she 'ad to go out an' do 'er bit an' earn something. An', wot's more, if she'd known I wasn't 'er mother she might 'ave stopped workin' for me-an' I couldn't 'ave made 'er, 'avin' lost my hold on 'er-an' I wasn't goin' to 'ave anything like that. Polly Wickes-Polly Wickes-the flower girl. Flowers-posies-pretty posies-that's where yer saw 'er—"

The woman's voice had thickened; her words, in snatches, were incoherent:

"Polly Wickes-Polly Wickes-Polly Gray-Polly Gray 'er name is-Polly Gray. I got the lines an' the birth paper. I kept 'em all these years. 'Ere! I got 'em 'ere."

"Where?" said Captain Francis Newcombe tersely.

"'Ere!" Mrs. Wickes plucked feebly at the edge of the bed clothing. "'Ere!"

Captain Francis Newcombe thrust his hand quickly in under the mattress. After a moment's search he brought out a soiled envelope. It bore a faded superscription in a scrawling hand. He picked up the candle from the chair and read it:

"Polly's papers which is God's truth,
Mrs. Wickes X her mark."

He tore the envelope open rather carefully at the end. It contained two papers that were turned a little yellow with age. Yes, it was quite true! His eyes travelled swiftly over the names:

"Harold Morton Gray....Elizabeth Pauline Forbes. Pauline Gray...."

There was a sudden sound from the bed-like a long, fluttering sigh. Captain Francis Newcombe swung sharply about. The woman's arm was stretched out toward him; dulled eyes seemed to be striving desperately in their fading vision to search his face.

"Polly!" Mrs. Wickes whispered. "For-for for Christ's sake-be-be good to Polly-be good to —"

The outstretched arm fell to the bed covering-and Mrs. Wickes lay still.

Captain Francis Newcombe leaned forward, holding the candle, searching the form on the bed critically with his eyes. After a moment he straightened up.

Mrs. Wickes was dead.

Captain Francis Newcombe replaced the papers in the envelope, and placed the envelope in his pocket. He set the candle back on the chair, blew it out, and walked across the room to the door.

"Gray, eh?" said Captain Francis Newcombe under his breath, as he closed the door behind him. "Polly Gray, eh? Well, it doesn't matter, does it? It's just as good an iron in the fire whether it's —Wickes or Gray!"

Three of Them

Twenty-five minutes later, Captain Francis Newcombe stood at the door of his apartment. Runnells admitted him.

"Paul Cremarre here yet?" demanded the ex-captain of territorials briskly.

"Yes," said Runnells. "Been here half an hour."

With Runnells behind him, Captain Francis Newcombe entered the living room of the apartment. A tall man, immaculately dressed, with a small, very carefully trimmed black moustache, with eyes that were equally black but whose pupils were curiously minute, stood by the mantel.

"Ah, monsieur!" He waved his arm in greeting. *"Salut!"*

"Back, eh, Paul?" nodded Captain Francis Newcombe, flinging himself into a lounge chair. "Expected you, of course, to-night. Well, what's the news? How's the fishing smack?"

Paul Cremarre smiled faintly.

"Ah, the poor *Marianne!*" he said. "Such bad weather! It is always the bilge. If it did not leak so furiously!" He lifted his shoulders, and blew a wreath of cigarette smoke languidly ceilingward.

"So!" said Captain Francis Newcombe. "Been searched again, eh?"

The Frenchman laughed softly.

"Two very charming old gentlemen who were summering on the French coast, and were so interested in everything. Could they come aboard? But, why not? It was a pleasure! Such harmless old children they looked–not at all like Leduc and Colferre of the Préfecture!"

"One more sign of the times!" commented Captain Francis Newcombe a little shortly. "And Père Mouche?"

"Ah!" murmured the Frenchman. "That is another story! I am afraid it is true that his back is really bending under the load. He has done amazingly, but though the continent is wide, it can only absorb so much, and there are always difficulties. He says himself that we feed him too well."

Captain Francis Newcombe frowned.

"Well, he's right, of course! Leduc and Colferre, eh? I don't like it! If we needed anything further to back us up in our decision lately that it was about time to lay low for a while, we've got it here. There is to-morrow night's affair, of course, that naturally we will carry through, but after that I think we should come to a full stop for, say —a six months' holiday. Personally, as you know, I'm rather anxious to make a little trip to America. I'll take Runnells along as my man for the looks of it. He can play at valeting and still enjoy himself if he keeps out of mischief–which I will see to it" —Captain Francis Newcombe's lips thinned —"that he does! That will account for the temporary closing up of this apartment here. And you, Paul —I suppose it will be the Riviera for you?"

The Frenchman shrugged his shoulders.

"Ah!" he said. "As to that I do not know, but what does it matter?" He laughed good-humouredly. "I have no attraction such as monsieur with a charming ward in America. I am of the desolate, one of the forlorn of the earth in whom no one has more than a passing interest."

"Except Scotland Yard and the Préfecture," said the ex-captain of territorials with a grim smile. He rose suddenly from his chair and paced once or twice the length of the room. "Yes," he said decisively, "we'd be fools to do anything else. It will give Père Mouche a chance to work down his surplus stock, and the police to lose a little of their ardour. It's getting a bit hot. Scotland Yard is badly flicked on the raw. London is becoming unhealthy. Even Runnells here, whom I would never accuse of having any delicate sense of prescience, has been uneasy of late as though he felt the net drawing in."

"You're bloody well right!" said Runnells gruffly. "I don't know how, but it's true. Let the coppers nose a cold scent for a while, I says. I can do with a bit of America whenever you're ready!"

"Quite so!" said Captain Francis Newcombe. "It's in the air. Like Runnells, I do not know exactly where it comes from, but I know it's there."

"Monsieur," said the Frenchman, "I have often wondered about the fourth-stragglers, I think you called us that night-about the fourth straggler."

"You mean?" demanded Captain Francis Newcombe sharply.

"Nothing!" said the Frenchman. "One sometimes wonders, that is all. The thought flashed through my mind as you spoke. But it means nothing. How could it? More than three years have gone. Let us forget my remark." He flicked the ash from his cigarette. "Well, then, as I am the only one left to speak, I will say that I too agree. For six months we do not exist so far as business is concerned-after to-morrow night." He made a wry face, and laughed. "Well, it will be dull! I fear it will be dull, and one will become *ennuyé*, but it is wise. So! It is decided. And so there remains only to-morrow night. I was to be here this evening to discuss the details-and here I am. Shall we proceed to discuss them? I have made a promise to the little Père Mouche that when I return he shall eat a *ragoût* from a veritable gold plate, and that Scotland Yard —"

The doorbell interrupted the Frenchman's words.

Runnells left the room to answer the summons. He was back in a moment with a card on a silver tray, which he handed to the ex-captain of territorials.

The card tray was significant. Captain Francis Newcombe glanced first at Runnell's face, frowned-then picked up the card. His eyes narrowed as he read it. On the card was written:

DETECTIVE-SERGEANT MULLINS
NEW SCOTLAND YARD

He handed the card coolly to Paul Cremarre.

"Everything all right so far as you are concerned?" he demanded in a low, quick tone.

The Frenchman smiled at the card in a curious way, handed it back, and lighted a fresh cigarette.

"Yes," he said.

"*Sure?*" said Captain Francis Newcombe.

"Absolutely!" replied the Frenchman in the same low tone.

"Very good!" said the ex-captain of territorials. "Don't look so damned white around the gills, Runnells. *And watch yourself!*" He raised his voice. "Show the sergeant in, Runnells!" he said.

A minute later, Runnells ushered in a thick-set, florid-faced man.

"Sergeant Mullins, sir!" he announced, and withdrew from the room.

The sergeant looked inquiringly from one to the other of the two men.

"I'm sorry to intrude, gentlemen," he said. "It's Captain Newcombe, I —"

Captain Francis Newcombe waved his hand pleasantly.

"Not at all, sergeant!" he said. "I am Captain Newcombe. What can I do for you?"

"Well, sir," said the man from Scotland Yard, "I'm not saying you can do anything, and then again maybe you can." He glanced at the Frenchman, and coughed slightly.

"Mr. Cremarre is a close friend of mine," said Captain Francis Newcombe quietly. "You may speak quite freely before him, so far as I am concerned."

"Very good, sir!" said Sergeant Mullins. "Well, then, even if the papers hadn't been full of it all day, you'd probably know about it anyway, being as how you were a friend of his. It's Sir Harris Greaves, sir-Sir Harris' murder."

Captain Francis Newcombe, as though instinctively, turned toward an evening paper that lay upon the table, its great headlines screaming the murder across the front page.

"Good God, sergeant-yes!" he exclaimed. "It's a shocking thing! Shocking!" He jerked his head toward the paper, and glanced at Paul Cremarre. "You've read it, of course, Paul?"

"I've never read anything like it before," said the Frenchman grimly. "The most wanton thing I ever heard of! Absolutely purposeless!"

"Don't you be too sure about that, sir," said Detective-Sergeant Mullins crisply. "Things aren't done purposelessly-leastways, not them kind of things."

"Exactly!" agreed Captain Francis Newcombe. "Right you are, sergeant! But you'll pardon me if I appear a bit curious as to why you should have come to me about it."

"Well, sir," said Sergeant Mullins, "that's simple enough. You are the last one as had any conversation with Sir Harris before he was murdered."

Captain Francis Newcombe stared at the Scotland Yard man in a puzzled way.

"I am afraid I don't quite understand, sergeant," he said a little helplessly. "According to the published accounts, Sir Harris was stabbed in his bed, presumably during the early morning hours, though no sound was heard, and the crime wasn't discovered until his man went to take Sir Harris his tea at the usual hour this morning. But perhaps the accounts are inaccurate?"

"No, sir," said Sergeant Mullins; "as far as that goes, they're accurate enough. The doctors say it must have been somewhere between two and three o'clock in the morning."

"Quite so!" said Captain Francis Newcombe. "That is what I had in mind. The last time I saw Sir Harris was yesterday evening at the club. Sir Harris left the club shortly before I did. I have no exact idea what the hour was, though the doorman would probably be able to say, but I am quite certain it could not have been later than half past eleven."

"It wasn't even as late as that, sir," said the man from Scotland Yard seriously. "Ten after eleven, it was, when Sir Harris left; and you, sir, at a quarter past. But I didn't say, sir, that you were the last one as *spoke* to Sir Harris alive. Conversation was what I said, sir-and a lengthy one too. One says a lot in an hour or so, sir."

"Oh, I see!" said Captain Francis Newcombe, with a smile. "Or, rather—I don't! What about this conversation, sergeant?"

"Well, sir, if you don't mind," said Detective-Sergeant Mullins, "that's what I'd like to know-what it was about?"

"Good Lord!" gasped the ex-captain of territorials feebly. "I'm not sure I know myself-now. What do men generally talk about over a Scotch and soda? I believe we started with the subject of democracy, and I'm afraid, in fact I'm certain, I talked a good bit of drivel, and incidentally settled several of the world questions and so on, and then we drifted from one thing to another in a desultory fashion."

"Yes, sir," said Sergeant Mullins. "And the things you drifted to-could you remember them, sir? It's very important, sir, that you should."

"Well, if it's important, I'll try," said Captain Francis Newcombe gravely. "The shows, of course, and the American Yacht race, horses, a hunting lodge Sir Harris had in Scotland, and-yes, I believe that's all, sergeant. But it's quite a range, at that."

Detective-Sergeant Mullins inspected the bottom button of his waistcoat intently.

"Sir Harris was a bit of a criminologist in his way, as perhaps you've heard, sir?" he said.

"Yes, I believe I have heard it said that was a hobby of his," nodded Captain Francis Newcombe. "But I wouldn't have known it from anything Sir Harris said last night, if that's what you mean. The subject wasn't mentioned."

"Nor any crime? And particularly any particular criminal?" prodded the Scotland Yard man.

Captain Francis Newcombe shook his head.

"Not a word," he said.

Detective-Sergeant Mullins looked up a little gloomily from his waistcoat button.

"I'm sorry for that," he said.

"So am I, if it would have helped any," said the ex-captain of territorials heartily. "But what's the point, sergeant?"

"Well, you see, sir," said the Scotland Yard man, "with all due respect to the dead, Sir Harris fancied himself a bit, he did, along those lines. Some queer notions he had, sir-and stubborn, as you might say. He's got himself into trouble more than once, and the Yard's had its own time with him. He's been warned, sir, often enough-and if he was alive, he wouldn't say he hadn't. It's what he's been told might happen. There's no other reason, as far as we've gone, why he should have been murdered. It looks the likely thing that he went too far this time, and got to know more than some crook took a notion it was safe to have him know."

Paul Cremarre smiled inscrutably at the Scotland Yard man.

"I take back what I said about it being a purposeless murder, sergeant," he murmured.

"Yes, sir," said Detective-Sergeant Mullins. "Well, I fancy that's all, gentlemen. We were hoping that if matters had reached as grave a state as that-that is, if Sir Harris ever realised how deep he'd got in-it would have been a bit on his mind, as you might say, and in the course of a long conversation with a friend, sir, a hint of it, even if he didn't go any further, might have cropped up." He buttoned his coat. "You're quite sure, Captain Newcombe, thinking it over, that there wasn't anything mentioned, even casually like, that would give us a clue?"

"Quite, sergeant!" said the ex-captain of territorials emphatically.

"Well, I'll be going, then," said the Scotland Yard man. "And sorry to have taken up your time, sir."

"You've done nothing but your duty," said Captain Francis Newcombe pleasantly. He rang the bell. "Runnells, bring Sergeant Mullins a drink!" And with a smile to the Scotland Yard man: "Will it be Scotch, sergeant?"

"Why, thank you very much, sir," said Detective-Sergeant Mullins. He took the glass from Runnells. "Here's how, sir!" He wiped his lips with the back of his hand. "Good-night, gentlemen!"

"Good-night, sergeant," said the ex-captain of territorials.

"Good-night, sergeant," said the Frenchman.

Detective-Sergeant Mullins' footsteps died away in the hall.

Captain Francis Newcombe's dark eyes rested unemotionally upon the Frenchman.

The Frenchman leaned against the mantel and stared at the end of his cigarette.

The front door closed, and Runnells came back into the room.

"Now, Runnells," said Captain Francis Newcombe blandly, "bring us *all* a drink, and we will talk about-to-morrow night."

IV
Gold Plate

A motor ran swiftly along a country road.

Two men sat in the front seat.

"My friend, Runnells," said one of the two quizzically, after a silence that had endured for miles, "what in hell is the matter with you to-night?"

"I don't know," said Runnells, who drove the car. "What the captain was talking about last night, maybe-the things you feel in the air."

"Bah!" said Paul Cremarre composedly. "If it is only the air! For three years we have found nothing in the air but good fortune."

"That's all right," Runnells returned sullenly. "But just the same that's the way I feel, and I can't help it. We're going to lay low for a spell after to-night, and maybe that's what's wrong too-kind of as though we were pushing our luck over the edge by sticking it just one night too many."

The Frenchman whistled a bar lightly under his breath.

"I should be delighted —*delighted*," he said, "to leave to-night alone-but not the Earl of Cloverley's gold plate! Have you forgotten that I told you I had made a promise to our little Père Mouche-to eat *ragoût* from a gold plate? I have never eaten from a gold plate. It is a dream!"

"You're bloody well right, it is!" said Runnells gruffly. "And I only hope it ain't going to be anything worse'n a dream to-night."

"It is evident," said Paul Cremarre, with a low laugh, "that, whatever you have eaten *from*, and whatever you have eaten *of*, to-night, my Runnells, it has not agreed with you! Is it not so?"

"Look here!" said Runnells suddenly. "If you want to know, I'll tell you. I know everything's fixed for to-night, maybe better than it's ever been fixed before-it ain't that. It's *last* night. It's damned queer, that bloke from Scotland Yard showing up in our rooms!"

"Ah!" murmured Paul Cremarre. "Yes, my Runnells, I too have thought of that. But you were at home the night before, when Sir Harris Greaves was murdered, you and the captain, were you not? It is nothing, is it? A mere little coincidence-yes? You should know better than I do."

"There's nothing to know," said Runnells shortly. "It's just the idea of a Scotland Yard man coming to *our* diggings. Like a warning, somehow, it looks."

"Yes," said Paul Cremarre. "Quite so! And the headlights now-hadn't you better switch them off? And run a little slower, Runnells. It is not far now, if I have made no mistake in my bearings."

Darkness fell upon the road; the motor slackened its speed.

"You were speaking of the visit from Scotland Yard," resumed the Frenchman calmly. "You were at home, of course, when Captain Newcombe returned from the club the night before last at-what time was it, he said?"

"Oh, that's straight enough!" grunted Runnells. "He came in about half past eleven, and we were both in bed by twelve. I've told you it ain't that. What would he have to do with sticking an old toff like Sir Harris that never done him any harm?"

"Nothing," said Paul Cremarre. "I was simply thinking that Sergeant Mullins' theory reminded me of something that you, too, may perhaps remember."

"What's that?" inquired Runnells.

"A rifle shot that was fired one night in a thicket when the Boche had us on the run," said Paul Cremarre.

Runnells swung sharply in his seat.

"Gawd!" he said hoarsely. "What d'you want to bring *that* up for to-night? I —damn it —I can see it out there in the black of the road now!"

The Frenchman remained silent.

Runnells spoke again after a moment.

"He's a rare 'un, all right, he is, is the captain," he said slowly; "but it wasn't him that did in Sir Harris Greaves. I'd take my oath on that. We was both in bed by twelve, as I told you, and he was still sleeping like a babe when I got up in the morning."

"And you, Runnells," inquired the Frenchman softly, "you too slept well?"

"You mean," said Runnells quickly, "that he slipped out again during the night?"

"Not at all!" said Paul Cremarre quietly. "How should I know? I mean nothing, except that Captain Francis Newcombe is a man like no other man in the world; that he is, as I once had the honour to remark-incomparable."

Runnells grunted over the wheel.

"I shan't ask him," he said tersely.

"Nor I," said Paul Cremarre.

Again there was silence; then the Frenchman spoke abruptly:

"Slower, Runnells. If I am not mistaken, we are arrived. The lodge gates can't be more than a quarter of a mile on, and the bit of lane that borders the park ought to be just about here-yes, there it is!"

Runnells stopped the motor; and then, with the engine running softly, backed it for a short distance from the main road down an intensely black, tree-lined lane.

"That's far enough," said Paul Cremarre. "We can't take any risk of being heard from the Hall. Now edge her in under the trees."

"What for?" grumbled Runnells. "It's so bloody dark, I'd probably smash her. She's right enough as she is. There's a fat chance of any one coming along this here lane at two o'clock in the morning, ain't there?"

"Runnells," said the Frenchman smoothly, "I quote from the book of Captain Francis Newcombe: 'Chance is the playground of fools.' Edge her in, my Runnells."

"Oh, all right!" said Runnells-and a moment later the lane was empty.

Still another moment, and the two men, each carrying two rather large-sized, empty travelling bags, began to make their way silently and cautiously through the thickly wooded park of the estate. It was not easy going in the darkness. Now and then they stumbled. Once or twice Runnells cursed fiercely under his breath; once or twice the Frenchman lost his urbanity and swore softly in his native tongue.

Five, ten minutes passed. And now the two reached the farther edge of the wooded park, and halted here, drawn back a little in the shadow of the trees. Before them was a narrow breadth of lawn; and, beyond, a great, rambling, turreted pile lay black even against the darkness, its castellated roof and points making a jagged fringe against the sky line.

Runnells appeared suddenly to find vent for his ill humour in a savage chuckle.

"What is it, Runnells?" demanded the Frenchman.

"I was just thinking that in the five or six years since I was here with Lord Seeton, you know, I ain't forgotten his nibs the Earl of Cloverley. I'd like to see his face in the morning! He's a crabbed old bird. My word! He'll die of apoplexy, he will! And if he don't, he won't be so keen on his 'ouse parties to visiting nabobs and cabinet ministers. He didn't send into London and get his gold service out of the bank for *us* when we were here."

"Perhaps," said the Frenchman gently, "he did not know that you were valeting Lord Seeton at the time-or perhaps it was because he did!"

"Aw, chuck it!" said Runnells gruffly. He stared at the black, shadowy building for a minute. Then abruptly: "It's two o'clock, ain't it? You looked, didn't you?"

"Yes," said Paul Cremarre. "I looked when we left the motor. The time's right. It was just ten minutes of two."

"Well, what the blinking 'ell's the matter now, then?" complained Runnells. "The place is as black as a cat. They're all in bed, aren't they?"

"That is not for me to say," replied the Frenchman calmly. "We will wait, Runnells."

Runnells, with another grunt, sat down on one of the bags, his back against a tree. The Frenchman remained standing, his eyes glued on the great house across the lawn.

"Aye," said Runnells after a moment, and chuckled savagely to himself again, "I'd give a bob or two, I would, to see the old boy in the morning! A fussy, nosey, old fidge-budget, that's what he is! A-poking of his sharp little nose into everything, and always afraid some 'un won't earn the measly screw he's paying for work he'd ought to pay twice as much for! It's no wonder he's rich!"

"You seem to have very pleasant recollections of your visit, Runnells," said the Frenchman slyly. "I wonder what he caught you at?"

"He didn't catch *me!*" said Runnells defiantly. "Though I'll say this, that if I'd known then that I was ever coming back now, I'd have kept my eyes peeled, and he'd be going into mourning for more'n his blessed gold plate to-night! He didn't bother me none, me being Lord Seeton's man, but at that I saw enough of him so that the talk that went on in the servants' hall wasn't in any foreign language that I couldn't tumble to. My eye!" said Runnells. "A rare state he'll be in!"

The Frenchman said nothing.

The minutes dragged along. Runnells too had relapsed into silence. A quarter of an hour passed. Then Runnells commenced to mutter under his breath and move restlessly on his improvised seat; and then, getting up suddenly, he moved close over beside the Frenchman.

"I say!" whispered Runnells uneasily. "I don't like this, I don't! What d'you suppose is up?"

"A great deal, I have no doubt, my Runnells," said the Frenchman imperturbably. "More perhaps than you and I could overcome in the same time-if at all."

"That's all right!" returned Runnells. "I'm not saying it ain't, but it's getting creepy standing here and staring your eyes out. I'm beginning to see the trees moving around and coming at you, and in every bit of breeze the leaves are like a lot of bloody voices whispering in your ears. I wish to Gawd you hadn't said anything about *that* night! It gives me the —"

"Look!" said the Frenchman suddenly.

From an upper window, out of the blackness of the building across the lawn, there showed a faint spot of light that held for a few seconds-and then, in quick succession, a series of little flashes came from the room within.

The two men stood motionless, intent, staring at the window.

The flashes ceased.

The Frenchman reached out and laid his hand on Runnells' arm.

"No need for a repeat," he said quickly. "You got it, didn't you?"

"My word!" exclaimed Runnells. "Two guards-butler's pantry-all clear! Strike me pink!"

The Frenchman laughed purringly under his breath.

"Did I not say he was incomparable? Come on, then, Runnells-quickly now!"

And now it was as though two shadows moved, flitting swiftly across the lawn, and along the edge of the building and around to the rear. And here they crouched before a doorway, and the Frenchman whispered:

"Don't be delicate about it, Runnells. This isn't any *inside* job! Nick it up badly enough so's a blind man could see where we got in."

"That's what I'm doing," said Runnells mechanically. His mind seemed obsessed with other things. "Two guards!" he muttered. And again: "Strike me pink!"

And after a moment, with both door and frame eloquent of the rough surgery that had been practised upon them, the door opened.

The two men entered, and closed the door silently behind them. An electric torch stabbed suddenly through the blackness and played for a moment inquisitively over its surroundings.

"'Tain't changed a bit, as I said when I saw the plan," commented Runnells.

They went on quickly. But where before there had been a steady play of the electric torch it winked now through the darkness only at intervals. A door opened here and there noiselessly; the footsteps of the men were cautious, wary, almost without sound. And then, as they halted finally, and the torch shot out its ray again, Runnells drew in his breath with a low, catchy, whistling sound.

The torch disclosed a narrow serving pantry, and, on the floor at one side, a great metal box or chest-obviously the object of their visit. But Runnells for the moment was apparently not interested in the chest.

"Look at that!" he breathed hoarsely-and pointed to the farther end of the pantry where a swinging door was ajar, and through which an upturned foot protruded.

The Frenchman set his bags down beside the metal chest, moved swiftly forward, pushed the swinging door open, and stepped silently through into what was obviously the dining room. And Runnells, beside him, whispered hoarsely again, but this time with a sort of amazed admiration in his voice.

"Gawd!" said Runnells. "Neat, I calls that! Neat! What?"

Two men lay upon the floor, gagged, bound and apparently unconscious. One, from his livery, was a servant in the house; the other was in civilian clothes.

Paul Cremarre pointed to the latter.

"The man that came out from London with the box from the bank," he observed complacently. He pushed Runnells back through the swinging door into the pantry. "Well, my Runnells, you were grumbling over a few minutes' delay, let us see if we can be equally as expeditious and efficient with infinitely less to do." He reached the chest and examined it. "Padlocks, eh? Let me see if I can persuade them!" He bent over the chest, and from his pocket came a little kit of tools.

Runnells stood silently by. There was no sound now save the breathing of the two men, and, as the minutes passed, an occasional faint, metallic rasp and click from Paul Cremarre at work.

And then the Frenchman flung back the lid, and straightened up.

"Quick now, Runnells-to work!" he said briskly. "Père Mouche is waiting for his *ragoût*!"

"My eye!" said Runnells with enthusiasm, as the electric torch bored into the interior of the box. "Pipe it! I've served with the swells, I have, and Lord Seeton was one of the biggest of 'em, but I never saw the likes of this before. Gold plate to eat off of! My eye!"

"They are very beautiful," said the Frenchman judicially; "but it would be a sacrilege against art to appraise them in haste and in a poor light. Work quickly, Runnells! And do not fill any one of the bags too full. You will find it heavy. The four will hold it all comfortably."

"Gawd!" said Runnells eagerly, as he bent to his task.

The men worked swiftly now, without words, transferring the Earl of Cloverley's priceless service of gold plate to the four travelling bags. The Frenchman, the quicker of the two, completed his task first, and locked his two bags. And then suddenly he touched Runnells on the shoulder.

"Listen!" he whispered. "What's that?"

Faintly, scarcely audible, there came a curiously padded, swishing sound-like slippered feet. It came from the direction, not of the swing door where the two guards lay, but from beyond the door through which Runnells and the Frenchman had entered the pantry.

"It's some one coming, all right," Runnells whispered back.

"But only *one*," said the Frenchman instantly. "Quick! Finish your job-but don't make a sound." There was a sudden, vicious snarl in his whisper. "Pull that hat of yours down over your eyes. I'll answer the door, as you English say!"

He moved back along the pantry with the noiseless tread of a cat, and took up his position against the wall at the edge of the closed door. From his pocket he drew a revolver. It was quite black, quite silent now-save for the approaching footsteps.

Perhaps a minute passed.

And then the door opened, and a light went on. A grey-whiskered little man in a dressing gown, with bare feet thrust into slippers, stood on the threshold. He cast startled eyes on a crouching figure in the centre of the pantry, the tell-tale travelling bags, the gaping treasure chest, and wrenched a revolver from the pocket of his dressing gown. But the Frenchman, reaching out, struck from the edge of the doorway. The revolver sailed ceilingwards from the other's hand, and exploded in mid-air. And coincidently the Frenchman struck again-with the butt of his own weapon-and the man went limply to the floor.

Runnells came staggering forward under the load of the bags.

"Strike me dead!" he gasped, "if it ain't the nosey old bird himself! Serves him proper-sneaking around to make sure he ain't paying money for nothing, and hoping he'll catch 'em asleep on sentry-go!"

The Frenchman snatched up two of the bags.

"Quick!" he said tersely.

Captain Francis Newcombe raised his head from his pillow, and propped himself up on his elbow. A door nearby suddenly opened. Other doors were being rapped upon. Voices came.

The ex-captain of territorials sprang from his bed, thrust his feet into slippers, threw a bathrobe over his pajamas, opened his door and stepped out into the hall. Some one had already turned on a light. He found himself amongst a group of fellow guests, whose number was being constantly augmented. From other doorways, wary of their extreme dishabille, women's faces peered out timidly-their voices, less restrained, demanding to know what was the matter, added an hysterical note to the scene.

"A shot was certainly fired somewhere in the house, though I couldn't place where it came from," declared some one. "I am quite sure of it."

"There is no question about it," corroborated another. "It woke me up, and I ran out here into the hall."

"The Earl is not in his room!" announced a third excitedly. "I've just been there."

"Ring for the servants!" screeched an elderly female voice. "Some one may be killed!"

"For God's sake!" snapped a man gruffly. "I didn't hear it myself, but if a shot was fired it's fairly obvious by now that it wasn't fired up *here*! What are you standing around like a pack of sheep for?"

"That's what I was wondering," said Captain Francis Newcombe softly to himself-and joined the now concerted rush down the stairway.

Lights were going on all over the house now, and the men servants began to appear. The rush scurried from one room to another. A cry went up from some one ahead. It turned the rush into the dining room, and there, in their motley garbs, chorusing excited exclamations, the crowd surrounded the two gagged and bound guards.

Then some one else shouted from the pantry that the metal chest had been broken open, and that the gold service was gone. There was another rush in that direction. Captain Francis Newcombe accompanied this rush. On the floor lay a revolver. The ex-captain of territorials picked it up.

"Hello!" he ejaculated. "It's rather queer this has been left behind-or perhaps it belongs to one of the two out there in the dining room."

"No, sir," said one of the servants at his elbow. "It's the Earl's, sir. I'd know it anywhere. And, begging your pardon, sir, it's a bit strange that *he* hasn't been seen since —"

"Here he is!" cried a voice from beyond the farther pantry door. "Here, lend a hand! The Earl's been hurt."

Captain Francis Newcombe aiding, the Earl was carried back to the dining room, and restoratives hastily applied. Here, the man in livery, released now, his voice weak and unsteady, was telling his story; his companion was still unconscious.

"...Gawd knows," the man was saying. "We was in the pantry, and Brown there 'e thought 'e 'eard a sound out 'ere in the dining room. And 'e gets up and pushes the swinging door open and goes through, and a minute later I 'ears what I thinks is 'im calling me. "Ere, quick, Johnston!' 'e says. And I goes through the door, and something bashes me over the 'ead, and I goes out. What 'appened though is as clear as daylight now. Brown goes through the door and gets hit on the 'ead, and I goes through the door and gets hit on the 'ead. And it wasn't Brown as called to me, it was the blighter that did us in, and —"

The Earl's voice broke in suddenly.

"I'm all right, I tell you!" he insisted weakly. "There were two of them ...one behind the door knocked the revolver out of my hand as I fired, and smashed me over the head with something ... bags, travelling bags for the plate ... that's the way they're carrying it ... I —"

The Earl's voice trailed off.

"It can't have been more than five minutes ago then," said the man with the gruff voice, "for they were therefore in the house when the shot was fired. They can't have got very far carrying that load. Quick now! We'll search the park."

"But they wouldn't attempt to carry it very far anyway," objected some one. "They'd have a motor, of course."

"Exactly!" retorted the other. "But not near enough to the house to be heard. Did any one hear a motor after that shot was fired? Of course, not! We may get them before they get their motor. Also, we'll use a motor too! Any one of the chauffeurs here?"

"Yes, sir," answered a man.

"Good! Any one armed?"

"I've got the Earl's revolver," said Captain Francis Newcombe.

"Well, there's the gun room," said the man who had assumed command. "And you servants get lanterns and things. Look lively, now! Sharp's the word!"

And for some reason Captain Francis Newcombe smiled grimly to himself, as he attached his person to the chauffeur, and, accompanied by three other pajama-clad guests, raced from the house.

At the garage Captain Francis Newcombe appropriated the front seat beside the chauffeur, his fellow guests scrambled into the tonneau, and a moment later the big car shot around the end of the house and began to sweep down the driveway. The ex-captain of territorials screwed around in his seat for a backward glance as they tore along. Every window in the great, rambling, castle-like edifice appeared to be alight; this caused a filmy, lighted zone without, and through this raced ghostly figures in bathrobes and dressing gowns that were almost instantly swallowed up in the shadows of the trees; and from amongst the trees, dancing in and out, like huge fireflies in their effect, there showed in constantly increasing numbers the glint of lanterns.

But now the motor was at the lodge gates, nosing the main road, and the chauffeur pulled up.

"Which way would you say, sir?" he asked anxiously.

"I'd vote for whichever is the shortest way to London-that's to the left, isn't it?" Captain Francis Newcombe responded promptly. He turned to his fellow guests. "I don't know what you think about it?"

"Yes," one of the others answered, "I'd say that's the way they'd most likely take."

"Very good, sir!" said the chauffeur. "Left, it is, and —" He broke short off. "There they are!" he cried excitedly. "Listen! They're coming out of that lane there, over to the right!" He swung the motor sharply into the straight of the main road. "There they are! See 'em!" he cried again, as the headlights brought the rear of a speeding motor into view. "The old general back there in the house was right. They didn't bring their motor any nearer for fear it would be heard. That's where it has been-up the lane there. But we've got 'em now! This old girl'll touch seventy and never turn a hair."

"Corking!" contributed Captain Francis Newcombe enthusiastically. "You're sure of the seventy, are you?"

"Rather!" exclaimed the chauffeur. "Look for yourself, sir. We're overhauling them now like one o'clock."

The ex-captain of territorials for a moment stared intently along the headlights' rays to where, gradually, the other motor was coming more and more into focus.

"By Jove, I believe you're right!" he agreed heartily-and from the pocket of his dressing gown produced the Earl's revolver.

The motor was lurching now with the speed. A hundred yards intervening between the flying cars diminished to seventy-five —to fifty. *Still closer*! The men in the tonneau clung to their seats. Twenty-five yards!

Captain Francis Newcombe shouted to his companions over the roar and sweep of the wind.

"I'll take a pot at the beggars, and see if that'll stop 'em!" he yelled. "Better chance over the top of the windshield, what?"

Captain Francis Newcombe stood up, swayed with the car, fired twice in quick succession and once after a short pause over the top of the windshield-but the ex-captain of territorials' mark seemed curiously comprehensive in expanse, for his eyes were at the same time searching the side of the road ahead. And now there showed at the end of the headlight's path a hedgerow bordering close against the side of the road. Captain Francis Newcombe fired again, but as the car lurched now the ex-captain of territorials seemed momentarily to lose his balance, and with the lurch swayed heavily against the chauffeur's arm.

There was a startled yell from the chauffeur; a vicious swerve-and the big motor leaped at the hedge. Came a crash of splintering glass as Captain Francis Newcombe was pitched head first against the windshield; a rip and rend and tear as the motor bucked and plunged and twisted in its conflict with the thick, heavy hedge; and then a terrific jolt that in its train brought a full stop.

And Captain Francis Newcombe, flung back and half out of the car, put his hands to his eyes and brought them away wet from a great gush of blood.

"Carry on! Carry on!" he cried weakly. "You'll never have a better chance to get them."

"My God!" screamed the chauffeur. "Carry on? We're a bally wreck!"

"What beastly luck!" murmured Captain Francis Newcombe-and lost consciousness.

V

"Dear Guardy"

Captain Francis Newcombe, a bandage swathing his head from the tip of his nose upward, groped out with his hand for a glass that stood on the bedside table, succeeded only in upsetting it, and swore savagely under his breath. At the same moment, he heard the front door of his apartment open and close.

"Runnells!" he shouted irritably. "D'ye hear, Runnells? Come here!"

A footstep came hurriedly along the hall, and the door of the bedroom opened.

Paul Cremarre stood on the threshold.

"It is not Runnells," said the Frenchman, staring at the bed. "I used my key. I saw Runnells and another man go out a few minutes ago."

"You, Paul!" exclaimed Captain Francis Newcombe quickly. "I did not expect you to return from France until to-morrow. I thought Runnells had forgotten something and come back. That was the doctor with him. Runnells has gone out for supplies. They've only just brought me back from Cloverley's this morning, and the place here was pretty well cleaned out of necessities."

The Frenchman moved over to the bedside, and grasped Captain Francis Newcombe's hand.

"Monsieur," he said earnestly, "I am desolated to see you like this. How am I to tell you of my gratitude? How am I to tell you what I owe you? We would have been caught. In two or three more little minutes, Runnells and I would have been *pouf*!"

"That seemed rather obvious," said Captain Francis Newcombe dryly.

"*Bon Dieu!*" ejaculated the Frenchman. "Yes! I heard from Runnells, of course-the whole story in code. There is only one man who would have done that. I, Paul Cremarre, will never forget it. Never! And I say again that I am desolated to see you like this. Runnells said your eyes were very badly injured."

"That is Runnells' lack of balance in the use of English," said the ex-captain of territorials. "There is nothing whatever the matter with my *eyes*. If I am blind for the moment, it is because my eyelids are kept shut by some damned medical method of torture, and because of this bandage. When I took a header into the broken windshield, I got a bit of a cut that beginning with the bridge of my nose had a go straight across on each side just under the eyebrows. They've made a bit of a fuss over it, wouldn't let me come home until now, and I must still be tucked up in bed, but —"

"It is more than you make out," said the Frenchman gravely. "I know that. But that your eyes are saved-that is luck!"

"Quite so!" Captain Francis Newcombe shrugged his shoulders. "And you? —speaking of luck."

"The best!" replied the Frenchman in a low, quick tone. "Père Mouche has had his *ragoût*, and afterwards another that was so hot that-would you believe it? —it melted the dishes. And, besides, he has had a stroke of good fortune in getting rid of some other stock, a lot of it, on the continent. There will be a nice bank account in a day or so-to-morrow, if you want any." His voice grew suddenly less buoyant. "But just the same, it is well that we are taking a holiday. It has caused a furor. The papers, the Earl, Scotland Yard-how they buzz! And the Prefecture more suspicious than ever! Your English journals are like spoiled children. They will not stop crying, and they are very bad tempered about it. This morning, for instance. I have one here. Shall I read to you what it says?"

"Good heavens-no!" expostulated Captain Francis Newcombe hastily. "Everybody from the Earl down to Runnells has read that stuff to me for a week! If you want to do anything that smacks of intelligence you can get me another drink in place of the one I knocked over when you came in-you know where the Scotch is; and if you want to do any reading see if there is any mail for me. I mentioned letters but the doctor said no. However, the doctor is gone, so look on the desk in the living room."

"All right," said the Frenchman, as he turned briskly away. *"Un petit coup* is decidedly in order this morning. I will have one with you."

He was back presently from his errand. He filled the glasses, and placed one in Captain Francis Newcombe's hand.

"Salut, mon capitaine!" he said. "Here's to the cash the little Père Mouche is getting ready for us —a fat, a very nice fat little dividend!"

"Good!" said the ex-captain of territorials. "How about the mail? Any letters?"

"I've got them here," Paul Cremarre answered. "There were only three."

"Well, what are they?" demanded Captain Francis Newcombe.

The Frenchman examined the first of the letters in his hand.

"A city letter from Hipplewaite, Jones & Simpkins, Solicitors —"

Captain Francis Newcombe chuckled.

"That's about a hen Runnells ran over a month or so ago. Extremely valuable fowl! Poultry show stock, and all that, you know. What has the price risen to now?"

Paul Cremarre tore the letter open.

"Two pounds, ten and six," he said.

"Still much too cheap!" grinned Captain Francis Newcombe. "The man is simply robbing himself. Chuck it away before Runnells sees it. He could have settled for a pound three weeks ago. What's next?"

The Frenchman examined another envelope.

"City letter again," he said. "From 'The Sabbath House.' "

"Ah, yes!" said Captain Francis Newcombe gravely. "Most worthy object. Gave 'em ten quid last month. A mission down in Whitechapel, you know. Elevation of the unelevated, and all that. Shocking conditions! I must see that your name goes on that list."

"Shall I tear it up?" drawled the Frenchman.

"Yes," said Captain Newcombe.

The Frenchman remained silent for a moment.

"Well?" prompted the ex-captain of territorials. "You said there were three."

"I have put the other on the table beside you," said the Frenchman. *"It is intime.* The stamp from America. The handwriting of a lady. You will read it yourself when you are able."

"Able!" echoed Captain Francis Newcombe, with sudden asperity. "I won't be able to do anything for another week, let alone read. Open it! You know damned well it's only from my ward in America. And since I'm going out there as soon as I'm fit again, I'm rather keen to know what her immediate plans are. She was going to a school friend's home for the summer. I've explained to you before that her mother did a rather big thing for me once, and I'm trying to repay the debt. Open it, and read it to me. There's nothing private about it."

"But, certainly!" agreed the Frenchman, as he opened the letter. "It is only that you are both young, and that the thought crossed my mind you —"

"Read the letter!" snapped Captain Francis Newcombe. "If there's any enclosure for her mother, you can lay that aside."

"There is no enclosure," returned the Frenchman good-humouredly. "Well, then, listen! I read:

> The Corals,
> Manwa Island, Florida Keys,
> Tuesday, June 30th.

DEAR GUARDY:

You knew, of course, I was going to visit Dora Marlin and her father, Mr. Jonathan P. Marlin, this summer, so you won't be altogether surprised at the above address. You see, we came here a little sooner than I expected, so that your last letter, forwarded on from New York, has just reached me.

I am wild with delight to know that you have decided to come out to America for a visit. I showed your letter at once to Dora and Mr. Marlin, and they absolutely insist that you come here as their guest. You will, won't you? You old dear! You'll have to, else you won't see me-so there! You see, we're on an island in the Florida Keys, and it's ever so far from the mainland, and there's no other place on it to stay except with us. I wonder, I wonder if you'll know me? I'm not the little Polly I was, you know.

Oh, guardy, it's simply wonderful here! The house is really a castle, and it's built mostly of coral, and is so pretty; and the foliage is a dream-the whole island, and it's really an awfully big one, is just like a huge garden. And, too, it's just like a little world all of your own. The servants are mostly negroes, with pickaninnies running around, and they live in jolly little bungalows, ever and ever so many of them, that peep out of the trees at you everywhere you go. And then there is the aquarium. It's Mr. Marlin's hobby. I couldn't begin to describe it. I never knew such beautiful and wonderful and queer creatures existed in the sea.

Dora's a dear, of course. I'm sure you'll lose your heart to her at once. And I've already grown so fond of Mr. Marlin, and the more so, perhaps, because Dora is frightfully worried about him. I am afraid there is something very serious the matter with his mind, though a great deal of the time he appears to be quite normal. I don't understand it, of course, because it is all about the financial conditions in the world; but anyway —

Paul Cremarre stopped reading aloud abruptly. There was a moment of silence while his eyes swept swiftly on to the end of the paragraph.

"Well?" inquired Captain Francis Newcombe. "What's the matter? Have you lost your place?"

The Frenchman drew in his breath sharply.

"*Bon Dieu!*" he exclaimed excitedly. "Listen to this! It is the lamp of Aladdin! It is the Isle of Croesus! We are rich! It is superb! It is magnificent! Listen! I read again:

—he has a great sum of money in banknotes here; half a million dollars, he said. He showed it to me. It was hard to believe there was so much. Why, you could just make a little bundle of it and put it under your arm. I asked him why he had it here, and he patted it and smiled at me, and told me it was the only safe thing to do. And then he tried to explain a lot of things to me about money that I couldn't understand at all.

Paul Cremarre looked up, and waved the letter about jubilantly.

"Yes, yes!" he cried. "I am awake! See! I pinch myself! It is amazing! In banknotes! In American money! *That* is valuable, eh? And a little bundle that one could put under one's arm!"

Captain Francis Newcombe's lips were a straight line under the bandages.

"I'm afraid I don't get the point," he said coldly.

"The point!" Paul Cremarre's face was flushed now, his eyes burned with excitement. "But, sacre nom, the point is —a half million dollars in cash. And so easy! It is ours for the taking.

The man is-ha, ha! —yes, I learned something in the war from the Americans-he is what they call a nut!" He tapped his forehead. "And from the nut we extract the kernel! Yes?"

"I think not!" said Captain Francis Newcombe evenly.

"Heh?" The Frenchman stared incredulously. "But it must be that you joke —a little joke of exquisite irony. Yes, of course; for what could be better-or suit us better? We were about to lay low for a while because it was becoming too hot for us on this side of the water-and, presto, like a gift of the gods, there immediately awaits us fortune on the other side!"

Captain Francis Newcombe suddenly thrust out a clenched hand toward the other.

"*No!*" he said in a low voice.

"*Bon Dieu!*" gasped the Frenchman helplessly. "But I do not understand."

"Then I'll try to make it plain," said Captain Francis Newcombe in level tones. "There are limits to what even I will do, and it is well over that limit here. To go there as a guest of —"

"Monsieur was a guest, I understand, of the Earl of Cloverley a few days ago," interrupted the Frenchman quickly.

"Yes!" said Captain Francis Newcombe tersely. "And the guest before that of many others. But I did not have a ward to consider upon whose reputation I was to trade, and which I would wreck. Do you understand that?"

"Damn!" said the Frenchman. "There is always a woman! Damn all women, I say!"

"You may damn them as much as you please," said Captain Francis Newcombe, a grim savagery in his voice; "but there'll be none of that sort of thing here. And you keep your hands off! Do you also understand that? There's going to be one decent thing in my life!" He stretched out his clenched hand again. "Curse these bandages! I wish I could see your face! But I tell you now that if any attempt is made to get that money I'll crush you with as little compunction as I would crush a snake. Is *that* plain?"

"But, monsieur-monsieur!" protested the Frenchman. "That is enough! Why should you say such things to me? I am distressed. And it is not just. You asked me to read a letter, and I read it. That was not my fault. And surely it was but natural, what I said. Has it not been our business to do that sort of thing together? I did not know how you felt about this. But now that I know it is at an end. I have forgotten it, my friend. It is as though it had never been."

"All right, then!" said the ex-captain of territorials in a softer tone. "As you say, that ends it."

"Shall I go on with the letter?" asked the Frenchman pleasantly.

"No," said Captain Francis Newcombe. "Give it to me. I've had enough of it for now." He smiled suddenly, as the Frenchman placed the letter in his hand. "I'm afraid I'm a bit off colour this morning, Paul. Sorry! The trip down from Cloverley's has done me in a bit, and my eyes hurt like hell. I'd give a hundred pounds for a few good hours of sleep."

"Try, then," suggested the Frenchman. "I'll be where I can hear you if you want anything. I won't go out until Runnells gets back."

"Good enough!" agreed Captain Francis Newcombe; and then abruptly, as the Frenchman rose from his chair: "Speaking of Runnells, Paul-you will *oblige* me by saying nothing to him of the contents of this letter."

"I will say nothing to any one, let alone Runnells," replied the Frenchman quietly. "It is already forgotten. Call, if you want anything."

"I will," said Captain Francis Newcombe.

The Frenchman's footsteps died away in an outer room.

Captain Francis Newcombe's fingers tightened around the letter he held in his hand, crushed it, and carefully smoothed it out again. He lay there motionless then, his face turned away from the door, his lips thinned, his under jaw outthrust a little.

"Three years in the planting!" he muttered to himself. "It has ripened well! Very well! Paul-bah! What does it matter, after all, that he read the letter? I am not sure but that he has already outlived his usefulness-and Runnells too!" He thrust the letter suddenly underneath his pillow. "Damn the infernal pain!" he gritted between his teeth. "If I could only sleep for a bit-sleep-sleep!"

And for a time he tossed restlessly from side to side, and then presently he slept.

Runnells, in response to a demand from the bedroom, brought in the luncheon tray.

"You've had a rare whack of sleep," he said, as he laid the tray down on the table beside the bed.

"What time is it?" inquired Captain Francis Newcombe.

"Three o'clock," said Runnells. "Here, sit up a bit, and I'll bolster the pillows in behind you."

"Where's Paul?" asked the ex-captain of territorials.

Runnells did not answer immediately. In arranging the pillows he had found a letter. He looked at it coolly. It ought to be worth looking at if Captain Francis Newcombe kept it under his pillow.

"Well?" snapped the ex-captain of territorials.

Runnells placed the letter on the table within easy reach beside the tray, pulled the table a little closer, and sat down on the edge of the bed.

"He went out after I got back," said Runnells. "Said he'd sleep here to-night, that's all I know. This is a bit of stew."

Runnells, with one hand presented a forkful of meat to Captain Francis Newcombe's lips, and with the other hand possessed himself of the letter again.

Runnells read steadily now. He conveyed food to Captain Francis Newcombe's mouth mechanically.

"Damn it!" spluttered the ex-captain of territorials suddenly. "Do you take me for a boa constrictor? I can't bolt food as fast as that!"

Runnells' eyes were curiously, feverishly alight.

"Yesterday you said I went too slow," he mumbled.

"In a great many respects, Runnells," said Captain Francis Newcombe tartly, "you are an irritating, tactless ass. But not to be too hard on you, and especially in view of the last week, I have to admit you possess one redeeming feature that I am bound to give you credit for."

"What's that?" Runnells was at the end of the letter now. He stared at the bandaged face with eyes a little narrowed, and with lips that twisted in a strange, speculative smile.

"A fidelity of the same uninitiative quality that a dog has," said Captain Francis Newcombe, motioning for more to eat. "And in that sphere you're a success. I hope you'll always stick to it."

Runnells made no answer. His eyes were on the letter again-re-reading it.

The lunch proceeded in silence.

At its conclusion, Runnells stood up, slipped the letter behind the pillow again, and gathered the various dishes together on the tray.

"America, eh?" confided Runnells to himself, as he carried the tray from the room. "So *that's* the bit of all right, is it? And Paul don't know anything about it! And the captain don't know —I know! Half a million dollars! Strike me pink!"

VI

The Writing on the Wall

It was a night of storm. The rain, wind driven, swept the decks in gusty, stinging sheets; the big liner rolled and pitched, disgruntled, in the heavy sea.

Within the smoking room at a table in the corner Captain Francis Newcombe turned from a companion who sat opposite to him to face a steward who had just arrived with a tray.

"How about this, steward?" he asked. "Is this weather going to delay our getting in? I understand that if we don't pass quarantine early enough they hold us up all night."

"So they do, sir," the steward answered. "But this isn't holding us up any, a bit nasty though it is. We'll be docked at New York by two o'clock to-morrow afternoon at the latest. Thank you, sir!" He pocketed a generous tip as he departed.

The young man at the opposite side of the table, dark-eyed, dark-haired, with fine, clean-cut features, a man of powerful physique, whose great breadth of shoulder was encased in an immaculate dinner jacket, lifted the glass the steward had just set before him.

"Here's how, captain!" he smiled.

"The same, Mr. Locke!" returned Captain Francis Newcombe cordially.

Howard Locke extracted a cigarette from his case, and lighted it.

"The end of as chummy a crossing as I've ever had," he said. "Thanks to you. And I've been lucky all round. Cleaned up well in London, and 'll get a pat on the back for it from dad-and a holiday, which, without throwing any bouquets at myself, I'll say I've earned. I think I'll do a bit of coast cruising in that little old fifty-footer of mine that I've filled your ear full of during the last few days. Wow! And not least of all my luck was Joyce introducing me to you at lunch that day in the club."

"It's very good of you to say so," said Captain Francis Newcombe.

"Good, nothing!" exclaimed the young American. "I mean it! You've made the trip for me. And now how about your plans? I know you're going on South somewhere, for you mentioned it the other day. But what about New York? You'll be a little while there, and I feel pleasurably responsible for the stranger in the strange land. The house is barred, for the family is away for the summer; but there are the clubs, and I'd like to put you up and show you around a bit."

Captain Francis Newcombe studied the young man's face for a moment-he smiled disarmingly as he did so. Howard Locke was the son of a man of great wealth, the head of a great financial house, and of a family whose social status left nothing to be desired-and America was the Land of Promise! But one could be *too* eager!

"I'd like to," he said heartily; "but I fancy I've still quite a little trip ahead of me, and I'm afraid I'm a bit overdue already. As you say, I mentioned that I was going South. To be precise, I'm going down Florida way-or do you call it up? —as the guest of a Mr. Marlin."

Howard Locke removed the cigarette from his lips.

"Marlin?" he repeated. "Not Jonathan P. Marlin, by any chance?"

Captain Francis Newcombe nodded.

"Whew!" The young American whistled softly under his breath.

Captain Francis Newcombe lifted his eyebrows inquiringly.

"You know him?" he asked.

"No," Locke answered. "Not personally. I know of him, of course. Everybody does. And I don't want to be nosey and butt in, and you can heave that glass at me by way of reply if you like, but how in the world do you happen to know him?"

Captain Francis Newcombe smiled.

"I don't," he said. "My ward, who has been over here at school for the past few years, has been a classmate of Miss Marlin, and she is spending part of the summer with them."

"Oh, I see!" Howard Locke tapped the end of his cigarette on the edge of an ash tray once or twice, and glanced in evident indecision at his companion.

"Go on!" invited Captain Francis Newcombe. "What is it?"

Howard Locke laughed a little awkwardly.

"Well, I don't know," he said. "Nothing very much. And I'm afraid it's not done, as you English put it, for me to say anything, since he is your prospective host; still, as you say you are not personally acquainted with him yourself, I think perhaps you ought to know just the same. I haven't anything definite to go on, no authoritative source of information, but it is rather generally understood that old Marlin's gone a bit queer in the head."

"Really!" ejaculated Captain Francis Newcombe. "Good lord! I had no idea of any such thing! And my ward's on this island of his in the Florida Keys, and —"

"There's nothing whatever to be alarmed about," said the young American hastily. "It's nothing like that. He's as harmless as you are, or as I am. It's only on one subject-money. I suppose he was one of the wealthiest men in America at the close of the war, and since then he's been wiped out."

"Wiped out?" Captain Francis echoed incredulously.

"Comparatively, of course," said Howard Locke. "I don't know how much he has got left-nobody does. It's been the talk of the financial district. There isn't a share of stock anywhere to be found standing in his name. He sold everything; and how much was used to cover losses, and how much remained to himself no one knows. You see, the last few years, to put it mildly, have been hell in a financial and business way. The foreign exchange situation has been a big factor in helping to play the devil with all sorts of holdings. Values have depreciated; the market has gone smash. Industries that were big dividend payers haven't been able to meet their overhead. You may not believe it, but hundreds and hundreds have taken their money out of the banks, and, insisting on being paid in American gold certificates, when they couldn't get the actual gold itself, have hoarded it in the safe deposit vaults. God knows why! Just instances the general panicky conditions everywhere, I suppose. The aftermath of the war! History repeating itself, so the writers on economics tell us. Small consolation! However! Marlin met with crash after crash. He lost millions. He's not a young man, you know, and it evidently got him finally in the shape of a monomania. Finance! You understand? He was on a dozen big directorates and his trouble began to show itself in the shape of an obsession that everything should be turned into cash, buildings, plants, everything-into American cash. Naturally he was quietly and unostentatiously dropped. Poor devil! Certainly, his losses were terrific. I don't know whether he's got anything left or not."

"By Jove!" said Captain Francis Newcombe gravely. "I'm glad you told me. Pretty rough that, I call it."

"Yes," said Locke. "It is! Damned rough! I think everybody was sorry for him. And so he's down there at this place of his now on an island in the Florida Keys, eh?"

"Yes," said Captain Francis Newcombe.

The young American selected another cigarette from his case, rolled it slowly between his fingers-and leaned suddenly across the table.

"Look here!" he said. "I've an idea. I'm going cruising somewhere-why not there? The Florida coast hits me down to the ground. How would you like to make the trip with me?"

Captain Francis Newcombe leaned back in his chair, and laughed a little.

"I'm afraid not," he said. "I —"

"Oh, come on, be a sport!" urged Howard Locke enthusiastically. "The more I think of it, the better I like it. I'll have good company on a cruise, and you'll enjoy it. And it's quite all right so far as my showing up there is concerned. It isn't as though I were foisting myself on their hospitality. The little old boat's my home; and, for that matter, I can drop you and sail solemnly away. You'll have the time of your life. What's the objection?"

"Time," said Captain Francis Newcombe. "It would take a long while, wouldn't it?"

"Well," said Howard Locke, "I wouldn't guarantee to get you there as fast as a train would, but what difference does a few days make? It isn't as though it were a business engagement you had to keep."

"No; that's so," acknowledged Captain Francis Newcombe. "And frankly I must admit it appeals to me; but"—he looked at his watch—"I don't know whether I can manage it or not. Anyway, I promise to sleep on it. It's after twelve, and time to turn in. What do you say?"

"That suits me," said Howard Locke, "so long as you promise to say 'yes' in the morning."

"We'll see," said Captain Francis Newcombe.

The two men rose from their chairs, and, crossing the room where several games of bridge were in progress, stepped out on the deck. And here, their respective cabins lying in different directions, they bade each other good-night.

But now Captain Francis Newcombe, despite the pitching of the ship and the general unpleasantness of the night, appeared to be in no hurry. He walked slowly. It was the lee side, and under the covered deck he was protected from the rain. He looked behind him. The young American, evidently in no mind for anything but the snugger shelter of his cabin, had disappeared. The deck was deserted.

The ex-captain of territorials stepped to the rail, and stared out into the murk, through which there showed, like pencilled streaks on a black background, the white, irregular shapes of the cresting waves. The howl of the wind, the boom and crash of the seas made thunderous tumult, conflict, turmoil. And he laughed. And spume, flying, struck his face. And he laughed again because a sort of fierce exaltation was upon him, and he found something akin in these wild, untramelled voices of the elements—a challenge, far-flung and savage, and contemptuous of all who would say them nay.

And then his eyes narrowed thoughtfully, and his fingers played a soft tattoo upon the dripping rail.

"I wonder!" said Captain Francis Newcombe to himself. "I wonder if it suits my book?"

His mind began to moil over the problem in a cold, unprejudiced, judicial way. Was the balance for or against the acceptance of the young American's offer? To arrive at Marlin's place in the company of a man of the standing of Howard Locke was an endorsation that spoke for itself. But he already had an unqualified endorsation. Polly supplied it. Still, he could not have too much of that sort of thing. Would, then, the man be in the way, a hindrance, a complication? He could not answer that off-hand, but it did not seem to be a vital point. What he proposed to do on Manwa Island in a general way he knew well enough; but just how he proposed to do it, and just how long he proposed to stay there, a week, or a month, or longer, only local conditions as he found them must decide.

He shrugged his shoulders suddenly. Neither Howard Locke nor any other man would make of himself a hindrance-hindrances were removed. But there was another point, an outstanding point. After Manwa Island there was-America. True, he had brought Runnells with him, while he had said good-bye to Paul Cremarre, who had departed for Paris, and thereafter for such destination as his fancy prompted, for the period, mutually agreed upon, of six months-but he, Captain Francis Newcombe, was not prepared to say when, or where, if ever, he intended to utilise, in the same manner as before, the services of either Runnells or the Frenchman again. Certainly not in America, if a lone hand promised better there! He proposed to play a lone hand at this Manwa Island. It might well be that he would continue to do so thereafter. And in America an intimacy with Howard Locke, such as this projected cruise offered, would help amazingly to spread and germinate the seed already sown by Polly Wickes. Polly Wickes was his private property!

Captain Francis Newcombe smiled confidentially at the angry waters.

"Yes," he said, "I think it is quite possible that he may be able to *persuade* me."

He turned abruptly away from the rail, making for his cabin, which was on the deck above and on the opposite side of the ship. And presently, halting in the lighted alleyway before his door, he turned the key in the lock and entered.

And then, just across the threshold, he stood for the fraction of a second like a man dazed-and the door, torn from his hand by a fierce gust of wind, slammed with a bang behind him. The cabin was on the windward side, the window was open, and outside the window, indistinct, shadowy, as though almost it might be an hallucination of the mind, a man's form suddenly loomed up. There was a flash, the roar of a revolver shot, muffled, almost drowned out in the thunder of the storm-and Captain Francis Newcombe lay flat upon the cabin floor.

The next instant he flung himself over beside the settee, and protected here from another shot, raised his head. The form had vanished from the window.

A cold fury seized upon the man. From his pocket he drew his own revolver, and covering the window as he backed swiftly for the door, wrenched the door open and made for the first egress to the deck. Too late, of course! The deck was deserted. He stood there, grim-faced, tight-lipped, straining his eyes up and down the length of the deck through the darkness, the rain beating into his face.

And then he began to run again-like a dog seeking scent. There were a dozen places up here where a man might hide-the juts of the superstructure, the great, grotesque, looming ventilators, the openings through to the other side of the deck. But he found nothing, no one-there was only the deserted deck, the drenching rain. And the howl of the wind metamorphosed itself into ironical shrieks.

Captain Francis Newcombe returned along the deck, and halted outside his cabin window. He examined it critically. It had been pried open from the outside-the marks were distinctly indented on the sill, as though a jimmy, or iron bar of some kind, had been used.

He stared at it, his jaws clamped. It was unpleasant. Some one on the ship had deliberately, premeditatively, attempted to murder him. There was something of hideous malignancy in it. To pry the window open, and wait there patiently in the storm for the sole purpose of ending a man's life! It hadn't succeeded because intuition, or, perhaps, better, an exaggerated instinct of self-preservation born of the years in which he had flaunted defiance of every law in the face of his fellow men, had prompted him, though taken unawares, to act even quicker than his assailant who lay in wait, and to fling himself instantly to the floor of the cabin.

Who was it? Why was it? Who, on board the ship, had any incentive, any reason, any cause to murder him? Save for Locke, the young American, he knew no one on board, barring Runnells, of course, except in the ordinary, casual way of shipboard acquaintanceship struck up since the ship had left Liverpool. It could not be any one of these-at least, not logically. And of them all, it certainly could not be Locke. The ship's company? Absurd! Runnells? Still more absurd! And so he had eliminated *everybody*, and yet *somebody* had done it!

He began to work with the window. Reaching inside he drew the curtains carefully together, and then lowered the window itself. When he re-entered his room, even providing he were still being watched, he would not be exposed in the same way as a target again!

He stood there now in the rain, his face hard, with savage, drooping lines at the corners of his mouth. Was he being watched now? Was there a cat-and-mouse game in play? Well, two could play at that! He, too, could prowl about the ship. His bed held little of invitation for him!

He went to Runnells' room. The man was in bed asleep. That definitely disposed of Runnells!

He returned and made another circuit of the upper deck; and then, forward, by one of the open companionways, he descended to the deck below. His mind was in a strange state of turmoil. It was not physical fear. It was as though a host of haunting shapes were being mar-shalled against him, were rising up out of the past to disturb him, jeering at him, mocking him, plaguing him with sinister possibilities. The past was peopled with shapes, shapes that had lived in the world of Shadow Varne; shapes which might well be accused of this attempt to do away with him, could they but take tangible form, could their presence but be reconciled with the here and now, with this ship, with these damp, slippery decks, with the drive and sting of the rain, with the scream and howl of the wind, with the plunge and roll of the great liner, the buffeting of the waves-if they could but be reconciled with *material* things. He clenched his hands. He was not as a man who could search his memory in vain for one who owed him such a debt as this; it was, rather, that his memory became crowded and confused with the *number* that came thronging in upon it, each vying with the others to shriek the loudest its boasted claim to the attempted retribution to-night.

He set his teeth. Where had he failed? When had he left ajar behind him the door of the past that allowed any one of these ghostly shapes to slip through upon his heels? Ghostly? There was little of the ghostly here! He *must* have been recognised by some one on board the ship. It seemed incredible, impossible-but it was equally incontrovertible. Who? And what did it portend? To-night he had won the first hand, but —

Locke! He was standing beside the smoking room window. Locke was in there, his back turned, standing beside one of the bridge tables, watching a game. It was a little strange! He had parted with Locke out here on the deck-and Locke was going to his cabin to turn in.

For an instant Captain Francis Newcombe held there, his brows knitted in a perplexed frown. Howard Locke! It was preposterous; it would not hold water; it was childish-unless the young American were some one other than he pretended to be, and there wasn't a chance in a thousand of that! His mind worked swiftly now. Locke had been introduced to him at lunch in the club by a fellow member a few days before they had sailed. That certainly vouched for the man sufficiently, didn't it? Locke had volunteered the information that he had booked passage on this ship, and they had not met again until here on shipboard. If Locke was what he passed for, if he was of one of the best families of America, the son of a millionaire, a clever, hard-working and ambitious young business man, it was untenable to assume for an instant that he was a potential murderer. It was even laughable. There wasn't even that one chance in a thousand that he could be any other than he seemed, not a chance in a million, and yet —

"Chance," said Captain Francis Newcombe, "is the playground of fools. We will see!"

He turned and ran swiftly along the deck. A minute later he was standing before one of the two doors of the young American's suite. A little metal instrument was in his hand, but it went instantly back into his pocket-the door was not locked. He stepped inside and closed the door behind him. Locke had one of the best and most expensive reservations on the ship —a suite of two rooms and a private bath, but there was a separate door from each of these rooms to the passageway without, since, naturally, they were not always booked en suite. And the room he stood in now was the one Locke used for his sitting room, and always as the entrance to the suite itself.

Captain Francis Newcombe was quick in every movement now. He ran through to the other room-the bedroom-closing the connecting door behind him. He switched on the light, and turned at once to the door that gave here on the passageway. The key was in the lock, and the door was locked. He unlocked it. The next instant he had a portmanteau open and was delving into its contents. It contained nothing but clothing-shirts, collars, ties, underwear, and the like. He opened another, and still another with the same result. Papers! It was the man's papers that interested him.

He snarled a little savagely to himself. There was nothing for it then but the steamer trunk under the couch-and Locke might be back at any moment. He dragged out the trunk-and snarled again savagely. It was locked. He began to work with it now, swiftly, deftly, with the little steel picklock. It yielded finally, and he flung back the lid. Yes, this was what he wanted! On the top lay a leather despatch case. But this also was locked. Again Captain Francis Newcombe set to work-and presently was glancing through a mass of papers and documents that the despatch case had contained: letters from the father's firm to the son, signed by Locke senior; a letter of credit in substantial amount; an underwriting agreement with a London house for the floating of a huge issue of bonds, signed and sealed, the tangible evidence of young Locke's successful trip, of which he had spoken. Incontrovertible evidence that Howard Locke was no other than he appeared to be, and —

Captain Francis Newcombe sprang for the electric-light switch, and turned off the light. There was Locke now! The pound of the ship, the noise of the storm, had of course deadened any sound in the passageway, but he could hear the other at the sitting room door. There was no time to replace the despatch case and push the trunk back under the couch, let alone attempt to lock either one. The man was coming now-across the other room. Captain Francis Newcombe laid the despatch case silently down on the floor, opened the door as silently, stepped out into the passageway and ran noiselessly along it.

He reached the door of his own cabin. His excursion to Locke's cabin and the evidence of intrusion he had been forced to leave behind him had put an end to any more "prowling" on his part to-night. Locke would probably kick up a fuss. There would be a very strict search for "prowlers!" He snapped his jaws together viciously. That did not at all please him. He would very much prefer that the would-be assassin should have another opportunity of showing his hand, that the man would be inspired to make a *second* attempt. He, Captain Francis Newcombe, would be a little better prepared this time!

He pushed open the door of his cabin cautiously-and for an instant stood motionless, a little back from the threshold, and at one side. There was always the possibility, remote though it might be, that while he had been out searching for the other, the man had slipped inside and, waiting, had made of the cabin a death trap which he, Captain Francis Newcombe, was now invited to enter. It was not likely. It would require a little more nerve than the firing of a shot through the window, and then running away. But, for all that, having failed the first time, the other might be moved to take what might possibly be considered more certain measures on the next attempt. And in that case-No; the cabin was empty! The light from the passageway, filtering in through the open door, showed that quite plainly.

Captain Francis Newcombe stepped inside, and, before closing the door, looked curiously over the woodwork near the door and on a line with the window. Yes, there it was! The writing on the wall! The bullet had splintered a piece of the wall panelling, and had embedded itself in the wall a little to the right of the door casing.

He closed and locked the door now, shutting out the light, and, with his revolver in his hand, sat down in the darkness, out of direct range himself, but where he could command the window. It was a bit futile. He was conscious of that. But there was always the possibility of the man's return, and there was no other possibility that promised any better-or, indeed, promised anything at all.

His mind began to weigh, and sift, and grope as through a maze, battling with the problem again. Not Locke! He was rather definitely prepared to set Locke apart from everybody else on board the ship, and say that it was not Locke. Who, then? Who had any —

He straightened up, suddenly even more alert. There was some one out in the passageway now-some one outside his door. There came a low, quick rap.

"Who's there?" demanded Captain Francis Newcombe sharply.

Locke's voice answered:

"It's Locke. May I come in?"

Captain Francis Newcombe crossed to the door, unlocked it, and flung it open.

"Hello!" ejaculated the young American, as the light from the passageway fell upon the other. "Not in bed, and in the dark! What's the idea? Why no light?"

"Because I fancy it's safer-in the dark," said Captain Francis Newcombe. "Come in."

"Safer!" Howard Locke stepped into the cabin, and closed the door behind him. "How safer? Say, look here! Some one's been turning my stateroom inside out-been going through my things."

"You're lucky!" said Captain Francis Newcombe tersely.

"Lucky!" echoed the young American quickly. "What do you mean?"

"That it wasn't anything worse," said Captain Francis Newcombe coolly. "Some one's been trying to put a bullet through me-only it went into the wall over there instead. Here, take a look!" He switched on the light. "See it-there by the door casing!"

"Good God!" exclaimed Locke. "Yes; I see it! When was this?"

"Shortly after I left you. As I opened the door here and stepped into the cabin, I was fired at through the window. And the window had been opened from the outside-there are marks on it-and whoever it was, was waiting for me."

"That's damned queer," said Howard Locke. "When I left you I went to my rooms, and everything was all right. I went back to the smoking room because I had left my cigarette case there. I stayed a few minutes watching several hands of bridge, and when I went back to my rooms again I found my steamer trunk open and a case of papers on the floor."

"Anything missing?" asked Captain Francis Newcombe.

"No; not so far as I know," Locke answered. "What do you think had better be done?"

"I think you had better switch that light off, and stand away from the line of the window."

The young American shook his head.

"No," he said. "It's hardly likely that the same game would be tried twice in the same night. Say, what do you make of it? It seems mighty queer that you and I should have been picked out for some swine's attentions! What should be done?"

"What *have* you done?"

"Nothing, so far," Locke replied. "I came here at once to tell you about it, and ask your advice. I suppose the commander ought to be told."

Captain Francis Newcombe sat down on the edge of his bunk.

"I can't see the good of it," he said slowly. "We're landing to-morrow. It would mean the shore police aboard, and no end of a fuss; and an almost certain delay, nobody allowed off the ship, and all that, you know. I can't see how it would get us anywhere. You haven't lost anything; and I —well, I'm still alive."

"That's true," said Locke. He was staring at the bullet hole in the wall. "And worst of all there'd be the reporters. Three-inch headlines! I'm not for *that*! I agree with you. We'll say nothing."

Captain Francis Newcombe inspected Locke's back.

"How much of a crew do you carry on this fifty-footer of yours?" he inquired softly.

"Why not necessarily any one but the two of us and your man, if you'll come along." Howard Locke turned around suddenly to face the other. "Why?"

"Well," said Captain Francis Newcombe quietly, "under those conditions, as the two victims of to-night, we'd form a sort of mutual protective society-and perhaps, if the offer is still open, it would be the safest way for me to reach my destination. There wouldn't be any windows for any one to fire through."

Howard Locke lighted a cigarette.

"That's a go!" he said. "I'm very keen to make the trip with you. And if all this has decided it, I'm glad it's happened. That's fine! And now-what are you going to do for the rest of the night?"

"Why, I'm going to bed," said Captain Francis Newcombe casually; "and at the risk of appearing inhospitable, I should advise you to do likewise."

"Right!" agreed Locke. "There's nothing else to do." He stepped toward the door, but paused, staring at the bullet mark in the wall again.

"That bullet hole seems to fascinate you," smiled Captain Francis Newcombe.

"Yes," said Locke, as he opened the door. "I was thinking what a rotten thing it was to be fired at cold-bloodedly in the dark. Good-night!"

The door closed.

Captain Francis Newcombe did not go to bed. With the light out again, he sat there on the bunk.

Long minutes passed; they drifted into hours.

The man's figure became crouched, became a shape that lost human semblance, that was like unto some creature huddled in its lair; and the face was no longer human, for upon it was stamped the passions of hell; and the head became cocked curiously sideways in a strained attitude of attention, as though listening, listening, listening, always listening.

And there came a time when he spoke aloud, and called out hoarsely:

"Who's that? Who's whispering there? Who's calling Shadow Varne ... Shadow Varne ... Shadow Varne...."

And in answer the ship's bell struck the hour of dawn.

Book II:
The Isle of Prey

I
The Spell of the Moonbeams

It was a night of white moonlight; a languorous night. It was a night of impenetrable shadows, deep and black; and, where light and shadow met and merged, the treetops were fringed against the sky in tracery as delicate as a cameo. And there was fragrance in the air, exotic, exquisite, the fragrance of growing things, of semi-tropical flowers and trees and shrubs. And very faint and soft there fell upon the ear the gentle lapping of the water on the shore, as though in her mother tenderness nature were breathing a lullaby over her sea-cradled isle.

On a verandah of great length and spacious width, moon-streaked where the light stole in through the row of ornamental columns that supported the roof and through the interstices of vine-covered lattice work, checkering the flooring in fanciful designs, a girl raised herself suddenly on her elbow from a reclining chair, and, reaching out her hand, laid it impulsively on that of another girl who sat in a chair beside her.

"Oh, Dora," she breathed, "it's just like fairyland!"

Dora Marlin smiled quietly.

"What a queer little creature you are, Polly!" she said. "You like it here, don't you?"

"I *love* it!" said Polly Wickes.

"Fairyland!" Dora Marlin repeated the word. "Wouldn't it be wonderful if there were a real fairyland just like the stories they used to read to us as children?"

Polly Wickes nodded her head slowly.

"I suppose so," she said; "but I never had any fairy stories read to me when I was a child, and so my fairyland has always been one of my own-one of dreams. And this is fairyland because it's so beautiful, and because being here doesn't seem as though one were living in the same world one was born in at all."

"You poor child!" said Dora Marlin softly. "A land of dreams, then! Yes; I know. These nights *are* like that sometimes, aren't they? They make you dream any dream you want to have come true, and, while you dream wide awake, you almost actually experience its fulfilment then and there. And so it is nearly as good as a real fairyland, isn't it? And anyway, Polly, you look like a really, truly fairy yourself to-night."

"No," said Polly Wickes. "You are the fairy. Fairies aren't supposed to be dark; they have golden hair, and blue eyes, and —"

"A wand," interrupted Dora Marlin, with a mischievous little laugh. "And if it weren't all just make-believe, and I *was* the fairy, I'd wave my wand and have *him* appear instantly on the scene; but, as it is, I'm afraid he won't come to-night after all, and it's getting late, and I think we'd better go to bed."

"And I'm sure he will come, and anyway I couldn't go to bed," said Polly Wickes earnestly. "And anyway I couldn't go to sleep. Just think, Dora, I haven't seen him for nearly four years, and I'll have all the news, and hear everything I want to know about mother. He said they'd leave the mainland to-day, and it's only five hours across. I'm sure he'll still come. And, besides, I'm certain I heard a motor boat a few minutes ago."

"Very likely," agreed Dora Marlin; "but that was probably one of our own men out somewhere around the island. It's very late now, and in half an hour it will be low tide, and they would hardly start at all if they knew they wouldn't make Manwa by daylight. There are the reefs, and —"

"The reefs are charted," said Polly Wickes decisively. "I know he'll come."

A little ripple of laughter came from Dora Marlin's chair.

"How old is Captain Newcombe, dear?" she inquired naïvely.

"Don't be a beast, Dora," said Polly Wickes severely. "He's very, very old-at least he was when I saw him last."

"When you weren't much more than fourteen," observed Dora Marlin judicially. "And when you're fourteen anybody over thirty is a regular Methuselah. I know I used to think when I was a child that father was terribly, terribly old, much older than he seems to-day when he really is an old man; and I used to wonder then how he lived so long."

Polly Wickes' dark eyes grew serious.

"It doesn't apply to me," she said in a low tone. "I wasn't ever a child. I was old when I was ten. I've told you all about myself, because I couldn't have come here with you if I hadn't; and you know why I am so eager and excited and so happy that guardy is coming. I owe him everything in the world I've got; and he's been so good to mother. I —I don't know why. He said when I was older I would understand. And he's such a wonderful man himself, with such a splendid war record."

Dora Marlin rose from her chair, and placed her arm affectionately around her companion's shoulders.

"Yes, dear," she said gently. "I know. I was only teasing. And you wouldn't be Polly Wickes if you wanted to do anything else than just sit here and wait until you were quite, quite sure that he wouldn't come to-night. But as I'm already sure he won't because it's so late, I'm going to bed. You don't mind, do you, dear? I want to see if father's all right, too. Poor old dad!"

"Dora!" Polly Wickes was on her feet. "Oh, Dora, I'm so selfish! I —I wish I could help. But I'm sure it's going to be all right. I don't think that specialist was right at all. How could he be? Mr. Marlin is such a dear!"

Dora Marlin turned her head away, and for a moment she did not speak. When she looked around again there was a bright, quick smile on her lips.

"I am counting a lot on Captain Newcombe's and Mr. Locke's visit," she said. "I'm sure it will do father good. Good-night, dear-and if they do come, telephone up to my room and I'll be down in a jiffy. Their rooms are all ready for them, but they're sure to be famished, and —"

"I'll do nothing of the sort!" announced Polly Wickes. "The idea of upsetting a household in the middle of the night! I'll send them back to their yacht."

"You won't do anything of the kind!" said Dora Marlin.

"Yes, I will," said Polly Wickes.

"Well, he won't come anyway," said Dora Marlin.

"Yes, he will!"

"No, he won't!"

They both began to laugh.

"But I'll tell you what I'll do," said Polly Wickes. "After he's gone I'll creep into bed with you and tell you all about it. Good-night, dear."

"Good-night, Polly fairy," said Dora Marlin.

Polly Wickes watched the white form weave itself in and out of the checkered spots of moonlight along the verandah, and finally disappear inside the house; then she threw herself down upon the reclining chair again, her hands clasped behind her head, and lay there, strangely alert, wide-eyed, staring out on the lawn.

She was quite sure he would come-even yet-because when they had sent over to the mainland for the mail yesterday there had been a letter from him saying he would arrive some time to-day.

How soft the night was!

Would he be changed; would he seem very different? Had what Dora had said about the viewpoint from which age measures age been really true? And if it were? *She* was the one who would seem changed-from a little girl in pigtails to a woman, not a very old woman, but a woman. Would he know her, recognise her again?

What a wonderful, glorious, dreamy night it was!

Dreams! Was she dreaming even now, dreaming wide awake, that she was here; a dream that supplanted the squalour of narrow, ill-lighted streets, of dark, creaking staircases, of lurking, hungry shapes, of stalking vice, of homes that were single, airless rooms gaunt with poverty —a dream that supplanted all that for this, where there was only a world of beautiful things, and where even the airs that whispered through the trees were balmy with some rare perfume that intoxicated the senses with untold joy?

She startled herself with a sharp little cry. Pictures, memories, vivid, swift in succession, were flashing, unbidden, through her mind —a girl in ragged clothes who sold flowers on the street corners, in the parks, a gutter-snipe the London "bobbies" had called her so often that the term had lost any personal meaning save that it classified the particular species of outcasts to which she had belonged; a room that was reached through the climbing of a smutty, dirty staircase in a tenement that moaned in its bitter fight against dissolution in common with its human occupants, a room that was scanty in its furnishings, where a single cot bed did service for two, and a stagnant odour of salt fish was never absent; a woman that was grey-haired, sharp-faced, of language and actions at times that challenged even the license of Whitechapel, but one who loved, too; the smells from the doors of pastry shops on the better streets that had made her cry because they had made her more hungry than ever; the leer of men when she had grown a few years older who thought a gutter-snipe both defenceless and fair game.

She had never been a child.

Polly Wickes had turned in the reclining chair, and her face now was buried in the cushion.

And then into her life had come-had come-this "guardy." He did not leer at her; he was kind and courtly-like-like what she had thought a good father might have been. But she had not understood the cataclysmic, bewildering and stupendous change that had then taken place in her life, and so she had asked her mother. She had always remembered the answer; she always would.

"Never you mind, dearie," Mrs. Wickes had said. "Wot's wot is wot. 'E's a gentleman is Captain Newcombe, a kind, rich gentleman, top 'ole 'e is. An' if 'e's a-goin' to adopt yer, I ain't goin' to 'ave to worry any more abaht wot's goin' into my mouth; an' though I ain't got religion, I says, as I says to 'im when 'e asks me, thank Gawd, I says. An' if we're a-goin' to be separated for a few years, dearie, wye it's a sacrifice as both of us 'as got to myke for each other."

They had been separated for nearly four years. As fourteen understood it, she had understood that she was to be taught to live in a different world, to acquire the viewpoints of a different station in life, in order that she might fit herself to take her place in that world and that station where her guardian lived and moved. To-day she understood this in a much more mature way. And she had tried to do her best-but she could never forget the old life no matter how com-pletely severed she might be from it, or how far from it she might be removed even in a physical sense; though gradually, she was conscious, the past had become less real, less poignant, and more like some dream that came at times, and lingered hauntingly in her memory.

The hardest part of it all had been the separation from her mother, but she would see her mother soon now, for Captain Newcombe had promised that she should go back to England when her education was finished in America. And her education was finished now-the last term was behind her. Four years-her mother! Even if that separation had seemed necessary and essential to her guardian, how wonderful and dear he had been even in that respect. How happy he had made them both! Indeed, her greatest happiness came from the knowledge that her mother, since those four years began, had removed from the squalour and distress that she had previously known all her life, and had lived since then in comfort and ease. Her mother could not read or write, of course, but —

Polly Wickes caught her breath in a little, quick, half sob. Could not read or write! It seemed to mean so much, to visualise so sharply that other world, to-to bring the odour of salt fish, the nauseous smell of guttering tallow candles. No, no; that was all long gone now, gone forever, for both her mother and herself. What did it matter if her mother could not read or write? It *had* not mattered. Even here guardy had filled the breach-written the letters that her mother had dictated, and read to her mother the letters that she, Polly, sent in her guardian's care. And her mother had told her how happy she was, and how comfortable in a cosy little home on a pretty little street in the suburbs.

Was it any wonder that she was beside herself with glad excitement to-night, when at any moment now the one person in all the world who had been so good to her, to whom she owed a debt of gratitude that she could never even be able to express, much less repay, would-would actually, *really* be here? For he would come! She was sure of it. After all, it wasn't so *very* late, and —

She rose suddenly from the reclining chair, her heart pounding in quickened, excited throbs, and ran lightly to the edge of the verandah. He was here now. She had heard a footstep. She could not have been mistaken. It was as though some one had stepped on loose gravel. She peered over the balustrade, and her forehead puckered in a perplexed frown. There wasn't any one in sight; and there wasn't any gravel on which a footstep could have crunched. All around the house in this direction there was only the soft velvet sward of the beautifully kept lawn. The driveway was at the other side of the house. She had forgotten that. And yet it did not seem possible she could have been mistaken. Imagination, fancy, could hardly have reproduced so perfect an imitation of such a sound.

It was very strange! It was very strange that she should have-No; she hadn't been mistaken! She *had* heard a footstep-but it had come from under the verandah, and some one was there now. She leaned farther out over the balustrade, and stared with widened eyes at a movement in the hedge of tall, flowering bush that grew below her along the verandah's length. A low rustle came now to her ears. Sheltered by the hedge, some one was creeping cautiously, stealthily along there under the verandah.

Her hands tightened on the balustrade. What did it mean? No good, that was certain. She was afraid. And suddenly the peace and quietness and serenity of the night was gone. She was afraid. And it had always seemed so safe here on this wonderful little island, so free from intrusion. There was something snakelike in the way those bushes moved.

She watched them now, fascinated. Something bade her run into the house and cry out an alarm; something held her there clinging to the balustrade, her eyes fixed on that spot below her just a few yards along from where she stood. She could make out a figure now, the figure of a man crawling warily out through the hedge toward the lawn. And then instinctively she caught her hand to her lips to smother an involuntary cry, and drew quickly back from the edge of the balustrade. The figure was in plain sight now on the lawn in the moonlight —a figure in a long dressing gown; a figure without hat, whose silver hair caught the sheen of the soft light and seemed somehow to give the suggestion of ghostlike whiteness to the thin, strained face beneath.

It was Mr. Marlin.

For a moment Polly watched the other as he made his way across the lawn in a diagonal direction toward the grove of trees that surrounded the house. Fear was gone now, supplanted by a wave of pity. Poor Mr. Marlin! The specialist had been right. Of course, he had been right! She had never doubted it-nor had Dora. What she had said to Dora had been said out of sympathy and love. They both understood that. It-it helped a little to keep up Dora's courage; it kept hope alive. Mr. Marlin was so kindly, so lovable and good. But he was an incurable monomaniac. And now he was out here on the lawn in the middle of the night in his dressing gown. What was it that he was after? Why had he stolen out from the house in such an extraordinarily surreptitious way?

She turned and ran softly along the verandah, and down the steps to the lawn, and stood still again, watching. There was no need of getting Dora out of bed because in any case Mr. Marlin could certainly come to no harm; and, besides, she, Polly, could tell Dora all about it in the morning. But, that apart, she was not quite certain what she ought to do. The strange, draped figure of the old man had disappeared amongst the trees now, apparently having taken the path that led to the shore. Mechanically she started forward, half running-then slowed her pace almost immediately to a hesitating walk. Had she at all any right to spy on Mr. Marlin? It was not as though any harm could come to him, or that he —

And then with a low, quick cry, her eyes wide, Polly Wickes stood motionless in the centre of the lawn.

II

The Voice in the Night

Captain Francis Newcombe, from the dock where he had been making fast a line, surveyed for a moment the deck of the *Talofa* below. His eyes rested speculatively on Howard Locke, who, with sleeves rolled up and grimy to the elbows, was busy over the yacht's engine; then his glance passed to Runnells on the forward deck of the little vessel, who was assiduously engaged in making shipshape coils of a number of truant ropes. Captain Francis Newcombe permitted a flicker to cross his lips. It was a new experience for Runnells, this playing at sailorman-and Runnells had earned ungrudging praise from Locke all the way down from New York. Runnells had taken to the job even as a child takes to a new toy. Well, so much the better! Runnells and Locke had hit it off together from the start. Again, so much the better!

He lit a cigarette and stared shoreward along the dock. Manwa Island! Well, in the moonlight at least it was a place of astounding beauty, and if its appearance was any criterion of its material worth, it was a — He laughed softly, and languidly exhaled a cloud of cigarette smoke. There was a lure about the place-or was it the moonlight that, stealing with dreamy treachery upon the senses, carried one away to a land of make-believe? That stretch of sand there like a girdle between sea and shore, as fleecy as driven snow; the restless shimmer of the moonbeams on the water like the play of clustered diamonds in a platinum setting; the trees and open spaces etched against myriad stars; the smell of semi-tropical growing things, just pure fragrance that made the nostrils greedy with insatiable desire.

He drew his hand suddenly across his eyes.

"What a night!" he exclaimed aloud. "It's like the eyes and the lips of a dream woman; like a goblet of wine of the vintage of the gods! No song of the sirens could compare with this! I'm going ashore, Locke. What do you say?"

Locke looked up with a grunt, as he swabbed his arms with a piece of waste.

"I'm done in with this damned engine!" he said irritably. "It's too late to go ashore. They'll all be asleep."

"I'm not going to ring the doorbell," said Captain Francis Newcombe pleasantly. "I'm simply going to stroll in paradise. You don't mind, do you?"

"Go to it!" said Locke. "I'm going to bed."

"Right!" said Captain Francis Newcombe.

He turned and walked shoreward along the dock. Over his shoulder he saw Runnells pause in the act of coiling rope to stare after him-and again an ironical little flicker crossed his lips. Runnells was no doubt prompted to call out and ask what this midnight excursion was all about, but Runnells in the eyes of Howard Locke was a valet, and Runnells must therefore be dumb. Runnells on occasions knew his place!

He nodded in a sort of self-commendatory fashion to himself, as, reaching the shore, he started forward along a roadway that opened through the trees. He was well satisfied with his decision to bring Runnells along on the trip. "Captain Francis Newcombe and man" looked well, sounded well, and was well-since Runnells, for once in his life, even though it was due to no moral regeneration on the part of Runnells, but due entirely to Runnells' belief that he was on an innocent holiday, could be made exceedingly useful in bolstering up his master's social standing without bagging any of the game!

"Blessed is he who expects little," murmured Captain Francis Newcombe softly to himself, "for he shall receive-still less!"

He paused abruptly, and stared ahead of him. Curious road, this! Like a great archway of trees! And all moon-flecked underfoot! Where did it lead? To the house probably! This was Manwa Island-the home of the mad millionaire! Queer freak of nature, these Florida Keys-if what he had been able to read up about them was true. Almost a continuous bow of islands, some fruitful, some barren, some big, some small-such a heterogeneous mess! —stretching along off the coast, some near, some far, for two hundred miles. Nothing but rocks on one;

tropical fruits and verdure in profusion on another! Well, the mad millionaire, if the night revealed anything, had picked the gem of them all!

He walked on again. The road wound tortuously through what appeared to be a glade of great extent. It seemed to beckon, to lure, to intrigue him the farther he went, to promise something around each moon-flecked turning. He laughed aloud softly. Promised what? Where was he going? Why was he here ashore at all? Was it possible that he had no ulterior motive in this stroll, that for once the sheer beauty of anything held him in thrall? Well, even so, it at least afforded him a laugh at himself then. This road, for instance, was like an enchanted pathway, and there was magic in the night.

Or was it Polly?

Captain Francis Newcombe shook his head. Hardly! Not at this hour! Thanks to the engine trouble that had delayed them, she would long since have given up expecting him to-night, even though he had written her that he would be here.

The house, then? A surreptitious inspection; an entry even?—there were half a million dollars there! Again he shook his head. He was not so great a fool as to *invite* disaster. To-morrow, and for days thereafter, he would be an inmate of the house when he would have opportunities of that nature without number, and without entailing any risk or suspicion-and time was no object.

He smiled complacently to himself. Things were shaping up very well-very well indeed. The seed so carefully planted years ago was to bear fruit at last. The greatest coup of his life was just within his grasp; and, if he were not utterly astray, that very coup in itself should prove but the stepping stone to still greater ones. Polly! Yes, quite true! The future depended very materially upon Polly. How amenable would she be to influence?—granting always that the said influence be delicately and tactfully enough applied!

He fell to whistling very softly under his breath. He had plans for Polly. And if they matured the future looked very bright-for himself. He wondered what she was like-particularly as to character and disposition. Was she affectionate, romantic-what? A great deal, a very great deal, depended on that. Not in the present instance-Polly had fully served her purpose in so far as a certain half million dollars in cash was concerned, and being innocent of any connivance must remain so-but thereafter. England was an exploited field; it had become dangerous; the net there was drawing in. Oh, yes, he had had all that in mind on the day he had first sent Polly to America, but only in a general way then, while to-day it had become concrete. Locke would make a most admirable "open sesame" to the New Land-if Locke married Polly. Polly, as Mrs. Locke, would step at once into a social sphere than which there was no higher —*or wealthier* —and, *ipso facto*, Captain Francis Newcombe would do likewise. And given a half million as stake money, Captain Francis Newcombe, if he knew Captain Francis Newcombe at all, would not fail in his opportunities! He had expected Polly in due course to make a place for herself in social America; that was what he had paid money for-but Howard Locke was a piece of luck. Locke conserved time; Locke opened the safety vault of possibilities immediately.

He frowned suddenly. Suppose Polly did not prove amenable? Nonsense! Why shouldn't she-if the man weren't flung at her head! Locke was the kind of chap a girl ought to like, and all girls *were* more or less romantic, and the element of romance had just the right spice to it here-the guardian she has not seen in years who is accompanied by a young man, who, from any standpoint, whether of looks, physique, manner or position, would measure up to the most exacting of young ladies' ideals! And to say nothing of the magic spells that seemed to have their very home in this garden isle —a veritable wooer's bower! There would be other moonlight nights. Bah! There was nothing to it-save to put a few minor obstacles in the way of the turtle doves!

Where the devil did this road lead to? Well, no matter! It was like a tunnel, dreamy black with its walls of leaves, dreamy with its sweet-smelling odours. In itself it was well worth while. It continued to invite him. And he accepted the invitation. His thoughts roved farther afield now. Locke ... the trip down on the fifty-foot *Talofa* ... not an incident to mar the days-nothing since the night that shot had been fired on shipboard through his cabin window.

His face for a moment grew dark-then cleared again. If, as through the hours thereafter when he had sat there in the cabin, it had seemed as though the shot had come from some ghostly visitor out of the past, there was no reason now why it should bother him further; for, granting such a diagnosis as true, Locke and the *Talofa* had thrown even so acute a stalker as a supernatural spirit off the trail. As a matter of fact, it had probably been some maniacal or drug-crazed idiot running for the moment amuck. To-night, with these soft, whispering airs around him, and serenity and loveliness everywhere in contrast with that night of storm, the incident did not seem so virulent a thing anyway; it seemed to be *smoothed* over, to be relegated definitely to where it belonged-to the realm of things ended and done with. Certainly, since that night nothing had happened.

And yet, now, his lips tightened.

It was unfortunate he had not caught the man. He would have liked to have seen the other's *face*; to have exchanged memory with memory-and to have slammed forever shut that particular door of the bygone days if by any chance he found he had been careless enough to have left one, in passing, ajar.

He swore sharply under his breath; but the next moment shrugged his shoulders. The incident was too immeasurably far removed from Manwa Island to allow it to intrude itself upon him now. Why think of things such as that when the very night itself here with its languor, its beauty, and-yes, again-its magic, sought to bring to the senses the gift of delightful repose and contentment? When the —

He stood suddenly still, and in sheer amazement rubbed his eyes. He had come to the end of the tree-arched road, and it seemed as though he gazed now on the imaginative painting of a master genius, daring, bold in its conception, exquisite in its execution. Either that, or there *was* magic in the night, and he had been transported bodily through enchantment into the very land of the Arabian Nights!

A few yards away, he faced what looked in the moonlight like a great marble balustrade, and rising above this, painted into a hue of softest white against the night, towered what might well have been a caliph's palace. It stretched away in lines unusual in their beauty and design; columns above the balustrade; little domes like minarets against the sky line; quaint latticed windows. And the effect of the whole was that of a mirage on a sea of emerald green; for, sweeping away from the balustrade, wondrous in its colour under the moonlight, was a wide expanse of lawn, level, unbroken until the eye met again the horizon rim beyond in the wall of encircling trees, a wall of inky blackness.

He moved forward out on to the lawn-and as suddenly halted again, as there seemed to float into his line of vision from around the corner of the balustrade, like some nymph of the moonlight, the slim, graceful figure of a girl in white, clinging draperies, whose clustering masses of dark hair crowned a face that in the soft light was amazingly beautiful. And he caught his breath as he gazed. And the girl, with a low cry, stood still-and then came running toward him.

"Oh, guardy! Guardy! Guardy!" she cried. "I knew you'd come! I knew it!"

It was Polly's voice. It hadn't changed. Was the nymph Polly? She was running with both hands outstretched. He caught them in his own as she came up to him, and stared into her face almost unbelievingly. Polly! This wasn't Polly! Polly's photographs were of a very pretty girl-this girl was glorious! She stirred the pulses. Damn it, she made the blood leap!

She hung back now a little shyly, the colour coming and going in her face.

He laughed. He meant it to be a laugh of one entirely in command both of himself and the situation; but it sounded in his ears as a laugh forced, unnatural, a poor effort to cover a suddenly routed composure.

"And is this all the welcome I get?" he demanded. He drew her closer to him. Gad, why not take his rights? She was worth it!

She held up her cheek demurely.

"I —I wasn't quite sure," she said coyly. "One's deportment with one's guardian wasn't in the school curriculum, you know-guardy!"

"Then I should have been more particular in my selection of the school," he said. It was strange, unaccountable! His voice seemed to rasp. He kissed her-then held her off at arm's-length. Polly! This bewitching creature was Polly! How the colour came and fled; and something glistened in the great, dark eyes-like the dew glistening in the morning sunlight.

"Oh, guardy!" she murmured. "It's so good to see you!"

"You waited up for me, Polly?" he asked.

"Yes," she answered. "Dora was sure you wouldn't come to-night because it was so late, and on account of it being low tide; but I was equally sure you would."

"Of course, I would!" said Captain Francis Newcombe glibly. "And I'm here. We're just in. I was afraid it was hopelessly late; but I didn't want to disappoint you in case you might still be clinging to what must have seemed a forlorn hope, and so I came ashore on the chance."

"Guardy," she said delightedly, "you're the only guardy in the world! But what happened? You were to have left the mainland to-day, and it's only five hours across."

"You'll have to ask Locke," he smiled. "That is, as to details-when he's in a better humour. In a general way, however, the engine broke down. We've been since one o'clock this afternoon getting over."

"Oh!" she exclaimed. "What perfectly wretched luck! And where's Mr. Locke now? And-no-first, you must tell me about mother. Is she changed any? Is she well, and quite, quite happy? And does she like her home? Is it pretty? And how —"

"Good heavens, Polly!" expostulated Captain Francis Newcombe with assumed helplessness. "What a volley!" But his mind was at work swiftly, coldly, judicially. To preface his visit with the announcement of Mrs. Wickes' untimely-or was it timely? —end, would create an atmosphere that would not at all harmonise with his plans. Polly in mourning and retirement! Locke! Impossible! Nor did it suit him to explain that Mrs. Wickes was not her mother. He was not yet sure when that particular piece of information might best be used to advantage. And so Captain Francis Newcombe laughed disengagingly. "I can't possibly answer all those questions to-night —we'd be here until daylight. The mother's quite all right, Polly-quite all right. You can pump me dry to-morrow."

"Oh, I'm so glad-and so happy!" she cried. She clapped her hands together. "All right, to-morrow! We'll talk all day long. Well, then, about Mr. Locke-where is he? And how did you come to make such a trip? You know, you just wrote that you were coming down from New York on his yacht. Who is he? Tell me about him."

Locke! Damn it, the girl was incredibly beautiful-the figure of a young goddess! What hair! Those lips! Fool! What was the matter with him? Polly was only a tool to be used; not to turn his head just because she had proved to be a bit of a feminine wonder. Fool! The downfall of every outstanding figure in his profession had been traceable to a woman. It was a police axiom. It did not apply to Shadow Varne! A girl-bah-the world was full of them! And yet — His hand at his side clenched, while his lips smiled.

"That's something else for to-morrow," he said. "You'll meet him then, and" —what was it he had said to himself a little while ago about slight obstacles in the way of the turtle doves? —"I hope you'll like him, though I've an idea that perhaps you won't."

"Why won't I?" demanded Polly instantly.

"Well, I don't know-upon my word, I don't," said Captain Francis Newcombe with a quizzical grin. "He certainly isn't strikingly handsome; and I've an idea he's anything but a ladies' man-though not altogether a bad sort in spite of that, you know."

"Oh!" said Polly Wickes, with a little pout that might have meant anything. "Well, who is he, then-and where did you meet him?"

"I met him at the club in London, and we chummed up on the way over. It's quite simple. He was off for a holiday with no choice as to where he went, whereas I wanted to come here-so we came down in his motor cruiser. As to who he is, he's just young Howard Locke, the son of Howard Locke, senior, the American financier."

"Oh!" said Polly Wickes again.

What a ravishing little pout! Where had the girl learned the trick? Was it a trick? Those eyes were wonderfully frank, steady, ingenuous-wonderfully deep and self-reliant. He wondered if he looked old in those eyes? *Young* Locke! Fool again! Go on, tempt the gods! Ask her if thirty-three fell within her own category of youth, or —

"Don't make a sound!" she cautioned suddenly. "Quick! Here!"

He found himself, obedient to the pressure on his arm, standing back again within the shadows of the tree-arched road.

"What is it, Polly?" he asked in surprise.

"Look!" she whispered, and pointed out across the lawn.

A figure was emerging from the trees some hundred yards away, and, in the open now, began to approach the house. Captain Francis Newcombe stared. It was a bare-headed, white-haired old man in a dressing gown that reached almost to his heels. The man walked quickly, but with a queer, bird-like movement of his head which he cocked from side to side at almost every step, darting furtive glances in all directions around him.

Captain Francis Newcombe felt the girl's hand tighten in a tense grip on his arm. Rather curious, this! The figure was making for that hedge of bushes that seemed to enclose the verandah from below. And now, reaching the hedge, and pausing for an instant to look around him again in every direction, the man parted the bushes and disappeared under the verandah.

"My word!" observed Captain Francis Newcombe tersely. "What's it about? A thief in the night-or what? I'll see what the beggar's up to anyway!"

He took a step forward, but Polly held him back.

"Keep quiet!" she breathed. "It's —it's only Mr. Marlin."

Captain Francis Newcombe whistled low under his breath.

"As bad as that, is he?"

Polly nodded her head.

"Yes," she said a little miserably. "I'm afraid so; though it's the first time I ever saw anything like this."

"But what is he doing under the verandah there at this hour?" demanded Captain Francis Newcombe.

Polly shook her head this time.

"I don't know," she said; "but I think there must be some way in and out of the house under there, for I am certain he was in bed less than an hour ago, because when Dora left me she was going to see that her father was all right for the night, and if she hadn't found him in his room, I am sure she would have been alarmed and would have come back to me. I —I saw him come out of there a little while ago. I was sitting on the verandah waiting for you. I started to follow him across the lawn, and then I thought I had no right to do so, and then I saw you, and-and I forgot all about him."

Captain Francis Newcombe was a master of facial expression. He became instantly grave and concerned.

"Well, I should say then," he stated thoughtfully, "that, from what I've just seen, and from what you wrote in your letter about the fabulous sum of money he keeps about him, he ought to have a good deal of medical attention, and the money taken from him and put in some safe place. Don't you know Miss Marlin well enough to suggest something like that?"

Polly Wickes shook her head quickly.

"Oh, you don't understand, guardy!" she said anxiously. "He has had medical attention. The very best specialist from New York has been here since I wrote you. And he says there is really absolutely nothing that can be done. Mr. Marlin is just the dearest old man you ever knew. It's just on that one subject, not so much money as finance, though I don't quite understand the difference, that he is insane. If he were taken away from here and shut up anywhere it would kill him. And, as Doctor Daemer said, what better place could there be than this? And anyway Dora wouldn't hear of it. And as for taking the money away from him, nobody knows where it is."

Captain Francis Newcombe was staring at the bushes that fringed the verandah.

"Oh!" he said quietly. "That puts quite a different complexion on the matter. I didn't understand. I gathered from your letter that the money was more or less always in evidence. In fact, I think you said he showed it to you —a half million dollars in cash."

"So he did," Polly answered; "but that's the only time I ever saw it; and I don't think even Dora has ever seen it more than once or twice. He has got it hidden somewhere, of course; but as it would be the very worst thing in the world for him to get the idea into his head that any one was watching him in an effort to discover his secret, Dora has been very careful to show no signs of interest in it. Doctor Daemer warned her particularly that any suspicions aroused in her father's mind would only accentuate the disease. Oh, guardy, it's a terribly sad case; and insanity is such a horribly strange thing! He never seems to —"

Polly was still talking. Captain Francis Newcombe inclined his head from time to time in assumed interest. He was no longer listening. Polly, the beauty of the night, his immediate surroundings, were, for the moment, extraneous things. His mind was at work. Incredible luck! The problem that had troubled him, that he had never really solved, that he had, indeed, finally decided must be left to circumstances as he should find them here and be then governed thereby, was now solved in a manner that far exceeded anything he could possibly have hoped for. To obtain the actual possession of the money from a fuddle-brained old idiot had never bothered him-that was a very simple matter. But to get away with the money after the robbery had been committed had not appeared so simple. Some one on the island must be guilty. The circle would be none too wide. He must emerge without a breath of suspicion having touched him. Not so simple! There would have been a way, of course; wits and ingenuity would have supplied it-but that had been the really intricate part of the undertaking. And now-incredible luck! He had naturally assumed that the household knew where the old madman kept his money; naturally assumed that there would be a beastly fuss and uproar over its disappearance-but now there would be nothing of the kind. It might take a few days to solve the old fool's secret, but in the main that would be child's play; after that, if by any unfortunate chance an accident happened to Mr. Jonathan P. Marlin, the whereabouts of the money would forever remain a mystery-save to one Captain Francis Newcombe. No one could, or would, be accused of having *taken* it!

"...Guardy, you quite understand, don't you?" ended Polly Wickes.

Captain Francis Newcombe smiled at the upturned, serious face.

"Quite, Polly! Quite!" he answered earnestly. "Very fully, I might say. It must be very hard indeed on Miss Marlin. I am so sorry for her. I wish there were something we might do. Your being here must have been a blessing to her."

The colour stole into Polly Wickes' cheeks.

"Guardy, you're a dear!" she whispered.

"Am I?" he said-and took possession of her hand.

What a soft, cool little palm it was! What an entrancing little figure! Who would have dreamed that Polly would develop into so lovely-no, not lovely-damn it, she was divine! Polly and a half million! Why Locke? Curse Locke! The eyes and lips of a dream woman, he had said; a half million-both his for the taking! Did he ask still more? He was not so sure about Locke having her. No, it wasn't the night drugging his senses and steeping his soul in fanciful possession of desires. It was real. If it pleased him, he had only to take, to drink his fill to satiation of this goblet of the gods. There was nothing to stay him. He had builded for it, and he was entitled to it; it wasn't chance. Chance! There was strange laughter in his heart. Chance was the playground of fools! Why shouldn't he laugh, aye, and boastingly! Who was to deny him what he would; this woman if he wanted her, the —

He stood suddenly like a man dazed and stunned. He let fall the girl's hand. Was he mad, insane, his mind unbalanced; was reason gone? It had come out of the night, a mocking thing, a voice that jeered and rocked with wild mirth.

His eyes met Polly's. She was frightened, startled; her face had gone a little white.

Imagination? As he had imagined that night in his cabin on board ship? A voice of his own creation? No; it came again now, jarring, crashing, jangling through the stillness of the night:

"Shadow Varne! Shadow Varne! Ha, ha! Ha, ha!" It rose and fell; now almost a scream; now hoarse with wild, untrammelled laughter. "Shadow Varne! Shadow Varne! Ha, ha! Ha, ha!" And then like a long, drawn-out eerie call: *"Shad-ow Va-arne!"*

And then the soft whispering of the leaves through the trees, and no other sound.

"What is it? What is it?" Polly cried out. "What a horrible voice!"

Captain Francis Newcombe's hand, hidden in his pocket, held a revolver. To get rid of the girl now! The voice had come from the woods in the direction of the shore. A voice! Shadow Varne! Who called Shadow Varne here on this island where Shadow Varne had never been heard of? He was cold as ice now; cold with a merciless fury battering at his heart. He did not know-but he *would* know! And then —

"You run along into the house, Polly." He forced a cool sang-froid into his voice. "It's probably nothing more than some of the negroes you spoke of in your letter cat-calling out there on the water; or else some one with a perverted sense of humour in the woods here trying to spoof us-and in that case a lesson is needed. Quick now, Polly! It's time you were in bed anyway. And say nothing about it-there's no use raising an alarm over what probably amounts to nothing. I'll tell you all about it in the morning."

She was still staring at him in a frightened, startled way.

"But, guardy," she faltered, "you —"

Damn the girl! She was wasting precious moments! But he could not explain that he had a *personal* interest in that cursed voice, could he?

He smiled reassuringly.

"I'll tell you all about it in the morning-if there's anything to tell," he repeated. "Now, run along. Good-night, dear!"

"Good-night, guardy," she said hesitatingly.

He watched her start toward the house; then he swung quickly from the road into the woods. He swore savagely to himself. She had kept him too long. There was very little chance now of finding the owner of that voice. Had there ever been? What did it matter, the moment or so it had taken to get rid of Polly? The odds were all with the voice, and had been from the start. He was not only metaphorically, but literally, stabbing in the dark. What did it mean? Again he swore, and swore now through clenched teeth. He knew well enough what it meant. It meant what he knew now that shot through his cabin window had meant. It meant that he was known to some one as he should be known to no one. It meant that of two men on this island, there was room for only *one*; otherwise it promised disaster, exposure-the end. A strangling, horrible end-on the end of a rope.

A door of the past ajar!

Who? *Who?*

He was making too much noise! Rather than stalking his game, he was more likely to be stalked. He had been stalked-when that voice had cried out. He halted-listened. Nothing! But it was somewhere in here that the voice had come from. He could swear to that.

He worked forward again. Damn the trees and foliage! How could one go quietly when one had to fight one's way through? And it was soggy and wet underfoot-one's feet made squeaky, oozy noises.

He came out on the beach —a long, curving stretch of sand, glistening white in the moonlight. He was amazed that he had travelled so far. How far had he travelled? His mind, like his soul, was in a state of fury, of fear; there was upon him a frenzy, the urge of self-preservation, to kill.

A structure of some kind, extending out into the sea, loomed up a distance away over to the right. He stared at it. It was a boathouse; and its ornate, exaggerated size stamped it at once as an adjunct to the mad millionaire's mansion. But the voice had not come from the boathouse-it had come from the woods back in here behind him.

Captain Francis Newcombe retraced his steps into the woods again, but now with far greater caution than before; and presently, his revolver in his hand, he sat down upon the stump of a tree. He held his hand up close before his eyes. It was steady, without sign of tremor. That was better! He was cooler now-no, cool; not cooler-quite himself. If he could not move here in the woods without making a noise, neither could any one else. And from the moment that voice had flung its threat and jeer through the night there had been no sound in the underbrush. He had listened, straining his ears for that very thing, even while he had manoeuvred to get Polly out of the road without arousing suspicion anent himself in her mind. He was listening now. It was the only chance. True, whoever it was might have been close to the beach, or close to the road, and had already escaped, and in that case he was done in; but on the other hand, the man, if it were a man and not a devil, might very well have done what he, Captain Francis Newcombe, was doing now, remained silent and motionless, secure in the darkness. If that were so then, sooner or later, the other must make a move.

Silly? Impossible? A preposterous theory? Perhaps! But there was no alternative hope of catching the other to-night. Why hadn't he adopted this plan from the start? How sure was he after all that, covered by the noise he himself had made, the other had not got away?

The minutes passed-five, ten of them. There was no sound. The silence itself became heavy. It began to palpitate. It grew even clamorous, thundering ghastly auguries, threats and gibes in his ears. And then it began to take up a horrible sing-song refrain: "Who was it? Who was it? Who was it?"

What would to-morrow bring? Shadow Varne! It was literally a death sentence, wasn't it? — unless he could close forever those bawling lips! He felt the grey come creeping into his face. He, who laughed at fear, who had laughed at it all his life, save through that one night on board the ship, was beginning to fight over again his battle for composure. Shadow Varne! Shadow Varne! Hell itself seemed striving to shake his nerve.

Well, neither hell nor anything else could do it! There were those who had learned that to their cost! And, it seemed, there was another now who was yet to learn it! His teeth clamped suddenly together in a vicious snap, and suddenly he was on his feet. Faintly there came the rustle of foliage-it came again. He could not place its direction at first. It might be an animal. No! The rustling ceased. Some one was *running* now on the road in the direction of the dock-but a long way off.

He lunged and tore his way through trees and undergrowth, and broke into the clear of the road. He raced madly along it. He could see nothing ahead because of those infernal moon-flecked turnings that he had been fool enough to rave over on his way to the house. Nothing! He drew up for a second and listened. Nothing! He spurted on again. A game of blindman's-buff-and he was blindfolded!

He came out into the clearing with the dock in sight. Again he stopped and listened. Still nothing!

His lips tightened. It was futile. He would only be playing the fool to grope further around in the darkness in what now could be but the most aimless fashion, robbed even of a single possible objective. He could not search the island! There was nothing left to do but go on board.

He started out along the dock-and then suddenly, as his eyes narrowed, his stride became nonchalant, debonair. He fell to whistling softly a catchy air from a recent musical comedy. Runnells had not gone to bed. Runnells was stretched out on his back on the deck of the yacht smoking a pipe, his head propped up on a coil of rope.

Captain Francis Newcombe dropped lightly from the wharf to the deck.

"Hello, Runnells," he observed, as he halted in front of the other, "the artistry of the night got you, too? Well, I must say, it's too fine to waste all of it at any rate in sleep."

"You're bloody well right, it is!" said Runnells. "Strike me pink, if it ain't! I've heard of these here places from the time I was born, but I wouldn't have believed it if I hadn't laid here smoking my pipe and saying to myself, this here's you, Runnells, and that there's it. London! I can do without London for a bit!"

"Quite so!" said Captain Francis Newcombe. He leaned over and ran his fingers along the sole of Runnells' upturned boot.

Runnells sat up with a jerk.

"What the 'ell are you doing?" he ejaculated.

"Striking a match," said Captain Francis Newcombe, as he lighted a cigarette. "You don't mind, do you? It saves the deck."

Runnells, with a grunt, returned his head to the comfort of the coiled rope.

"Locke turned in?" inquired Captain Francis Newcombe casually.

"About ten minutes after you left," said Runnells. "That engine did him down, if you ask me. I mixed him a peg, and he was off like a shot."

"Well, I don't know of anything better to do myself," said Captain Francis Newcombe.

He turned and walked slowly toward the cabin companionway; but aft by the rail he paused for a moment, and, flinging his cigarette overboard, watched it as it struck the water, and listened as it made a tiny hiss-like a serpent's hiss.

His face for an instant became distorted, then set in hard, deep lines.

Who was it?

The sole of Runnells' boot was dry-quite dry.

III

The Mad Millionaire

"It's an amazing place!" said Howard Locke.

"Yes; isn't it?" said Polly Wickes. "But, come along; you haven't seen it all yet."

"Is there more?" Howard Locke asked with pretended incredulity. "I've seen a private power plant; an aquarium that contains more varieties of fish than I ever imagined swam in the sea; a house as magnificent and spacious as a palace; stables; gardens; flowers; bowers of Eden. More! Really?"

"I think guardy was right," observed Polly Wickes naïvely.

"Yes?" inquired Howard Locke.

Polly Wickes arched her eyebrows.

"He said you weren't a ladies' man."

"Oh!" said Howard Locke with a grin. "So he's been talking behind my back, has he?"

"I'm afraid so," she admitted.

"And may I ask why you agree with him-why I am condemned?"

"Because," said Polly Wickes, "it would have been ever so much nicer, instead of saying what you did, to have expressed delight that the tour of inspection wasn't over-something about charming company, you know, even if everything you saw bored you to death."

"Unfair!" Locke frowned with mock severity. "Most unfair! I *was* going to say something like that, and now I can't because you'll swear you put the words into my mouth and I simply parroted them."

"Sir," she said airily, "will you see the bungalows and the pickaninnies next, or the boathouse?"

"I am contrite and humble," he said meekly.

Polly Wickes' laughter rippled out on the air.

"Come on, then!" she cried, and, turning, began to run along the path through the grove of trees where they had been walking.

Locke followed. She ran like a young fawn! He stumbled once awkwardly-and she turned and laughed at him. He felt the colour mount into his cheeks-felt a tinge of chagrin. Was she vamping him; did she know that if his eyes had been occupied with where he was going, and not with her, he would not have stumbled? Or was she just a little sprite of nature, full to overflowing with life, buoyant, and the more glorious for an unconscious expression of the joy of living? Amazing, he had called what he had seen on this island since he had been installed here as a guest that morning, but most amazing of all was Newcombe's ward. Newcombe's ward! It was rather strange! Who was she? How had a girl like this come to be Captain Newcombe's ward? Newcombe had not been communicative save only on the point that since she had gone to America to school Newcombe had not see her. Rather strange, that, too! He was conscious that she piqued him one moment, while the next found him possessed of a mad desire to touch, for instance, those truant wisps of hair that now, as she stood waiting for him on the edge of the shore, a little out of breath, the colour glowing in her cheeks, she retrieved with deft little movements of her fingers.

Her colour deepened suddenly.

"*That's* the boathouse over there," she said.

"I —I beg your pardon," said Locke in confusion. And then deliberately: "No; I don't!"

Polly Wickes stared. Again the colour in her cheeks came and went swiftly.

"Oh!" she gasped; then hurriedly: "Well, perhaps, that is better! Don't you think those two little bridges from the rocks up to the boathouse are awfully pretty?"

"Awfully!" laughed Locke.

"You're not looking at them at all," said Polly Wickes severely.

"Yes, I am," asserted Locke. "And just to prove it, I was going to ask why that amazing structure-you see, I said amazing again-that looks more like the home of a yacht club than a private boathouse, is built out into the water like that, and requires those bridges at all? Is it on account of the tide? I see there's no beach here."

"I'm sure I don't know," said Polly Wickes. "But they are pretty, aren't they? —and the place *does* look like a clubhouse. And it looks more like one inside-there's a lovely little lounging room with an open fireplace, and I can't begin to tell you what else. Shall we go in?"

"Yes, rather!" said Locke.

He was studying the place now with a yachtsman's eye. It was built out from the rocky shore a considerable distance, and rested on an outer series of small concrete piers, placed a few feet apart; while, by stooping down, he could see, beneath the overhang of the verandah, a massive centre pier, wide and long, obviously the main foundation of the building. At the two corners facing the shore were the little bridges, built in shape like a curving ramp and ornamented with rustic railings, that she had referred to. These led from a point well above high water mark on the shore to the verandah of the boathouse itself.

"Mr. Marlin must be an enthusiast," he said, as he followed his guide across one of the bridges.

Polly Wickes did not answer at once, and they began to make the circuit of the verandah.

Howard Locke glanced at her. Her face had become suddenly sobered, the dark eyes some-how deeper, a sensitive quiver now around the corners of her lips. His glance lengthened into an unconscious stare. She could be serious then-and, yes, equally attractive in that mood. It became her. He wondered if she knew it became her? That was cynical on his part. Was he trying to arm himself with cynicism? Well, it was easily pierced then, that armour! It was a very wonderful face; not merely beautiful, but fine in the sense of steadfastness, self-reliance and sincerity. He was a poor cynic! Why not admit that she attracted him as no woman had ever attracted him before?

They had reached the seaward side of the verandah. Here a short dock was built out to meet a sort of sea-wall that gave protection to any craft that might be berthed there-but the slip was empty of boats.

She looked up at him now, as she answered his observation.

"He was," she said slowly; "but all the boats are stowed away inside now. Poor Mr. Marlin!" She turned away abruptly, her eyes suddenly moist. "Let's go inside."

They found a cosy corner in the little lounging room of which she had spoken, and seated themselves.

Locke picked up the thread of their conversation.

"You're very fond of him, aren't you, Miss Wickes?" he said gently.

"Yes," she said simply.

"It's a very strange case," said Howard Locke.

"And a very, very sad one," said Polly Wickes. "I don't know how much Dora-Miss Marlin-has said to you, or perhaps even Mr. Marlin himself, for he is sometimes just like-like anybody else, so I don't —"

"I hardly think it could be a case of trespassing on confidences in any event," Locke inter-rupted quietly. "It's rather well known outside; that is, in what might be called the financial world, you know. What I can't understand, though, is that, having lost all his money, a place like this could still be kept up."

Polly Wickes shook her head thoughtfully.

"Guardy was speaking about the same thing," she said; "but I don't think it costs so very much now. You see, it is almost in a way self-supporting —the vegetables, and fruit, and fuel and all that. And the servants all have their little homes, and have lived on the island for years, and the wages are not very high, and anyway Dora has a fortune in her own name-from her mother, you know; and, besides, thank goodness, dear old Mr. Marlin hasn't lost all his money anyway."

"Not lost it?" ejaculated Locke. "Why, that was the cause of his mind breaking!"

Polly Wickes looked up in confusion.

"Oh, perhaps, I shouldn't have said that," she said nervously. "But-but, after all, I don't see why I shouldn't, for you could not help but know about it before very long. Indeed, I shouldn't be a bit surprised if Mr. Marlin showed it to you himself, just as he did to me, for he seems to have taken a great fancy to you. He hardly let you out of his sight this morning."

"He knows of my father in a business way," said Locke. "I suppose that's it. Do you mean that he showed you a sum of money here on this island?"

"Yes," said Polly Wickes slowly, "after I had been here a little while; a very large sum-half a million, he said."

"Good heavens!" exclaimed Locke. "That's hardly safe, is it? I know the peculiar form his disease has taken is an antipathy to all investments, but can't Miss Marlin persuade him to deposit it somewhere?"

"That's exactly what guardy said," nodded Polly Wickes. "But it's quite useless. Dora has tried, but her father won't even tell her where he keeps it."

Howard Locke rose from his chair, walked over to the empty fireplace, and, standing with his back to Polly Wickes, opened his cigarette case.

"Captain Newcombe, of course, is quite *au fait* with the conditions?" he observed casually.

"Of course," said Polly Wickes ingenuously. "I naturally wrote him all about it."

"Naturally!" agreed Howard Locke.

He stooped over, and, striking a match on the edge of the fireplace, lighted his cigarette. So Captain Francis Newcombe had known all about it, had he, even before he had left England? And yet Captain Francis Newcombe in the smoking room of the liner on the way across had been densely in ignorance, and even alarmed for his ward's safety at the first intimation that her host was a monomaniac! It was rather peculiar! More than peculiar!

Locke turned, and, leaning against the mantel over the fireplace, faced Polly Wickes. His mind was working swiftly, piecing together strange and apparently irrelevant fragments, that, irrelevant as they appeared, seemed to make a most suggestive whole. Captain Newcombe had lied that night on board the liner. Why? Who was it that had invaded his, Locke's stateroom and had searched through his belongings? And why? Why was it that now for the first time in four years Captain Newcombe should have come to visit his ward in America? He had more than Newcombe's word for that-Polly here had said so herself; and Miss Marlin had referred to it in the most natural way when welcoming Newcombe that morning. What had an insane old man, who hid away a half-million dollars on a little island in the Florida Keys, got to do with the letter received in London and containing those facts that Polly Wickes had just admitted she had written? What did it mean? Was a certain, insistent deduction to be carried to a logical conclusion, or was he hunting a mare's nest in his mind? Was it a mere coincidence in life, where far stranger coincidences were daily happenings-or was it a half-million dollars? And Polly Wickes, here? Captain Francis Newcombe-and his ward! Was it a bird of paradise in cahoots with a vulture? No, he wouldn't believe that! It was preposterous! There weren't any grounds for it anyway. He was an irresponsible fool. He became angry with himself. He was worse than a fool-he was a cad! The girl's very ingenuousness in what she had said put to rout any possibility of connivance. But, damn it-Captain Newcombe's ward! How? What was the explanation of that? And if—

Polly Wickes' small foot beat the floor in a sharp little tattoo.

Locke straightened up with a start. In his fit of abstraction he had been gazing at the girl with abominable rudeness.

"I forgot to say," said Polly Wickes severely, "that besides saying you were not a ladies' man, guardy said something else about you."

"No! Surely not!" Locke forced a mock dismay into his voice. "What was it?"

Polly Wickes took a critical survey of the toe of her spotless white shoe.

"He said he didn't know whether I would like you or not."

Locke took a step forward from the fireplace.

"And do you?" he demanded.

"I do not," she said promptly; "at least not when I am utterly ignored for a whole five minutes, except to be stared at as though I were a specimen under a microscope."

"I'm awfully sorry," said Locke contritely; "really I am. I was thinking of what we had been saying about Mr. Marlin, and —"

She suddenly lifted a warning finger.

"There he is now," she said in a low voice.

Locke turned around. His back had been to the door, leading to the seaward side of the verandah, which they had left open behind them. Mr. Marlin was peering cautiously around the jamb of the door-and now, as the blue eyes under the silvered hair, which was rumpled and astray, caught his, Locke's, the old man thrust a beckoning finger into view.

Locke glanced at Polly Wickes.

"I think," she said in a whisper, "that he has been acting more strangely just of late than ever before. He wants you for something. Of course, you must go and see what it is."

"All right," said Locke.

He walked quietly across the room, and out on to the verandah.

"You wanted to speak to me, Mr. Marlin?" he said pleasantly.

It was a queer, strangely contradictory figure, that of the little, stoop-shouldered, old man, who now seized his arm in feverish haste and led him hurriedly away from the door. And quite a different figure from the Mr. Marlin of the morning! The white clothes were spruce and immaculate, but he wore no hat, and, as Locke had already noted, his hair was dishevelled. The thin, almost gaunt face, a rather fine old face, had lost the calm and composure that had marked it, for instance, a few hours ago at lunch, and there was now a furtive, hunted look in the eyes, a spasmodic twitching of the facial muscles, a sort of pathetic tearing aside of the veil that had so jealously striven to hide the man's affliction; and yet too, and perhaps even more pathetic in this particular, there seemed to cling intangibly about the old financier a certain dignity of manner and bearing-the one heritage possibly of the days when he had been a power, his name a talisman in the money markets of the world.

"I don't want her to hear," said Mr. Marlin mysteriously. "I can't trust her, Locke."

"Can't trust her!" repeated Locke. "You can't trust Miss Wickes? Why, surely, Mr. Marlin, you are making a mistake. Why can't you trust her?"

"Because," said the old man sharply, "she is the ward of Captain Newcombe."

Locke stared into the other's face. A half angry, half-yes, that was it-cunning gleam had come into the blue eyes.

"What is the matter with Captain Newcombe?" he asked bluntly.

"He's a philanthropist," snapped Mr. Marlin. "A philanthropist! And all philanthropists are fools-with money."

"Oh!" said Locke a little helplessly. "So that's it, is it? Yes, of course! But I did not know Captain Newcombe was a philanthropist."

"What else is he?" demanded Mr. Marlin fiercely. "Polly Wickes herself proves it. Do you know who Polly Wickes is? No; you don't! I'll tell you! I heard her tell Dora. She was a poor girl-sold flowers on the street corners in London. Newcombe spends his money like water on her-education-clothes-thousands. He is a philanthropist, that is enough!"

"Good Lord!" muttered Locke to himself. The man hadn't been anything like this during the several hours that, off and on, he had been in the other's company that morning. The man had seemed almost, if not wholly, rational then. It was one of the idiosyncratic phases of the disease, of course. There was nothing to do but humour him. Captain Francis Newcombe a philanthropist! Five minutes ago he had come to quite another conclusion!

"Yes; I see," he said seriously. They had walked around the corner of the verandah, and now halfway down the side he halted. "But there was something you wanted to speak to me about, Mr. Marlin, wasn't there?"

"Yes," said the old man eagerly. He looked cautiously around him in all directions. "I put great faith in you as your father's son. I have never met your father; but I know of him. I know a great deal about him. He is a power. You must influence him. The world is facing a crisis, but we may yet save it from ruin. I must have a conference with you where no one can hear or see. No one must *see* —do you understand? That is most important. Some people think I am a little touched in the head; but they are the fools. I shall show you, my boy, for I shall have with me the proof that I am in earnest, and the evidence that I practise what I preach. You shall see for yourself who is the fool. To-morrow night" —he fumbled in the pocket of his coat, and drew out a little book —"what day is to-day, and what is the date? Yes, yes, of course; this is Tuesday, isn't it?"

"Yes," said Locke gravely; "to-day is Tuesday."

"Tuesday, the twenty-fifth," mumbled the old man, as he consulted the book. "Yes, yes!" He returned the book to his pocket. "Very well, then, to-morrow night. Meet me in the aquarium to-morrow night at a quarter past two."

Locke, for the sake of nonchalance, carefully selected another cigarette from his case and lighted it. A quarter past two to-morrow night! If it were not pitiable, it would be absurd that the old man should have come down here in this manner to the boathouse to make an appointment for to-morrow night, when in the natural course of events he would have been afforded an endless number of infinitely more convenient opportunities to make the same request! And why to-morrow night, other than to-night, or this afternoon, or even now? And why at such an hour? It was useless to ask the question for it found its answer simply in the workings of a poor, unhinged mind-and yet Locke found himself asking the question mechanically.

"That's a rather unusual hour, isn't it, Mr. Marlin? And why to-morrow night? Why not to-night, for instance?"

The old man came close, and gripped Locke's arm again with feverish intensity. He looked all around him, then placed his lips to Locke's ear.

"I'll tell you why," he whispered. "Since last night I have been watched and followed-watched and followed all the time, all the time, all the time. They think I am mad, that my reason is gone. Ha, ha, can you imagine that, young man? Well, they will see! And so it cannot be to-night, for I must be very careful, and I must have time to prepare. And the hour? You do not understand that? Well, I will tell you something else. The hour is fixed; it cannot be altered; it cannot be changed. It is fixed." He gripped suddenly with a fiercer pressure on Locke's arm. "Ha! Did I not tell you I was always being watched and followed?" he breathed excitedly. "Listen! Listen! There is some one coming now!"

The old man was trembling violently. Locke laid his hand reassuringly upon the other's shoulder. It was quite true that there was distinctly the sound of some one's footsteps coming across one of the little bridges from the shore, the one on the far side of the boathouse from where they stood obviously, for the one on this side was in plain view.

"Why, Mr. Marlin," Locke smiled, "it's only some one coming to the boathouse. That's quite natural. There's nothing to cause you alarm in that. But just to set your mind at rest we'll go and see who it is."

"No, no!" whispered Mr. Marlin fiercely. "No one must know that I suspect anything. I can elude them-they're around on the other side now. You stay here. Don't move! I'm going now. But remember! To-morrow night! You will remember?"

"Yes; of course, Mr. Marlin," Locke replied soothingly.

The old man laid his finger to his lips.

"And not a word about it! No one must know! Keep silent! You will see! You will see! But I must be quick now! I will elude them. Keep silent-not a word!"

The old man was running at top speed along the verandah.

Locke leaned against the railing, his face strangely set, as he watched the flying figure cross the bridge, and, with head constantly jerking around to peer first over one shoulder and then the other, disappear finally along the shore.

"Good Lord!" muttered Locke to himself again. "And this morning he appeared to be as sane as I am!" He frowned suddenly. "Queer obsession, that-of being constantly watched! Since last night! I wonder!"

He straightened up abruptly, and drew a letter from his pocket. He read it slowly, carefully, several times, as though almost he were memorising it; and then he began to tear it into little pieces.

"I guess it's safer," he confided to himself; and then with a grim smile: "Perhaps it's just as well I didn't have anything like this with me that night on board ship!"

He threw the pieces over into the water, but one fluttered back through the railing. And, staring at this, he laughed a little shortly as his eyes deciphered the typewritten fragment on the verandah floor:

> ll reports approved. Use
> w Scotland Yard fully pre

He picked it up, tore it into minute shreds, searched carefully to make sure there were no other wayward scraps, and then started slowly back along the verandah to rejoin Polly Wickes.

His mind seemed in confusion, coherence smothered in a multitude of thoughts that impinged one upon the other, each vociferating its right to sole consideration. There was Newcombe and that smoking room scene on the liner, and a letter advising about a half-million dollars, and a madman, and-no-there was something else, something that was gradually gaining priority over the rest. Yes-Polly Wickes! Well, Polly Wickes, then ...a flower girl in London ... a lady four years later in America ...how old had she been when this had happened ...how old had she been ...confound it, what did he mean by that ...what did he mean ...she couldn't have been more than a child ...a mere child....

He halted, abruptly at the sound of his own name. Unconsciously he had almost reached the door leading into the lounging room of the boathouse. Polly Wickes was talking to some one-to whoever it was, of course, whose arrival at the boathouse had frightened old Mr. Marlin away a few minutes ago. Ah, yes! Newcombe! That was Newcombe laughing now.

"But just the same," said Polly Wickes, "it *does* seem a little strange to me that Mr. Locke would make such a trip with you on so short acquaintance."

"Nonsense!" replied Captain Francis Newcombe. "There's nothing strange about it. You don't know that type of young American, that's all. The 'short acquaintance' end of it is purely the insular English viewpoint. He had a holiday on his hands, as I told you, and he meant to spend it on his boat somewhere. We hit it off splendidly together coming over, and-well, we've hit it off splendidly ever since. That's all."

"Let's change the subject, then," said Polly Wickes.

Captain Francis Newcombe laughed complacently.

"I was going to," he said. "I want to speak to you about last night."

"I don't care for your choice," said Polly Wickes in what seemed to Locke like sudden agitation. "I haven't been able to get that horrible cry out of my mind all day, and I hardly slept at all when I went to bed."

"But, my dear, that is utterly absurd!" Captain Francis Newcombe returned, with another laugh. "I can only repeat what I said to you this morning-that it must have been some boatmen out on the water cat-calling to each other. I was startled myself at first, and a bit angry, I'll admit, at the thought that some one was taking liberties with us; but I am quite sure now it was nothing of the kind. You mustn't give it another thought-really. It isn't worth it! But I wasn't going to refer to that again. What I wanted to know was whether or not you told Miss Marlin about seeing her father out there at that hour of night?"

"Yes," said Polly Wickes. "I told her; and she said she knew he sometimes went out night after night for a number of nights, and that, strangely enough, he'd go out later each night until finally it would be just before daybreak when he left the house-and then, after that, for a long while he wouldn't go out at all. She said she had never given her father an inkling that she knew, and had never put any restraint upon him. As I have told you, what the doctors have warned her about, and what she is more afraid of than anything else, is arousing any suspicion in her father's mind that he requires watching or is being watched. There is the danger that he might become violent. In fact, it is almost certain that he would under such conditions, Doctor Daemer said."

"H'm!" commented Captain Francis Newcombe.

A chair creaked within; a footstep sounded on the floor approaching the door.

And Howard Locke retreated quietly around the corner of the boathouse.

IV
The Unknown

It was dark in the room, save where the moonlight stole in through the window and stretched a filmy path across the floor until, in a strange, nebulous way, it threw into relief a cheval-glass that stood against the opposite wall. And in the glass a shadowy picture showed: The reflection of a man's figure seated in a chair, but curiously crouched as though about to spring, the shoulders bent a little forward, the head outthrust, the elbows outward, strained with weight, the hands clenched upon the arms of the chair. And then suddenly, with a low, snarling oath, the more vicious for its repression, the figure sprang from the chair, and stood with face thrust close against the mirror.

It was Captain Francis Newcombe.

He stared into the glass, his fists knotted at his sides. It was as though the two faces flung a challenge one at the other, each mocking the other in a sort of hideous imitation of every muscular movement. They were distorted-the lips drawn back, displaying teeth as beasts might do; and in the shadows the eyes were lost, only the sockets showing like small, black, ugly, cavernous things.

The minutes passed-long minutes. A metamorphosis was taking place. The faces became more composed; they became debonair, suave-and finally they smiled at one another as though a truce had been proclaimed.

Captain Francis Newcombe swung back to the chair, and flung himself down in it again. It was over for the moment. For the moment! Yes, that was it-for the moment! But it would come again. Last night in his bunk on the *Talofa* he had lain awake, and lived through hell. To-day, behind his mask of complaisance, fear had gnawed. Fear! And it had been his boast that fear and he were strangers.

His lips grew tight.

Well, his boast still held good! What man had ever stood before him, and taunted him with fear! This was fear in a different sense. It was a fear of the intangible, of what he could not reach, or see, of what he could not materialise into actual form. It was the fear of the *unknown*.

He was on his feet again.

"Damn you!" he snarled. "Come out into the open and fight! You hell-hound, you spawn of the devil, come out, show your face —"

No! Quiet! That would not do! He was in control of himself again, wasn't he? It was a game of wits against wits, of cunning matched against cunning. But against whom-and what was the stake this unknown, who had come to plague and torment him, played for? Revenge? The law? A Nemesis rising up out of forgotten things?

His mind prodded and sifted and strove, and in its striving seemed to jar and jangle and crunch like the parts of some machinery in motion, which, out of gear, threatened at any moment to demolish itself.

If he went mad-like Mr. Marlin! Ha, ha!

"By God!" he muttered grimly. "This is bad —a bad bit of nerves. If it was the same blighter who fired at me on shipboard, and it must have been, why didn't he fire at me again last night when he had an even better chance, instead of yowling through the darkness?"

That was better! It was the one trump card in his hand; the card that, as he had watched the daylight creep in through the tiny portholes of the *Talofa* that morning, had determined him, not only to carry on, but to make it serve as a trap to put an end to this skulking familiar who had fastened itself upon his trail. That wasn't fear, was it?

Shadow Varne! Who was the fool who dared to challenge Shadow Varne!

He was smiling now-but his lips were thin and merciless.

It could no longer be held attributable to some crazed, irresponsible act, that shot on shipboard, which chance had elected should be fired through his stateroom window rather than through any other. Logic now denied that. The man who had fired that shot, and the man who had screamed out in taunting mockery at him last night, were one and the same. Well, who was it, then, who had been on the liner, and was now on Manwa Island?

There were only two. Runnells and Locke!

Had Runnells had time to change his shoes, or, granting the time, had cunning enough to have thought of doing so? No; the chances were a thousand to one against it. Locke, then? But Runnells had said that Locke hadn't left the *Talofa*. Were Runnells and Locke in cahoots together? They had been extremely friendly on the way down. But Locke-it was preposterous! He knew who Locke was —a young American business man of good family. It was curious, though, that Polly should have made that remark to-day —about a trip like this on such short acquaintance. No; there was nothing in that. It had happened too naturally. Locke had a good many pairs of shoes. Like Runnells', none of them had been wet; but he was not sure he had found all of them in the darkness in the cabin with Locke-supposedly at least-asleep there on the opposite bunk. Locke could easily have hidden a tell-tale pair; and Locke was decidedly the kind of man who would have had the intelligence to do so.

But how could Locke know him as Shadow Varne?

Well, there was Runnells!

His jaws set with a snap. Was it Runnells? There was one way to find out-within the next ten minutes-with his hands at Runnells' throat! No; that would not do-not yet-save as a last resort. If it were not Runnells, then any act like that on his part would disclose his hand, arouse Runnells' suspicions that this trip to Manwa Island was perhaps, after all, not entirely a holiday jaunt!

He began to pace up and down the room-but noiselessly, without sound. His subconscious mind imposed the necessity for silence.

His hands clenched until the nails bit into the palms. Who was it? What did it mean? What was at the bottom of it? There was no answer that solved the question even to the satisfaction of a tormented brain that would have grasped with eager relief at even a plausible conclusion. The law? If the law had proof that he was Shadow Varne, he would not be an instant at liberty-though he would never be taken alive again-not even under the helpless condition that had done him down in Paris for the first and only time, as that old busybody, Sir Harris Greaves, the fool who loved to play with lighted matches over a powder cask, had so unctuously set forth. But perhaps the law did not have proof, had only suspicion-was only playing a game to trip him into disclosing his identity. Revenge? Then why not another shot last night, as on the liner; why —

The cycle! The infernal and accursed cycle again!

Well, whoever it was, they would play with Shadow Varne, would they? Fools! Did they think he was one, too-that he could not see the weak spot in their attack? Something was holding them back here on the island from a shot as on the liner; here, for some reason, an attempt to inspire fear was evidently being resorted to instead. Something kept them from coming out into the open; something necessitated this cat-and-mouse game. Something, if exposure were actually within their power, prevented them from exposing him.

That was it! That was it exactly-the one point on which he would stake everything and play out the game. Curse them and their childish tricks to frighten him! Exposure was the only thing he feared, because that would ruin every chance of success here; but if he was safe from exposure, or if exposure were only delayed long enough-and it need not be very long delayed, at that-he would have got, as he meant to get, in spite of God, or man, or the devil, what he had come for!

There was another angle. What had transpired might not have anything to do with what had brought him here.

Of course not! Why should it-essentially? But it was a menace, a hideous thing. It made him think of a picture he had seen somewhere —a gibbet at a bleak, wind-swept, dark-skyed cross-road with a figure dangling from it. One of those damned steel-plate engravings of the highwaymen days in England!

The unknown!

For a moment he stood still-and then suddenly both fists were raised above his head. That was a reason above all others why he should go on. The stakes were on the table. It was not merely a question of old Marlin's money. Win or lose here, the menace of that voice that shrieked the name of Shadow Varne for all to hear now hung over his whole future. It must either be removed, or he, Shadow Varne, promised with ghastly certainty to take the place of that dangling, swaying thing upon the gibbet chain. The menace was *here*. What better chance was there to fight it than here and now? Who was the more cunning? Who would misplay a card?

Not Shadow Varne!

A grim and cold composure came. He had two birds to kill with one stone now-that was all! Frighten Shadow Varne away? Bah! They did not know Shadow Varne-save only as a name to be screeched out from some safe retreat in the darkness! What might transpire in the secret recesses of his heart, the purely human fact that dismay and fear might prey at ugly moments upon him, was one thing; to halt him, to make him even hesitate, was another! He had never hesitated; he had but moved the more quickly, speeded up his plans, for time was a greater object now. He was at work at this very moment-waiting until the house was quiet for the night.

Well, it was time now, wasn't it?

A small flashlight played on the dial of his wrist watch.

Just midnight!

He nodded his head sharply, slipped across the room, and, with the door ajar, stood listening. A minute passed-another. There was no sound. He stepped out into the great, wide hall, and closed his door softly behind him.

It was like a shadow moving now.

That was Locke's room there; Polly's here-Dora Marlin's opposite. He passed them by, silently descended the great staircase, made his way back along another wide hallway, and finally halted before a door. This was Mr. Marlin's room. He listened intently. The sound of regular breathing, as of one asleep, was distinctly audible from within.

He smiled grimly as he turned away, and cautiously let himself out through a French window in the living-room which opened on the verandah. From here, he dropped lightly to the lawn.

The money was not hidden in the house. He was spared from the start any loss of time in an abortive search of that kind. There was too much significance attached to the old maniac's act of creeping stealthily in and out under his own verandah in the dead of night; especially when added to this had been the information gleaned from Polly that Mr. Marlin was in the habit of stealing out of the house at intervals for a succession of nights on end, though at a later hour each night. It was the obvious! But why a later hour each night? Rather queer! But the man's brain was queer! Why try to square insanity with the rational?

It was the secret under the verandah that interested him.

But his mind, as he made his way noiselessly along the edge of the bushes that fringed the verandah, reverted with a certain disturbing insistence to Polly. The girl hadn't stopped talking about going back to England! She said he had promised her she should when her education was finished. Well, perhaps he had-as one makes a promise to quiet a child! She wanted to be with her mother. Quite natural! But she hadn't any mother; and, if things went right here, *he* was rather inclined to believe that hereafter he preferred America to England as a permanent place of residence. He had reiterated his promise, of course. He couldn't afford to do anything else-yet. Sooner or later, he would have to "explain" to Polly; but when that time came, unless he had lost a certain facility in explanations that had never failed him yet, he should be able to turn even the fact that he had kept Mrs. Wickes' death from her to his own account. And tell the truth, even if somewhat inverted, at that! Solicitude would be the keynote-that, since Mrs. Wickes was not really her mother, her visit here need not be spoiled by ill news that would keep. Solicitude-and all that sort of idea. It was a good thing Mrs. Wickes was dead. Polly wouldn't want to live in England now. Mrs. Wickes' death settled that problem, which, otherwise, he would have had to find some other way of settling.

A minor matter! Very minor! Why should it even have crossed his mind? There was first the money; then, as a corollary, when that was found, the distressingly fatal *accident* that would overtake poor old Mr. Marlin-and, woven into the warp and woof of this, the twisting of a certain windpipe that would screech its indiscretions for the last time to a far different tune!

Ah, that was more like Shadow Varne!

He parted the bushes and slipped in under the verandah. This was the spot where the old madman had disappeared from view last night. His flashlight was switched on now. It showed a well-defined path, if it could be called a path, where through much usage the earth and gravel had been pressed down close up against the side of the house. It led toward the rear. He followed it. It took him around the corner of the house, and here, under a flight of steps that led to the verandah above, he found himself confronted with a basement door. Captain Francis Newcombe smiled. He had never ranked the task of probing the old fool's actions as one that demanded much ingenuity, or as presenting any particular difficulty. It was simply a question of watching the other without being seen himself; and with the man's mode of exit and entry from and into the house already known, the rest would almost automatically take care of itself.

He opened the door and stepped inside. The flashlight disclosed an ordinary basement store-room, and, at one side, a flight of stairs. Captain Francis Newcombe moved quickly, but without sound now. He crossed the basement and crept up the stairs. Here, at the top, another door confronted him. With the flashlight out, he opened this door cautiously-and again a smile touched his lips. He had rather expected it! The door opened on the lower hall, and almost directly opposite Mr. Marlin's room.

He stepped across the hall and listened again at the old man's door. There still came from within the sounds of occupancy; but instead now of the regular breathing as of one asleep, it was the sound as of one moving softly around within.

Captain Francis Newcombe retreated to the stairs, closed the door behind him, descended the stairs, left the basement, and selected a spot amongst the trees at the edge of the lawn where he could command a view of the shrubbery bordering the verandah. It was still a little earlier than the hour last night when, according to Polly, Mr. Marlin had gone out, and if, in the bizarre workings of a warped brain, a later hour each night added to secretness and security, Mr. Marlin was not yet to be expected for a little while. Quite so! He, Captain Francis Newcombe, had formulated his own timetable on that basis. There was nothing to do now but wait.

He frowned suddenly. Suppose, though, Mr. Marlin did not come out at all? This might well be one of the nights when — No! He shook his head decisively. To begin with, he had just heard the man moving around in his room after having previously been, or pretended that he had been, asleep; and if Polly's report was based on fact, as it undoubtedly was, the old maniac, once started on his period of peregrinations, kept it up until, on the basis of a later hour each night, his final sortie was made just before daybreak-and taking into account the hour at which the old man had been out last night, Mr. Marlin ought at present to be in the thick of one of those periods of nocturnal activity that would endure for a number of consecutive nights to come.

In a sort of grim mirth, he laughed softly now to himself. *One* night, not a number of nights, would be all that was required! It did not entail any distressingly laboured mental effort to understand *why* the old man went out-it was simply a question of *where* he went.

The minutes dragged along. A quarter of an hour went by; it became half an hour-and then Captain Francis Newcombe drew back silently a little deeper in amongst the trees. Yes, there was the old maniac now, dressing gown and all, and cocking his head to and fro in all directions as he parted the bushes in emerging from under the verandah. A moment later, the old man scurried across the lawn to a spot not far from where he, Captain Francis Newcombe, was standing. The woods here surrounding the house were full of little paths and walks, and the grotesque figure with the flapping gown now disappeared along one of these paths a few yards away.

Captain Francis Newcombe's lips twisted a little ironically as he took up the chase. The head that kept cocking itself around so idiotically would avail its owner little in the shape of protection! Apart from it being too dark to see more than a few feet in any direction now in the wooded path, he, Captain Francis Newcombe, had not the slightest intention of trying to keep the other in sight, much less run any risk of being seen himself. The sense of sound was quite sufficient-entirely adequate! Twigs and dried pine needles snapped eloquently under Mr. Marlin's feet. Captain Francis Newcombe's ironical smile deepened. His own rubber-soled yachting shoes, combined with a little precaution, might be relied upon to cause the old maniac no alarm!

The chase led on, following the turnings and twistings of the path for perhaps three hundred yards, and then turned into a narrow intersecting by-path at the right. Here again Captain Francis Newcombe followed the sound of the other's footsteps for perhaps another hundred yards-and then suddenly he halted. The footsteps had ceased abruptly.

For a moment Captain Francis Newcombe remained motionless, listening; then with extreme caution he went forward again. He came presently to where the path ended at the edge of a small clearing; and here, though shadowy and indistinct, he could make out just in front of him the outline of what looked like a little *cabane*, or hut. He nodded his head complacently. From inside the hut he caught the sound of movement again. So this was where Mr. Marlin went at nights, was it!

He crept forward on hands and knees now, careful to make not the slightest noise, made the circuit of the little hut, and halted again-this time on the side opposite from the door and beneath the single window that the place possessed. From what he had been able to make out in the darkness, the hut appeared to be in a more or less tumble-down and neglected condition. It was probably an old tool house or something of the sort. Well, that mattered very little!

With his head well at one side of the window frame to guard against any possibility of being seen from within, he brought his eyes to a level with the sill, and peered in. At first he could distinguish nothing; then gradually a shadowy figure took form in one corner and kept moving up and down with a motion, which, more than anything else that suggested itself to him, re-sembled the motion of a woman assiduously at work over a washboard. This was accompanied by a scraping sound.

Mr. Marlin was digging!

Captain Francis Newcombe quietly sat down on the ground beneath the window. It was quite hopeless to expect to see anything more than he had seen-for the present! One would have asked a good deal to have asked more! The spot where the old maniac was at work was close up against the wall at the right of the door and almost directly opposite the window!

The digging ceased. Another sound took its place —a sort of crooning, a sing-song droning sound. Words, snatches of sentences, became audible:

"...All! All here! ...In the darkness where no one can see....And I do not need to see —I feel....Night after night I feel, and my fingers count....Money! Money! ...Ha, ha-and they do not understand....Fools! All fools! ...You will multiply yourself a hundred, a thousandfold....Fools! Blind fools! ...They would not listen....They called me mad...."

The crooning went on.

Captain Francis Newcombe with cool nonchalance made himself more comfortable now by propping his back against the side of the hut. When the old fool was through with his puling, and the fondling of that half million in banknotes that he imagined was so safely hidden, the next move would be in order. Until then there was nothing to do except to exercise what degree of patience he could.

Patience! He stirred suddenly. Why exercise patience? Was it, after all, absolutely necessary that he should? A moment's work would do away with that senile old idiot now. Mr. Marlin would be found, but the money would not be found. That was the plan in its actual essence, wasn't it?

He snarled, then, angrily at himself under his breath. That was the method of the "cusher," which, on a certain occasion, he had branded with so much contempt! The record of Shadow Varne was marred by no such crudeness as that. A cusher without art! It brought him a sense of intense irritation that the thought should even have entered his mind.

Why had it?

He shook his head. Was it impatience, or perhaps, rather, a prescience prompting him to be through and done with this with the least possible delay? Were the events that had happened since he had left England insidiously taking effect upon him to the detriment of his customary cold and measured judgment? Well, he would see to it that nothing of that sort should happen! Crime was a science; its procedure was calculated, methodical, orderly, denying scruples. He had always approached it as a science; he proposed never to approach it in any other way. The case in point, for instance: Once he knew exactly where this hidden half-million was, where he could lay his hands on it whenever he desired at an instant's notice-and he would locate its precise position inside the hut there as soon as the old maniac returned home to his bed-Mr. Marlin would be removed. But that must be accomplished apparently through an accident-and the accident must be such as to serve as *proof*, so to speak, that Captain Francis Newcombe could not possibly have had any part in it. This became the more essential now in view of that infernal voice last night. The nature of the accident itself was a mere detail. The choice was legion. There had been others who, becoming encumbrances in the path of Shadow Varne, had met with accidents. What folly to go in there now-and have the whole island aroused by the crime of murder and invaded by the police; with the crime itself proclaiming the fact that the murder had been done for the money the old madman was known to have had somewhere, but which was now obviously in the possession of *some one*, to wit, the murderer!

Bah! What was the matter with him? Did he need to rehearse the obvious? Mr. Marlin's secret would die with him; and, being unable to find the money, they would give the old maniac more credit for cunning and originality than was due to the moss-eaten method of selecting a hiding place under the floor of an old hut! The pitiful fool! Under the floor! That was where the treasure was always hidden-in every book he had ever read!

The crooning continued. It began to get a little on his nerves. It was interminable. Would the man stay here until daylight? No; that was hardly likely-not if he ran true to form. Old Marlin hadn't stayed out until daybreak last night when Polly and he, Captain Francis New-combe, had watched the other go in under the verandah.

It might have been an hour, though it seemed two, when at last Captain Francis Newcombe rose silently to his feet. The crooning had finally ceased, and in its place there came now a series of low, thudding sounds, as though soft earth were being tamped into place; and then he heard the door creak a little as it was opened and closed. An instant later the footsteps of the old man died away along the path by which he had come.

Captain Francis Newcombe stepped quickly around to the other side of the hut, and tried the door. It was unlocked. He smiled in a sort of grim humour as he pushed it open, and, entering, closed it again behind him. That was the first sign of intelligence-no, applied to a maniac, it could hardly be termed intelligence! —well then, craftiness that measured up in at least a little way to the intensive order of cunning with which the insane in general were popularly credited. An unlocked door was no mean safe-guard. The last place one would expect to find, or look for, a half-million dollars would be behind an unlocked door!

His flashlight threw an inquisitive circle of light around the interior. Whatever the place had been used for at one time, it was decidedly neglected and in disuse now. The flooring was in an advanced state of decay. His eyes followed the ray of the flashlight as it held on a spot on the flooring near the door. Yes, knowing beforehand that some pieces of the flooring there had been lifted, he could see that such was the case in spite of the fact that the pieces had been very neatly replaced.

The flashlight continued its tour of inspection. There was a pile of rubbish and some old barrels over in the far corner. He stepped quickly across to these and nodded his head sharply in satisfaction, as, tucked in behind the barrels, he found what he had been looking for. Mr. Marlin had been digging. Exactly! Here was the spade. He lifted it up and examined it. Particles of fresh earth still clung to it.

Captain Francis Newcombe stood still now for an instant to listen. And as he listened his brows gathered in a savage frown of annoyance. Why this exaggerated precaution? What did he expect to hear? What sound could there be? The old fool was finished for the night. There wasn't the slightest chance that he would return. Why should he, Captain Francis Newcombe, waste time now, when with a moment's work he could satisfy himself that the half-million dollars that had brought him to Manwa Island was definitely within his reach? Was that it? Was it psychological? Was it that *voice* he was listening for again?

He swore fiercely under his breath in a sudden flood of blind rage at himself; and, crossing the hut, stood the spade up against the wall within reach, and knelt down on the floor with the flashlight playing on the two or three sections of board that the old man had removed. Yes, they were quite loose. His fingers worked their way into a crack between two of them. The old maniac's half-million! Hidden under the flooring! It was child's —

What was that?

He was on his feet, the flashlight out, every muscle tense, his revolver outflung before him.

In God's name, what was that?

It seemed to crash and thunder through the stillness.

Only a knock upon the door?

Again!

Once more-sharp, imperative!

He stood motionless-his jaws clamped like iron. What was he to do? If he answered the summons-what then? How explain the presence here of Captain Francis Newcombe, the guest, who at this hour should be peacefully asleep in his bed? Who was it out there who had knocked upon the door? Not the old fool himself who might have come back. Old Marlin wouldn't have knocked. Who, then?

Strange! A full minute must have passed. Why were the knocks not repeated? There was no sound from without. He had heard no one approach-he had heard no one go away. Only the knocks upon the door.

He was listening now, every faculty alert. Was some one standing outside there, as tense, as silent, waiting-as he stood tense and silent, waiting, here within? If so, then, that was another angle to the situation. It must be so! There was not a sound out there-there had not been a sound. He had heard no one go away. Well, two could play at a game like that! And it would be the other who would show his hand!

He moved softly toward the door. In the darkness he felt out with his hand. It touched the panel of the door, crept down until it clasped the knob-and then suddenly, even as he moved swiftly to one side out of the direct line, he flung the door wide back upon its hinges.

And where the door had stood, there showed now but an oblong of filmy, hazy murk, scarcely more penetrable to the eye than the black interior of the hut. Nothing more! No, that was not true. There was something else-something white, a small white fluttering thing that seemed to drift and flutter downward to the ground. No sound from without-save the night sounds of the woods: The leaves talking to one another; the stir in the grasses; the low, faint, never-ending chatter of insects.

The watch ticking on Captain Francis Newcombe's wrist became a loud, discordant thing. It ticked away the minutes before he moved again.

His eyes became accustomed to the murk outside the open door. There was no one there.

That white thing lying by the threshold was an envelope. It had been stuck in the door. He reached out now, and picked it up. And now he closed the door again, and, with the flashlight on, he tore the envelope open.

He stared at the sheet of paper it contained. The single line of crude, printed letters seemed to leap out at him from the white sheet, scorching, burning, searing its message into his consciousness. He raised his hand and drew it across his forehead. It came away wet with sweat. He looked around him, snarling like a beast at bay. A thousand minions of hell here in the hut were screeching in his ears the words he had just read:

"Who murdered Sir Harris Greaves?"

V

The Gutter-snipe

A clock somewhere in the house chimed the hour.

Midnight!

Polly Wickes rose hastily from the corner of the big leather-upholstered Chesterfield in which her small figure had been tucked away.

"Oh!" she exclaimed. "I had no idea it was so late. Every one else has been in bed ages ago."

"I think," said Locke gravely, "that it is our duty to stand by that last log. It's been a rather jolly fire, you know. I —"

"That is the second one you have put on after having made the same remark twice before," she accused him severely.

"I know," said Locke. "I'm guilty-but think of the extenuating circumstances."

Polly Wickes laughed.

"No," she said.

"This is positively the last," pleaded Locke. "There may not be any excuse for a grate fire to-morrow night. Have you thought of that? The wind is still howling, but the rain has stopped and the moon is coming out, and —" His tongue was running away with him inanely. He stopped short.

"Yes?" inquired Polly Wickes demurely.

The great dark eyes were laughing at him-teasing a little.

"Well, confound it," he blurted out, "I don't want you to go! This has been a day and an evening that I shall never forget-very wonderful ones for me. I don't want them to be only memories-yet."

He met the dark eyes steadily now. The laughter had gone from them. He found them studying him for an instant in an almost startled way-and then the eyelids drooped and covered them, and she turned her head a little, facing the portièred window beside the fireplace of the living room in which they stood, and the colour crept softly upward from the full, bare throat, and stole into her cheeks.

He caught his breath. He felt his pulse stir into a quicker beat. She was very lovely as she stood there with the soft, mellow glow of the rose-shaded lamp and with the flicker of the flames from the firelight playing upon her.

"Just this last one," he pleaded again.

She hesitated for an instant, then sat down slowly on the Chesterfield once more. And as he watched her, there seemed to have come a curious quiet upon her. She did not look at him now-she was staring at her hands, which were tightly clasped together in her lap.

"Very well," she said in a low voice. "I think that I, too, would like to have-that last log. There is something that I want to say-that I meant to say this afternoon on the yacht. I —Mr. Locke, do you know who I am?"

She would not look up. He could not see her face. He knew what she meant-Mr. Marlin's words of the day before flashed upon him. There was something of dreariness in her voice, something that strove to be very bravely defiant but was only wistful, and an almost uncontrollable impulse fell upon him to touch her face and lift it gently, and make her eyes meet his again. There would be an answer there-an answer that he had not yet dared put in words. What right had he to do so? A day of dreams on the yacht to-day —that, and yesterday. Two days! He had known her longer than that....

He found himself answering her question automatically.

"What a strange question!" He was laughing-speaking lightly. "Of course, I know who you are."

"Yes," she said gravely, "you know that my name is Polly Wickes-but do you know anything about me?"

He came and stood a little closer to her.

"I think I know *you*." His voice had lost its lighter tone.

A little flood of colour came as she shook her head.

"Did guardy tell you anything about me on your trip down here?"

"No," he said.

"I didn't think he had," she said. "He has always been opposed to either of us saying anything about it to any one. Dear guardy! I know it is for my sake and that he believes it makes it easier for me, and generally it does; but-but sometimes it doesn't." She stopped and looked up suddenly. "But I do think it is more than likely that Mr. Marlin, in his queer way, has said something. Has he?"

"Look here," said Locke impulsively, "does it really matter-does it even matter at all? Mr. Marlin did say something, as a matter of fact-yesterday, down there at the boathouse, you know."

"What did he say?" she demanded.

"Why," Locke smiled, "something about London, and selling flowers."

"Well, it is quite true," she said slowly. "That is exactly what I was —a flower girl in London- on the street corners."

"I sell bonds-when I can-and wherever I can." Locke was laughing again-he was not quite sure whether he was striving the more to put her or himself at ease. "I can't see any difference on the basis of pure commerce between the two-except perhaps that the flowers are the more honest offering of the two. Bonds sometimes are not always what they seem."

She shook her head.

"That's very nice of you, Mr. Locke," she said. She was studying her clasped hands again. "But-but of course, as you quite well know, that has nothing whatever to do with what I am saying. You know London, don't you?"

"Why, yes; a bit," he answered.

"Yes," she said. "I think you do. Indeed, from what you have said to-day, I am sure you know it better than any American I have ever met before; and, indeed, far better than most people who live there all their lives. And so-and so" —her voice broke a little, then steadied instantly —"it is not necessary to go into any details, for you will understand quite well when I say that I lived in Whitechapel, and even there where only the cheapest room was to be found, and that when I sold flowers I did not have any shoes-and to the police I was known as a gutter-snipe."

He was beside her, bending over her.

"My God, Miss Wickes-Polly," he burst out, "why do you hurt yourself like this!"

He had called her "Polly." The name had come unbidden to his tongue. It had brought no rebuke-or was it that she had not noticed it?

"I would hurt myself more," she said steadily, "if I felt that those around me could have any justification in believing that I was purposely masquerading in order to deceive. That would be hypocrisy-and I hate that!" She flung out her hands suddenly with a queer, little helpless gesture. "Oh, I wonder if you understand what I mean; I wonder if I am explaining myself-and if you won't at once think that I am utterly inconsistent when I say that at school no one knew anything about my former life? But, you see, I have never felt that I was called upon to make the intimate things in my life a matter of public knowledge. And in that respect I can quite understand guardy's attitude in wishing me to say nothing about it, for, in so many cases, and especially at school, it would have just supplied a fund for gossip, and-and that would have been abominable."

"Of course, it would!" There was savage assent in Locke's voice. "It's nobody's business but your own."

"Oh, yes, it is," she answered instantly. "It's Miss Marlin's business-if I come here as a guest."

"Yes," said Locke quickly; "but you *have* told her, and —"

"Wait!" she interrupted. "Yes, I have told her; and now I have told you. But your two cases are entirely different, and I am not altogether sure that my reason for telling you is entirely to my credit, because it-it is perhaps like the child who confesses when he knows he is sure to be found out. You couldn't be here with poor Mr. Marlin very long before you knew. Do you understand? I couldn't bear the thought of you, or any one, thinking I was deliberately trying to hide the truth, or that, when there was reason to do so, I was afraid or ashamed to speak out myself."

"I wish you hadn't added that 'any one,'" he said in a low voice.

She did not answer. She was staring now into the fire. And he too stared into it now. It was full of pictures-strange, drab pictures. He knew Whitechapel-its stark, hopeless realism; he knew its children-without shoes. Was that what she saw there now? The fire was dying-beneath the one remaining log, almost burned through now, there were only embers. They glowed here and there and went out-black. Like some memories!

He looked at her again. Her face, that he could see now, seemed strangely pinched and drawn. Her hand toyed nervously with a frill of her dress. And something seemed suddenly to choke in his throat, and a great yearning came-and it would not be denied.

"Polly!" he whispered, and, leaning over, caught her hand in his.

With a quick, sharp indrawing of her breath as of one in sudden pain, she rose to her feet and drew her hand away.

"Oh, why did you do that?" she cried out.

"Because," he said, "I love —"

"No, no!" she cried out again. "Don't answer me! I didn't mean that you should answer. It is only that *now* there is something else that I must say. I —I —" Her voice broke suddenly.

"Don't!" he said huskily. "Polly, there is nothing to take to heart. What could it ever matter, those days? They are gone now forever. You exaggerate any possible bearing they could have on to-day. Suppose you were a flower girl, that you have known poverty in its bitterest sense-would that matter, could it possibly matter to any one who was not a contemptible snob, or to —"

"There is something else now that I must say." She was repeating her own words, almost as though she were unconscious of any interruption. "You-you make me say it. I —I never knew who my father was."

She was gone.

He had had a glimpse of a face pitifully white, of dark eyes that fought bravely against a mist that sought to blind them; and then before he could move or speak she had run from the room-and he stood alone before the fireplace.

And in the fireplace the last log fell spluttering, throwing out its dying rain of little sparks, and lay a broken thing between the dogs.

VI
The Man in the Mask

Again a clock somewhere in the house chimed the hour. And again.

One o'clock.

Two o'clock.

The embers in the fireplace had long since turned to black charred things. Locke raised his head. Two o'clock! He had not been conscious of it when the last little glow had died away. He had turned out the light when Polly had gone-and had sat there staring at the dying fire. He had not put on another log. The fire was dead now-quite dead. He had been staring into a black fireplace-that was as black as the room itself.

Two o'clock!

He stood up, and, going to the windows, flung back the portières. It was still blowing hard; but the moon was beginning to show through the scudding clouds. He brushed his hand heavily across his eyes. It was very still in the house; but the stillness itself seemed a disquiet, untranquil, chaotic thing. Polly! Yes, Polly had filled his thoughts during those two hours-Polly, and Captain Francis Newcombe. But he had not forgotten withal the bizarre appointment he was to keep with Mr. Marlin in the aquarium-at a quarter past two. One would not be likely to forget so extraordinary a thing in any case, no matter what might meanwhile have intervened-even if Mr. Marlin had not been so grotesquely persistent in his reminders. A dozen times that day the old man had plucked significantly at his, Locke's, coat sleeve, or had signalled mysteriously with his finger to his lips; and twice, with a childish titter, the old man had come upon him unexpectedly and had said exactly the same thing on each occasion.

"Tee-hee, tee-hee!" the old man had tittered. "It is all right for to-night, my boy-you will see-you will see. And they thought I was a fool. Do not say a word. Keep quiet-keep quiet-you will see."

What would he see? What would he learn? Much-or little? Would it be only the babble of a sick brain? Queer, strange, almost impossible conditions in this house! Where would they climax-and how? Whose hand held the trumps?

His eyes fixed suddenly on a spot across the lawn. Something seemed to have moved there. Fancy, perhaps; or a shadow cast by the swaying branches. The moon was just coming out from under the edge of a cloud-another moment and he would be able to tell if anything were there. Yes! A woman emerging from the path that led to the shore. The figure began to cross the lawn, approaching the house.

And then Locke's eyes narrowed suddenly in astonishment. It wasn't a woman at all; it was a man wearing a long gown, a dressing gown. It was Mr. Marlin. And the man kept cocking his head from side to side; and he appeared to be carrying something under the dressing gown-at least his arm was crooked up as though he held a bundle there.

Locke smiled now a little grimly, as the old man finally disappeared around the corner of the house. It was almost a quarter past two. He would find Mr. Marlin in the aquarium.

He drew the portières together again, and, leaving the room, went out into the reception hall beyond. There was no light showing anywhere and he was obliged to feel his way along. The aquarium was in, or, rather, composed in itself, a little wing built at the rear of the house, but connected therewith by a short, covered passageway. He knew the way quite well-he had been there with Polly on that first day.

That *first* day! That was only yesterday ... it was incredible, impossible.... His mind was running riot as he groped his way to the rear of the main staircase and into the wide passage that ran parallel with the length of the house. But then the whole place was incredible! The house itself was like a great hotel with its corridors and its endless number of rooms! This was Mr. Marlin's room here at his right, and —

He stood still. A door on his left had opened. It shut again instantly-and then he could hear it being cautiously reopened a little way.

"Don't you move!" said a voice in a fierce whisper. "Don't you move! I can see you! If you move I will shoot you!"

Locke found his muscles, that had suddenly grown tense and strained, as suddenly relaxed. He could see nothing-the door wasn't wide enough open-but it was the old madman's voice. Strange, though! How had the man got there? That wasn't Mr. Marlin's room-Mr. Marlin's room was on the opposite side of the hall. Yes, of course, there must be an entrance into the house there of some sort.

"It's Locke," he announced quietly. "That's you, Mr. Marlin, isn't it?"

"Hah!" ejaculated the other. "You, my boy, eh? Well, that's quite different. Of course, it's you. You know the value of being prompt. Excellent! Excellent! Be very quiet-but hurry! Follow me. We have only a little time."

Locke could just make out the old man's form now as the other came through the door-and then in the darkness it was lost again. But the patter of footsteps ahead of him, hurrying along, served as a guide. He followed the other to the end of the hall, turned into the covered passageway, and was halted again by the old man, this time at the door of the aquarium.

"Tee-hee!" tittered the maniac. "They think they are dealing with a fool. Wait! Wait, young man, I will see that the window shades are all down before we turn on the light-though there will be no one here to-night except ourselves-tee-hee! —they will be somewhere else!"

The old man opened the door and disappeared. And now Locke, as he waited, and though he listened, could not hear the other moving around inside-what sound the old man made was drowned by the noise of running water through the pipes that fed the tanks, and, added to this, the low, constant drip and trickle that pervaded the place.

Presently the lights went on.

"Here!" cried the old man. "Come over here!"

Locke blinked a little in the light as he stepped forward. It reflected bewilderingly from the glass faces of the tanks that were everywhere about. He joined the old man in the centre of the aquarium. Here there was an open space from which the tanks radiated off much after the manner of the spokes of a wheel, and this space was utilised as a sort of luxurious observation point, so to speak, for a heavy oriental rug was on the tiled floor, and ranged around a table were a number of big easy chairs.

From under his dressing gown now the old man took a package that was wrapped in oiled silk, and laid it on the table.

"Money!" he cried out abruptly. "Hah! We know its power, young man, you and I!" He began to fumble with the cord that was tied around the package; and then suddenly commenced to titter again. "Did I not tell you I was being followed, always being followed? Well, last night they followed a wrong scent. Tee-hee! Tee-hee! I told you you would see who was the fool! They are there to-night —digging-digging-digging. Tee-hee! Tee-hee! They will dig the place all up before they are sure it is not there."

Money! That package! Locke's lips tightened a little. Was this, as he had more than half expected, what he was to "see" —the half-million dollars at last that Polly had seen? And what did the man mean by "wrong scent"? And "digging"?

"Yes, of course, Mr. Marlin," said Locke quietly. "Of course, they will! But who is it that is following you?"

The old man dropped the package from his hands and leaned across the table, his eyes suddenly ablaze.

"If I knew, I would kill them!" he whispered. "It is everybody-everybody!"

"Perhaps you are mistaken." Locke spoke in a soothing tone. "Did you see anybody following you last night?"

"It is not necessary to see" —the old madman's whisper had become suddenly confidential — "I know. They were there-they are always there-watching-eyes are always watching." He broke into his insane titter once more. "Tee-hee, yes, yes; and we are being watched by thousands of eyes to-night —look at them-look at them-the pretty things-see them swimming all around you-but they look and they say nothing-and they do not follow me." His voice was rising shrilly; he began to gesticulate with his hands, pointing with darting little motions at one tank after another. "Do you hear? You need not be afraid because they watch. They will not follow us."

Locke sat down leisurely in a chair facing the other across the table. He was rather curious about this mysterious digging of last night, a little more than curious-but, also, it was necessary to calm the old maniac's growing excitement.

"I am quite sure of that, Mr. Marlin," he agreed heartily. "We should be perfectly safe here, especially as you say that you have succeeded in making whoever was following you watch somewhere else. That was very clever of you, Mr. Marlin."

The old man put his finger to his lips.

"I'll tell you where it was, young man," he said. "The old hut in the woods behind the house. They think it's there. They think that's where I hide the money. And they'll keep on looking there. It will take them a long while. They will be looking there to-night —and perhaps to-morrow night, too. And then they will begin to follow me again. But it will be too late-too late for many, many days, because the time-lock will be set-ha, ha-God supplies the time-lock, young man-you do not understand that-but can you imagine any one opening a time-lock that God has made?"

Locke took refuge in a cigarette. Apart from some mare's nest in an old hut, it was quite hopeless! The old maniac's condition was growing steadily worse. There was a marked change in even the last twenty-four hours. It did not require any professional eye to discern that.

"I think," suggested Locke conversationally, "that you were going to show me something in that package, Mr. Marlin."

"Yes," said the old madman instantly, and as though quite oblivious of any digression. "That is why you are here. Listen! You will tell your father about it. I do not ask others to do what I do not do myself. Your father must do the same. He must get all the great capitalists of America to do likewise-it is the only thing that will save the country from ruin and disaster. Look!" The old man ripped off the cord and wrapper, and there tumbled out upon the table, each held together with two or three elastic bands, a half dozen or more small bundles of bank notes. "See! See! Do you see, young man?"

Locke with difficulty maintained an impassive countenance. He had expected something of the sort, but it seemed somehow incredible that a sum so great as Polly had named should be represented by those few little bundles scattered there on the table in front of him. He picked one of them up and riffled the notes through his fingers. It contained perhaps a hundred bills, each one of the denomination of a thousand dollars-one hundred thousand dollars. He laid the bundle back on the table. Others were of like denomination; others again of five hundred. The full amount was undoubtedly there.

"Do you know how much is there?" demanded the old madman sharply.

Locke regarded the money thoughtfully. To name the exact amount offhand might aggravate the old maniac's already suspicious frame of mind.

"I can see that there is a very large sum," he answered cautiously.

"A large sum!" echoed the madman aggressively. "And what do you call a large sum, young man?"

"Well, at a guess," said Locke quietly, "and basing it on that package I have just examined, I should say in the neighbourhood of half a million dollars."

The old maniac thrust his head forward across the table, stared for an instant, and then suddenly burst into a peal of wild, ironical laughter.

"Half a million!" He rocked upon his feet, his peals of laughter punctuating his words. "Bah! There are five millions, ten millions, fifty millions there!" He shook his finger under Locke's nose. "Do you hear what I say, young man?"

The blue eyes had become alight with a mad blaze; hectic spots began to burn in the old madman's cheeks. Locke nodded his head in a slow, deliberate manner-as the most effective thing he could think of to do by way of calming the other. The whole place, the surroundings, the grotesque shapes swimming around in the tanks everywhere he looked, the eyes of the queer sea creatures that all seemed to be fascinated by that fortune which lay upon the table, the constant drip and trickle of water, the crazed old man who rocked upon his feet and laughed, were eerily unreal. That sea-horse in the tank that faced him from just beyond the other side of the table, for instance, seemed to be a most bizarre and unnatural creature both in shape and actions even for one of his own species! Half-past two in the morning, in an aquarium with a madman and a half-million dollars! Again, by way of appeasing the other, he nodded his head.

"Listen!" cried the old maniac fiercely. "You must help me. Men are blind, blind, blind! Europe is crumbling, nations are bankrupt-chaos-chaos-chaos is everywhere. Everything else is decreasing in value; only the American dollar climbs up and up and up. Sell, sell, sell while there is time! Commercial houses are tottering, dividends are not being paid, the employment of labour becomes less and less-the end is near. And fools cling to their business enterprises; and their capital shrinks and is swallowed up and lost. Lost!" The man was working himself into a frenzy. His voice rose in a shriek. "*Lost*! Do you not see? Do you not understand? Money alone has any value. And the less money there is left in the world, and the more that is lost, the greater will be the value of what remains. It will multiply itself by the thousandfold. Look! Look what is on the table here! It will become a wealth beyond counting in any case, and if no one will believe me then the more it will be worth because there will be the less money to compete against it. Millions! Millions! Hundreds of millions! But I am not selfish. I do not wish to see the ruin of the world. And you —*you*! You will now be responsible. They will not listen to me because they say I am mad —I, who alone have the vision to see, and the courage to act. But your father will listen to you and he will believe you, and the great financiers of America will follow your father, and —"

Subconsciously Locke was aware that the old maniac was still talking, the crazed words rising in shrieks of passionate intensity-but he was no longer paying any attention to the other. He was staring again at the glass tank, behind and a little to one side of the old madman, that contained the sea-horse. The creature was most strange! It was only a small and diminutive thing, but, unless he were the victim of an hallucination, it had taken on an extraordinary appearance. It seemed to possess *human* eyes; to assume almost the shape of a face-only there was a shadow across it. The water rippled a little. The sea-horse moved to the opposite corner of the tank-but the eyes remained in exactly the same original spot.

Locke leaned nonchalantly back in his chair, though his lips were compressed now into a thin, grim line. They were human eyes, and the shadow across the face was a mask. Where did it come from? He began trying to figure out the angle of reflection. The face of each glass tank, of course, with the deeper-hued water behind it, was nothing more or less than a reflecting mirror. What was that dark straight line above the eyes? To begin with, the reflection must come from somewhere behind him, and well to one side of him. Taking into consideration the position in which Mr. Marlin stood, it must be the left-hand side. The tanks, then, that would seem to answer that requirement became instantly limited in number-it must be either the first or second tank of those that formed the left-hand side of the alleyway nearest to where he sat, and that, like the spoke of the wheel, led obliquely to the wall. He could not see the wall, but — Yes, he had it now. There was a window there. That dark line above the eyes was the window shade-raised six inches or so from the sill. It could easily have been accomplished-even if the old madman had carefully drawn every shade and shut every window in the place, as presumably he had. The drip and trickle, the running water, would have deadened any little sound made in forcing the window, and after that to reach in and manipulate the shade would have been but child's play.

Locke's eyes shifted now to the old madman. What was to be done? The other, still rocking and swaying upon his feet, still flinging his arms about in mad gestures, his facial muscles twitching violently as he shrieked out his words, was already verging on a state of acute hysteria. Even to hint at the possibility that they were being watched would not only have a probably very dangerous effect upon the maniac, but would in itself defeat any chance of turning the tables on that watcher outside the window! Whose eyes were those, whose face was that behind the mask? Intuitively he felt he knew–the trail went back, broad and well defined, to London. Newcombe! Captain Francis Newcombe! Who else could it be? His jaws clamped hard together now. How turn intuition into a practical, visible certainty–by stripping that mask from the other's face?

The eyes were still there in the tank.

His mind was working keenly, swiftly now. Suppose he made some excuse to leave the aquarium and stole around outside to that window? No; that would not do. In the first place, he probably could not get away from the old madman; and, if he could, he dared not, for the length of time it would take him to accomplish any such purpose, leave the other alone with that money on the table and subject to attack from an open window only a few feet away. There was only one thing to do. The man outside the window there, unaware that his presence was known, would naturally not consider that he, Locke, was a factor to be reckoned with when, say, the old madman left the aquarium here to return the money to its hiding place, wherever that might be; and therefore, if he, Locke, could manage to keep ward over Mr. Marlin without being seen himself, the man out there would almost certainly rise to the bait and bring about his own downfall. The money was in evidence for the first time; its whereabouts known–and the man in the mask would be illogical indeed if he allowed it to be restored to the security of a secret hiding place without making an attempt to get it when an opportunity such as this apparently presented itself. But against this was a certain risk to which the old man would be subjected; if not a physical risk, then a mental one–which latter, to one in Mr. Marlin's condition, would probably be the more dangerous of the two. And then there was the chance, too, that if luck turned an ugly trick the money itself might be in jeopardy. The old maniac's unconscious co-operation must be secured. The hiding place was somewhere outside the house. That was obvious, both from Mr. Marlin's nocturnal habits, and from the even more significant fact that the old madman, in coming to this appointment here to-night, had brought the money with him from somewhere outdoors. Also it seemed to be no secret that Mr. Marlin roamed abroad at night. Polly had spoken of it without reserve. It was therefore but fair to presume that one as interested as was the man outside the window, and particularly if it were Newcombe, was in possession of this knowledge, and being in possession of it was equally capable of putting two and two together, and would expect the old maniac to go out again to-night —with the money. If then, without unduly alarming him, Mr. Marlin could be persuaded to remain in the house with his money to-night, it would not only be the safest thing the old madman could do, but would afford him, Locke, if he were right in his supposition, an excellent chance to trap the man in the mask while the latter waited for his prey to come out.

Locke, leaning forward now, crossed his arms on the table, and nodded his head earnestly at the old maniac. One corner of the table at least was distinctly visible from where the window would be along that little alleyway between the rows of tanks, but he was careful not to glance in that direction. The reflection of the masked face still showed in the same place. What was the old madman saying? Well, it didn't matter, did it? He interrupted the other now.

"You are right, Mr. Marlin," he said gravely. "I agree with everything you have said. It is a most serious situation. I had no idea that there existed any such vital and immediate necessity of realising cash for every description of asset that we can lay our hands upon. And I had no idea of the immense potential value that this money here on the table, for instance, possesses. As you say, when the crash comes it will be worth untold millions —a fabulous amount."

"Yes, yes!" agreed the old man excitedly. He began to pat and fondle the bundles of bank notes. "Millions! Millions! Hundreds of millions!"

"The amount is so vast," said Locke, still earnestly, "that I cannot help thinking about what you said in reference to being followed out there in the woods last night. I don't think you should risk any chance of being followed to-night when you have all this great wealth with you, even though you are quite sure you have put whoever it may be off the scent, and that he, or they, will be busy somewhere else. I don't think, if I were you, I would go out of the house again to-night."

The old madman straightened up, and for a moment stared at Locke; and as he stared the red spots began to overspread his cheeks, and the pupils of the blue eyes seemed to enlarge and darken. And then with a sudden sweep of his arms he gathered the bundles of bank notes together, wrapped them up frantically in the oiled-silk covering, and thrust the package under his dressing gown.

"Hah!" His voice rose in a wild and savage scream. "You think I should stay in the house, do you? Hah! I see! I see! That is what you want me to do, is it? You want to trick me! You are one of them-one of them-one of them! You could never find the money where I hide it! You could never open God's time-lock! So you want me to keep it in the house to-night where you can get it! And you think that I am a madman and cannot see what you are after! You are one of them-one of them that follows-follows everywhere-and watches-and watches!"

He burst into a wild peal of laughter-another and another. He clutched fiercely at the package under his dressing gown. His face was distorted. His free hand pounded the table; saliva showed at the corners of his lips.

"For God's sake, Mr. Marlin," cried Locke, "listen —"

"One of them! One of them!" screamed the old man-and, turning suddenly, dashed for the door.

Locke's chair overturned with a crash as he sprang to his feet, and, darting around the table, started to follow-but the old maniac by now was already at the door. He saw the other's hand snatch at the electric-light switch. The aquarium was in sudden darkness. He heard the door slam. He groped his way to it, and wrenched at it.

The old madman had locked it on the outside.

VII
The Fight

For a moment, grim-lipped, Locke stood there at the door. He had accomplished exactly the opposite to what he had intended-the old man, the money, were both in infinitely greater peril now than under almost any other circumstances of which he could conceive. He did not blame himself-the vagaries, the impulses, the irrational promptings of an insane mind were beyond his control or guidance. It was the last thing he had expected the old maniac to do. But it was done now; it was too late to consider that phase of it. There was work for his own brain to do-he hoped more logically.

He turned sharply now, and began to make his way as best he could in the darkness toward the window at the end of that aisle of tanks outside of which he knew the masked man had stood. He dared not show any light here, though by so doing he would have been able to move more swiftly. The man who had been at the window was almost certainly gone now-to watch for the old maniac's appearance outside the house. And Mr. Marlin would assuredly, and as quickly as he could, scurry outside to hide his money away again. And even if the man in the mask had had no previous knowledge of the old madman's strange nightly movements, which would be a very unsafe assumption on which to depend, he would have *heard* enough at the window, if not to know, then, at least, to expect that the old maniac's one thought now would be to secrete his money, and that the hiding place, this time-lock that God had made, as the old man had called it, was somewhere outside the house. But the watcher's new lurking place might still embrace a view of the window, and if he, Locke, climbed out with the light behind him —

He was at the window now. He smiled grimly. He was pitted against no fool-but then he never had been fool enough himself ever to place Captain Francis Newcombe in that category! The man in the mask had left no tell-tale evidence of his presence behind him. The shade was drawn down; the window closed.

Locke lifted the shade now, raised the window quietly, and stood for an instant listening, staring out. He could see little or nothing, other than the swaying branches of trees against the sky line; and there was no sound save the sweep of the wind which was still blowing half a gale. And now he swung himself over the window sill, dropped the few feet to the ground-and crouched against the wall, listening, staring again into the blackness.

Nothing! The moon, burrowing deeper under the clouds, made it even blacker than it had been a moment ago. He straightened up and began to run toward the front of the house. It was perhaps a case of blindman's-buff, but there was not an instant to lose, and, deprived of any aid from the sense of either sight or hearing, he was left with only one thing to do. From the living room window a little while ago, he had seen Mr. Marlin *coming* toward the house from across the lawn, after having presumably just unearthed his money from its hiding place; the chances were that it was by the same route the old maniac would *return* now.

Locke ran on, stumbling, half groping his way through what seemed a veritable maze of out-buildings here at the rear of the house. The minutes seemed to be flying-wasted. The old maniac, if he had left the house the moment he had run from the aquarium, must by now have had a good three minutes' start; and if the man in the mask had at once picked up the trail, then —

No; he was not too late! He had reached the front corner of the house now, and across the lawn, where in the open space it was a little lighter, something, a blacker thing than the darkness, moving swiftly, caught his eye. It was the figure of a man running toward the trees in the direction of the path that led to the shore, and from which old Mr. Marlin had emerged earlier in the evening. And now the figure was gone-lost in the trees.

But he, Locke, too, was running now, sprinting for all he knew across the lawn. It was perhaps sixty yards. There was no time to use caution and circuit warily around the edge of the woods. He might be seen-but he had to take that chance. He would not be heard-the soft grass and the whine of the wind guaranteed him against that. It was a little better than an even break. The figure he had seen was not, he was sure, that of the old maniac. The long, flapping dressing gown would, even in a shadowy way, have been distinguishable. If he were right, then, in his supposition, the figure he had seen was the man in the mask, and old Mr. Marlin was already in there on the path leading through the woods to the shore. A cry, sudden, like a scream that was strangled, came with the gusting wind. It came again. From the edge of the lawn now, Locke leaped forward along the path. Black, twisting shapes loomed up just ahead of him. He flung himself upon them.

A low, startled, vicious snarl answered his attack. After that there was no sound while perhaps a minute passed, save the rustle of leaves and foliage, the *snip* of broken twigs under swiftly moving, straining feet. Locke was fighting now with merciless, exultant ferocity. It was the man in the mask he was at grips with-it was not the dressing gown alone, the *feel* of it, that distinguished one from the other; he had even in that first plunging rush in the darkness felt his hand brush against the mask on the man's cheek.

It was all shadow, all blackness. To this side and that, close locked together, he and his antagonist now swayed madly. The man's one evident desire was to break away from his, Locke's, encircling arms; his, Locke's, purpose not only to prevent escape, but to unmask the other-the moon might come out again at any instant-filter through the branches-just enough light to see the other's face if the mask were off.

A peal of laughter rang out. It was the old madman. Locke, as he fought, more sensed than saw the old man's form close to the ground, as though the other were groping around on his hands and knees. The peal of laughter came again; and then the old maniac's voice in a triumphant scream:

"I've got it! I've got it! Money! Money! Money! Millions! Millions! Millions! It's all here! I've got it! It's all —"

The voice was dying away in the distance. Locke laughed a little with grim, panting breath. Whether it had been dropped or had been snatched from him in the first attack, old Marlin had now obviously recovered his package of bank notes. He was gone now-running to hide it again, of course. In any event, the old maniac and his money were safe, and —

His antagonist had wrenched free an arm. Locke's head jolted back suddenly from a wicked short-arm blow that caught the point of his chin. A sensation of numbness seemed to be trying insidiously to creep upward to his brain-but it did not reach that far-not quite that far-only it loosened his grip for an instant and the shadowy form that he had held appeared to be floating away from him. And then, as his brain cleared, he shot his body forward in a low, lunging tackle. The other almost eluded him, but his hands caught and clung to the man's arm-both around one of the other's arms. The man wrenched and squirmed in a savage frenzy to tear himself free. There was a sound of the ripping and rending of cloth-something showed white in the darkness-the other's sleeve had torn away at the armpit.

A white shirt sleeve! It was a beacon in the blackness. The man would not get away now. There was something more tangible than a shadow-something to see. In a flash Locke shifted his hold, and his arms swept around the other, pinioning the man's hands to his sides-tighter-tighter. Neither spoke. The only sounds were hoarse, rasping gasps for breath. Tighter! He was bending the man backward now-slowly-surely —a little more. No-the man was too strong-the pinioned arms were free again, and Locke felt them grip together like a vise around the small of his own back.

They lurched now, swaying from side to side like drunken men. The mask! To get at the mask! They were locked together, the chin of one on the other's shoulder-straining until the muscles cracked. Locke began to raise his head a little. The hot breath of the other was on his cheek now-and now his cheek rubbed against the other's mask.

An oath broke suddenly from the man-quick, muttered, the voice unrecognisable in its laboured breathing; and the other, seeming to sense his, Locke's, intention, suddenly relinquished his grip, snatched for a throat-hold instead, and, missing, began then to tear at Locke's arms in an effort to break away.

And then Locke laughed again grimly. It would avail nothing to snatch at the mask and get it off in the darkness here, if by so doing, with his own hold on the other gone, the man should get away. There was another way to get the mask off-and still maintain his grip upon the other!

They were holding now, seemingly as motionless as statues, the strength of one matched against the other in a supreme effort. The sweat broke out in great beads on Locke's forehead; his arms seemed to be tearing away from their sockets. He could feel the muscles in the other's neck, as it hugged against his own, swell and stand out like great steel ridges. And then slowly, inch by inch, he forced his own head around until his face was against the other's cheek. He could just feel the mask now with his lips-another inch-yes, now he had it-his teeth closed on the lower edge of the mask, chewed at it until he had a still firmer grip-and then he suddenly wrenched his head backward.

The mask came away in Locke's teeth. He spat it out. The other was a man gone mad with fury now; and with a new strength that fury brought he strove only to strike and strike again-but Locke only closed his hold the tighter. To strike back was to take the chance of the other breaking loose. It was too dark to see the man's face, though the mask was off now-but it could only be a few yards along the path to the open space of the lawn out there-and the moon would not always be fickle-it would break through the clouds, and —

They were rocking, lurching, twisting, swaying in their mad struggle-and now they circled more widely-and branches snatched and tore at them, and broke and fell from the trees at the sides of the path. And here Locke gave a step, and there another, working nearer and nearer to the edge of the lawn.

And then suddenly there came a half-choked cry from the other. The man had tripped in the undergrowth. Locke swung his weight to complete the fall-tripped himself-and both, with their balance gone, but grappling the fiercer at each other, pitched headlong with terrific force into the trees at the side of the path.

And Locke was for an instant conscious of a great blow, of streaks of fiery light that smote at his eyeballs with excruciating pain-and then utter blackness came.

When he opened his eyes again a moonbeam lay along the path, and a figure in a long dressing gown was passing by. He was dreaming, wasn't he? There was a sick sensation in his head, a giddiness-and besides that it gave him great pain. He raised himself up cautiously on his elbow, fighting to clear his mind-and suddenly his lips tightened grimly. There was something ironical in that moonbeam-something that mocked him in disclosing a figure in a dressing gown instead of a face that had been unmasked yet still could not be seen. He looked around him now. He was lying a few feet in from the edge of the path, and against the trunk of a large tree. Yes, he remembered now. His head had struck against the tree and he had been knocked unconscious. And the man who had been masked was gone.

He rose to his feet. He was very groggy-and for a moment he leaned against the tree trunk for support. The giddiness began to pass away. That was old Mr. Marlin who had just gone by. Well, neither the old madman nor his money had come to any harm, anyway! He stepped out on the path, and from there to the edge of the lawn. The old madman was just disappearing around the corner of the verandah.

Locke put his hands to his eyes. How his head throbbed! How long had he lain there unconscious? He took out his watch. His eyes seemed blurred-or was it the meagreness of the moonlight? He was not quite sure, but it seemed to be ten minutes after three. It wasn't very easy to figure backward. He did not know how long he and the old maniac had been together in the aquarium, but, say, half an hour. Starting then at the hour of the rendezvous, which had been at a quarter past two, that would bring it to a quarter of three; then, say, ten minutes for what had happened afterward, including the fight, and that would make it five minutes of three. He must therefore have been lying in there unconscious for at least fifteen minutes.

The man who had worn the mask was gone now-naturally. But perhaps it would not be so difficult to pick up the trail. Captain Francis Newcombe's room offered very promising possibilities-and there was a torn coat sleeve that would not readily be replaced in fifteen minutes!

He made his way now across the lawn, and up the steps to the verandah. He tried the front door. It was locked. Of course! He had forgotten that he had left the house by crawling out of the aquarium window. There was no use going back that way because the old madman had locked the aquarium door. Mr. Marlin, though, had some means of entrance-and if that door through which the man had so suddenly appeared in the back hall meant anything, the entrance the old man used was likely to be somewhere in the rear. But Mr. Marlin would probably have locked that, too, behind him.

He looked up and down the now moon-flecked verandah-and began to try the French windows that opened upon it from the front rooms of the house. The first two were locked as he had expected. It was only a chance, but he might as well begin here as anywhere else. He tried the third one almost perfunctorily. It opened at a touch.

"I'm in luck!" Locke muttered, and stepped inside.

He turned the knob to lock the French window behind him, and found the bolt already thrown. Queer! He stood frowning for an instant, then stooped and felt along the inside edge of the threshold. The socket that ordinarily housed the bolt-bar was gone. The same condition therefore obviously existed at the top, as the long bar had a double throw.

He straightened up, a curious smile twitching at his lips now, and, making his way silently to the stairs, he reached the upper hall, stole along it to the door of his own room, and entered. Here, from one of his bags, he procured a revolver; and a moment later, his ear to the panel, listening, he stood outside Captain Francis Newcombe's door.

There was no sound from within. Softly he began to turn the door handle-the door would hardly be locked; that would be a misplay; one didn't lock one's bedroom door when a guest in a private house. No; it was not locked. He had the door ajar now. Again he listened. There was still no sound from within. Was the man back yet, or not? The absence of any sound meant nothing, save that Newcombe was probably not in the sitting room of his suite-he might easily, however, be in either the bathroom or the bedroom beyond.

Locke swung the door a little wider open, stepped through, and closed it noiselessly behind him. Again he stood still, his revolver now outthrust a little before him. The moonlight played across the floor. It disclosed an open door beyond. Still no sound.

Locked moved forward. He could see into the bedroom now. The bed was not only empty, but had not been slept in. He turned quickly and opened the bathroom door. The bathroom, too, was empty.

Captain Francis Newcombe had not, then, as yet returned. With a grim smile Locke thrust his revolver into his pocket. It was perhaps just as well-the time while he waited might possibly be used to very good advantage! Captain Francis Newcombe's baggage was invitingly at one's disposal-the *Talofa*, with its confined quarters, and where, on the little vessel, it was always *crowded*, as it were, had offered no such opportunity!

Locke opened one of the bags. His smile now had changed to one of irony. Barring any other justification, turn about was no more than fair play, was it? He possessed a moral certainty, if he lacked the actual proof, that Captain Francis Newcombe had not hesitated to invade his, Locke's, cabin on the liner and go through his, Locke's, effects.

He laughed a little now in low, grim mirth. He wondered which of the two, Newcombe or himself, would be the better rewarded for his efforts?

There was little light, but Locke worked swiftly by the sense of touch, with fingers that ignored the general contents, and that sought dexterously for *hidden* things. His fingers traversed every inch of the lining of the bag, top, bottom and sides. He disturbed nothing.

Presently he laid the bag aside, and started on another-and suddenly he nodded his head sharply in satisfaction. This one was what was generally known as a Gladstone bag, and under the lining at one side his fingers felt what seemed like a folded paper that moved under his touch. The lining was intact, of course, but there must be some way of getting in underneath it-yes, here it was! Rather clever! And ordinarily quite safe-unless one were actually looking for something of the sort! There was a flap, or pocket, at the side of the bag, the ordinary sort of thing, and at the bottom of the flap Locke's fingers, working deftly, found that the edges of the lining, while apparently fastened together, were made, in reality, into a double fold-the lining being stiff enough, even when the edges were displaced, to fall back of its own accord into place again.

He separated the edges now, worked his fingers into the opening, and drew out an envelope. It had been torn open at one end, and there was a superscription of some sort on it in faded writing which, in the semi-darkness, he could not make out. He stood up, and went quickly to the window to obtain the full benefit of the moonlight. He could just decipher the writing now:

> "Polly's papers which is God's truth,
> Mrs. Wickes X her mark."

For a moment he stood there motionless-but his eyes had lifted from the envelope now and were fixed on the lawn below. The window here gave on the side of the lawn with the trees at the rear of the house in view. A man had just stepped out from the shadow of the trees and was coming toward the house.

Locke stared, even the envelope in his hand temporarily forgotten, as a frown of perplexity that deepened into amazed chagrin gathered on his forehead. The figure was quite recognisable, even minutely so. It was Captain Francis Newcombe. It accounted for the missing sockets on that French window perhaps-but the man was as perfectly and immaculately dressed as he had been that night at dinner. There was no torn coat-on missing coat sleeve. The man he had fought with, the man in the mask, had not been Captain Francis Newcombe.

He laughed now-not pleasantly. He had obviously been waiting here for the wrong man. There was no need of waiting any longer-unless he desired to be caught himself! Queer! Strange! But there was the envelope. Polly's papers! What was it that was "God's truth"? At least, he would find that out!

He thrust the envelope into his pocket, closed the bag, and returned to his own room. He switched on the light, hurriedly took the envelope from his pocket again, and from it drew out two documents. He studied them while minute after minute passed, then dropping them on the table before him, he stood with drawn face and clenched fists staring across the room. Polly's birth certificate! The marriage certificate of her parents! He saw again the agony in the dark eyes, he heard again the agony in the voice that had proclaimed a parentage outside the pale. And a great oath came now from Locke's white lips.

He flung himself into a chair beside the table. He fought for cool, contained reasoning. These papers-Newcombe! Did it change anything, place Newcombe in any better light, because it was some other man who had worn that mask to-night? He shook his head in quick, emphatic dissent. It did not! He was sure, certain of that. The trail led too far back, was too well defined, too conclusive. And even to-night! What was Newcombe doing out of the house at three o'clock in the morning? Ah, yes-he had it! The old maniac's words came back with sudden and sure significance: "Digging-digging-digging.... The wrong scent.... The hut in the woods at the rear of the house."

Locke gnawed savagely at his lips. That was where Newcombe had come from-the woods at the rear of the house. It meant that Newcombe was the one who had been tricked by the old madman's cunning, which could never have happened if Newcombe had not been stealthily trying to find the hidden money; it simply meant that Newcombe was the one who had been on the wrong scent-and that some one else had been on the right one!

His face was set in lines like chiselled marble now. Who was this "some one else"? Was the question very hard to answer? The field was very limited —*significantly* limited now! He wasn't wrong, was he? He couldn't be wrong! And there was always the torn sleeve!

Locke's eyes fixed upon the two documents on the table again. Captain Francis Newcombe! No; it did not make Newcombe any the less a guilty man because it was not he who had worn the mask to-night. Newcombe stood out sharply defined against the light of evidence which, if only circumstantial, was strong enough to damn the man a thousand times over for what he was.

And here, adding to that evidence, was the proof that Polly's identity had been, and was being, deliberately concealed from her. It opened a vista to uglier and still more evil things-things that only a soul dead to decency, black as the pit of hell, could have conceived and patiently put into execution. A child —a gutter-snipe, Polly had called herself—*rescued* from naked poverty and the slums of Whitechapel by a man such as Newcombe, whose only promptings were the promptings of a fiend! Why? Was there room to question further why Captain Francis Newcombe had years ago adopted such a ward-when now before one's eyes those years were bearing their poison fruit? Polly's introduction into this family here was even at this moment being traded upon to effect the theft of half a million dollars. That was too obvious now to permit denial. Newcombe was making of a girl, high-minded, pure-souled, a hideous cat's-paw. Yes, yes! All that was clear enough! But why should Polly have been deprived of her rightful name, her claim to honest parentage? Was it to weld a stronger bond of gratitude-or make her the more helpless, and therefore the more dependent upon her guardian? Where were these parents? Dead or living? There was Mrs. Wickes-Mrs. Wickes, who had posed as the mother! Well, there were certain quarters in London where those who strayed outside the law could be made to talk. Mrs. Wickes should be able to furnish very interesting information. It was not far to Whitechapel and London-by cable.

His mind, his brain, worked on-but now suddenly in turmoil and misery despite all effort of his to hold himself in check.

Polly! Polly *Gray!*

She loved this monster-that she thought a man, and called her guardian. Not the love of a maid for lover; but with the love, the honour, the respect and gratitude that she would give a cherished father.

The truth would break her heart. The love her friends had given her, turned to their own undoing! The shame would be torture; the self-degradation, the abasement that she would know, would be beyond the bearing. Her faith would be a shattered thing!

Locke's clenched hands lay outspread across the table. He drew them suddenly together and dropped his head upon them.

"And you love her," he whispered to himself. "Do you know what that is going to mean? You did not count on that, did you? Do you know where that will lead? Do you know the consequences?"

He answered his own questions.

"No," he said numbly; "I don't know what it is going to mean. I know I love her."

VIII

The Message

Polly Wickes, from her pillow, stared into the darkness. There had been no thought of sleep; it did not seem as though there ever could be again. She had undressed and gone to bed-but she had done this mechanically, because at night one went to bed, because she had always gone to bed.

Not to sleep!

The tears blinding her eyes, she had groped her way up the stairs from the living room where she had left Howard Locke, and somehow she had reached her room. That was hours and hours ago. Surely the daylight would come soon now; surely it would soon be morning. She wanted the daylight, she wanted the morning, because the darkness and the stillness seemed to accentuate a terrible and merciless sense of isolation that had come so swiftly, so suddenly into her life-to overturn, to dominate, to stupefy, to cast contemptuously aside the dreams and thoughts and hopes of happiness and contentment. And yet, though she yearned for the morning, she even dreaded it more. How could she meet Howard Locke-at breakfast? She couldn't. She wouldn't go down to breakfast.

The small hands came from under the coverings, and clasped themselves tightly about the aching head-and she turned and buried her face in the pillow. She might easily, very easily evade breakfast-and postpone the inevitable for a few minutes, even a few hours. Why did she grasp at pitiful subterfuges such as that?

She was nameless.

That phrase had come hours ago. It had scorched itself upon her brain-as a branding iron at white heat sears its imprint upon quivering flesh, never to be effaced, always to endure. She was nameless. It wasn't that she had not always known it-she always had. But it meant now what it had never meant before. Until now it had been as something that, since it must be borne, she had striven to bear with what courage was hers, and, denying its right to embitter life, had sought to imprison it in the dim recesses of her mind-but now in an instant it had broken its bonds to stand forth exposed in all its ugliness; no longer captive, but a vengeful captor, claiming its miserable right from now on to control and dominate her life.

She had thought of love-it would have been unnatural if she had not. But she had never loved, and therefore she had thought of it only in an abstract way. Dream love-fancies. But she loved now-she loved this man who had so suddenly come into her life-she loved Howard Locke. And happinesss, greater than she had realised happiness could ever be, had unfolded itself to her gaze, and, love had become a vibrant, personal thing, so wonderful, so tender and so glad a thing, that beside it all the world was little and insignificant and empty; but even as the glory of it, and the joy of it had burst upon her, she had been obliged to turn away from it-not very bravely, for the tears had scalded her as she had run from the living room-because there was no other thing to do, because it was something that was not hers to have.

She could never be the wife of any man.

She was nameless.

Why had she ever found it out! It might so easily have been that she would have never known. That-that no one need ever have known! She was sure that even her guardian did not know.

She smothered her face deeper in the pillow as she cried out in anguish. She could have had happiness then-and-and it would have been honourable for her to have taken it, wouldn't it?

She lay quiet for a little while. No; that was cowardly, selfish. If she really loved this man, she should be glad for his sake that she knew the truth, glad now of the day when she had found it out. She remembered that day. It seemed to live more vividly before her now than it ever had before. Mrs. Wickes-her mother-had-had been drinking. The words had been a slip of the tongue; a slip that her mother, owing to her condition at the time, had not even been conscious of. Mrs. Wickes had been garrulously recounting some sordid crime that had remained famous even amongst its many fellows in Whitechapel, and, in placing the date, had stated it was two years after Mr. Wickes had died. Later on, in the same garrulous account, she had again referred to the date, but had placed it this time by saying that she, Polly, was a baby not more than a month old when it had happened.

And on that day when she had listened to her mother's tale she had still been but a child-in years. She could not have been more than twelve-but she was very old for twelve. The slums of London had seen to that. And so, the next day, when her mother had been more herself, she had asked Mrs. Wickes, more out of a precocious curiosity perhaps than anything else, for an explanation. Mrs. Wickes had flown into a furious rage.

"Mind yer own business!" Mrs. Wickes had screamed at her. "The likes of you a-slingin' mud at yer mother! Wot you got to complain of? Ain't I takin' care of you? If ever you says another word I'll break yer back!"

She had never said another word. In one sense she had not been different from any other child of twelve then, and it had not naturally caused any change in her feelings toward her mother; nor in the after years, with their fuller light of understanding, had it ever changed or abated her love for the mother with whom she had shared hardship and distress and want. She thanked God for that now. Her mother might have been one to inspire little love and little of respect in others; but to her, Polly, when she had parted from her mother to come here to America, she had parted from the only human being in all the world she had ever loved, or who, in turn, had ever showed affection for her. She had never ceased to love her mother; instead, she had perhaps been the better able to understand, and even to add sympathy to love and to know a great pity, where bitterness and resentment and unforgiveness might otherwise have been, because she, too, had lived in those drab places where the urge of self-preservation alone was the standard that measured ethics, where one fought and snatched at anything, no matter from where or by what means it came, that kept soul and body together-because she could look out on that life, not as one apart, but with the eyes of one who once had been a —a guttersnipe.

And now?

Now that this crisis in her life had come-what now? She did not know. She had been trying to think calmly, but her brain would not obey her-it was crushed, stunned. It ached even in a physical way, frightfully, and —

She raised her head suddenly from the pillow in a sort of incredulous amazement-and immediately afterward sat bolt upright in bed. The telephone here in her room was ringing. At this hour! Her heart suddenly seemed to stop beating. Something-something must be wrong-something must have happened-Dora-Mr. Marlin!

It was still ringing-ringing insistently.

She sprang from the bed, and, running to the 'phone, snatched the receiver from its hook.

"Yes, yes?" she answered breathlessly. "What is it?"

A voice came over the wire; a man's voice, rising and falling creepily in a sing-song, mocking sort of way:

"Is that you, Polly-Polly Wickes-Polly Wickes-Polly Wickes-Wickes-Wickes —P-o-l-l-y W-i-c-k-e-s?"

It frightened her. She felt the blood ebb from her cheeks. There was something horribly familiar in the voice-but she could not place it. Her hand reached out to the wall for support.

"Yes" —she tried to hold her voice in control, to answer steadily —"yes; I am Polly Wickes. Who are you? What do you want?"

She heard the sound as of a gust of wind from a door that was suddenly blown open, the beat of the sea, then the slam of a door-and then the voice again:

"Polly-Polly Wickes." The words seemed to be choked now with malicious laughter. "Why don't you dress in black, Polly Wickes-Polly Wickes-for your mother, Polly Wickes?"

"What do you mean?" she cried frantically. "Who are you? Who are you? What do you mean?"

There was no answer.

She kept calling into the 'phone.

Nothing! No reply! The voice was gone.

She stood there staring wildly through the darkness. Black ...for her mother ...dead! No, no ...it couldn't be true! That voice ...yes, it was like the horrible voice that had called out the other night ...she knew now why it was familiar....

Terror-stricken, the receiver dropped from her hand.

Dead! Her mother dead! It couldn't be true! She began to grope around her. The chair-her dressing gown. Her hands felt the garment. She snatched it up, flung it around her, and stumbled to the door and along the hall to Captain Francis Newcombe's room. And here she knocked mechanically, but, without listening for response, opened the door, and, stumbling still in a blind way, crossed the threshold.

"Guardy! Guardy! Oh, guardy!" she sobbed out.

Captain Francis Newcombe was not asleep. Quite apart from the fact that he had only got to bed but a very short while before, the cards that night had gone too badly against him, and there was a savage sense of fury upon him that would not quiet down. And now, as he heard his door open and heard Polly call, he was out of bed and into a dressing gown in an instant. Polly out there in his sitting room-at half-past four in the morning! And she was sobbing. She sobbed now as he heard her call again:

"Guardy! Guardy! Oh, guardy!"

This was queer-damned queer! His face was suddenly set in the darkness as he crossed the bedroom floor-but his voice was quiet, cool, reassuring, as he answered her: "Right-o, Polly! I'm coming!"

He switched on the light as he entered the sitting room. It brought a quick, startled cry over the sobs.

"Oh, please, guardy!" she faltered out. "I —I —*please* turn off the light."

"Of course!" he said quietly-and it was dark in the room again.

He had caught a glimpse of a little figure crouching just inside the door —a little figure with white, strained face, with great, wondrous masses of hair tumbling about her shoulders, with hands that clasped some filmy drapery tightly across her bosom, and small, dainty feet that were bare of covering. And as he moved toward her now across the room, another mood took precedence over the savagery he had just been nursing —a mood no holier. It might be queer, this visit of hers; but that glimpse of her, alluring, intimate, of a moment gone, had set his blood afire again-and far more violently than it had on that first occasion when he had seen her here on the island two nights ago. It brought again to the fore the question that, through a cursed nightmare of happenings, had almost since that time lain dormant. Was he going to let Locke have her-or was he going to keep her for himself? How far had she gone with Locke? They had been a lot together. Well, that mattered little-if he wanted her for himself he would *make* the way to get her, Locke and hell combined to the contrary! The woman-against her potential value as somebody else's wife! Damn it, that was the wonder of her-that she could even hold her own when weighed on such scales. There were lots of women.

He had reached her now, and touched her, found her hand and taken it in his own. "What is it, Polly?" he asked gently. "What's the matter?"

"It's —it's mother," she whispered brokenly. "The telephone in my room rang a few minutes ago, and some one —a man-and, oh, guardy, I'm sure it was the same voice that we heard when we were in the woods the night before last-asked me why I didn't wear black for my mother. It-it couldn't mean anything else but-but that mother is dead. Oh, guardy, guardy! How could he know, guardy? How could he know?"

Captain Francis Newcombe made no movement, save to place his arm around the thinly clad shoulders, and draw the little figure closer to him. It was dark here, she could not have seen his face anyway, but it was composed, calm, tranquil. Perhaps the lips straightened a little at the corners-nothing more. But the brain of the man was working at lightning speed. Here was disaster, ruin, exposure if he made the slightest slip. Again, eh? This was the fourth time this devil from the pit had shown his hand! The reckoning would be adequate! But how was he to answer Polly? Quick! She must not notice any hesitation. Tell her that Mrs. Wickes was dead? He had a ready explanation on his tongue, formulated days ago, to account for having withheld that information. Seize this opportunity to tell her that Mrs. Wickes was not her mother? No! Impossible! He had meant to use all this to his advantage, and in his own good time. It was too late now. He was left holding the bag! If he admitted that Mrs. Wickes was dead, he admitted that there was some one on this island whose mysterious presence, whose mysterious knowledge, must cause a furor, a search, with possible results that at any hazard he dared not risk. Polly would tell Locke-Dora-everybody. It was impossible! But against this, sooner or later, Polly must know of Mrs. Wickes' death, and — Bah! Was he become a child, the old cunning gone? He would keep her for a while from England-travel-anything-and, months on, the word would come that Mrs. Wickes was dead, and found in the old hag's effects would be Polly's papers. The one safe play, the *only* play, was not alone to reassure the girl now, but to keep her mouth shut. Above all to keep her mouth shut! But-how? How? Yes! He had it now! His soul began to laugh in unholy glee. His voice was grave, earnest, tender, sympathetic.

"He couldn't have known, Polly," he said. "That is at once evident on the face of it. How could any one on this little out-of-the-way island possibly know a thing like that when I, who am the only one who *could* know, and who have just come direct from England, know it to be untrue. Don't you see, Polly?"

He had drawn her head against his shoulder, stroking back the hair from her forehead. She raised it now quickly.

"Yes, guardy!" she said eagerly. "I —I see; and I'm so glad I came to you at once. But-but it is so strange, and-and it still frightens me terribly. I don't understand. I —I can't understand. Why should any one ring the telephone in my room at this hour, and-and tell me a thing like that if it were not true?"

"Or even if it were true-at such an hour, or in such a manner," he injected quietly. "Tell me exactly what happened, Polly."

"I think I've told you everything," she said. "I don't think there was anything else. When I answered the 'phone, the voice asked if I were Polly Wickes, and kept on repeating my name over and over again in a horrible, crazy, sing-songy way, and then I heard a sound as though a door had been blown open by the wind, and I could hear the waves pounding, and then the door was evidently slammed shut again, and the voice said what I —I have told you about wearing black for my mother. And then I couldn't hear anything more, and I couldn't get any answer, though I called again and again into the 'phone. Oh, guardy, I can't understand! I —I'm sure it was the same voice as that other night. What does it mean? Guardy, what should we do? Who could it be?"

A door blown open by the wind! The pound of the waves! Where was there a telephone that would measure up to those requirements? Not in the house! Captain Francis Newcombe smiled grimly in the darkness. The private installation was restricted to the house and its immediate surroundings. Therefore the boathouse! The boathouse had a 'phone connection. And there was still an hour or more to daybreak! But first to shut Polly's mouth.

"Polly," he said gravely, measuring his words, "I haven't the slightest doubt but that it was the same voice we heard in the woods; in fact, I'm quite sure of it. And I'm equally sure now that I know who it is."

She drew back from him in a quick, startled way.

"But, guardy, you said it was only some one catcalling to —"

"Yes; I know," he interrupted seriously. "But I did not tell you what I was really suspicious of all along. With what I had to go on then, it did not seem that I had any right to do so. It's quite a different matter now, however, after what has happened to-night."

"Yes?" she prompted anxiously.

"There can be only two possible explanations," he said. "Either some one is playing a cruel hoax; or it is the work of an unhinged mind, an irrational act, a phase of insanity that —"

"Guardy!" she cried out sharply. "You mean —"

"Yes," he said steadily; "I do, Polly. And there can really be no question about it at all. Can you imagine any one doing such a thing merely from a perverted sense of humour? —any one of us here? —for it must have been some one of us who is connected with the household in order to have had access to a telephone. It is unthinkable, absurd, isn't it? On the other hand, the hour, the irresponsible words, their 'crazy' mode of expression, as you yourself said, the motiveless declaration of a palpable untruth, all stamp it as the work of one who is not accountable for his actions-of one who is literally insane. And then the fact that you recognised the voice as the one we heard two nights ago is additional proof, if such were needed, which it very obviously is not. You remember that we had seen Mr. Marlin in his dressing gown disappear under the verandah a few minutes before we heard the calls and cries and wild, insane laughter. My first thought then was that it was Mr. Marlin, and I was afraid that either harm had, or might, come to him. I sent you at once back to the house, and I ran into the woods to look for him. I did not find him; and, therefore, as there was always the possibility then that I had been mistaken, I felt that I should not alarm any of you here, and particularly Miss Marlin, by suggesting that Mr. Marlin's condition was decidedly worse than even it was supposed to be. Is it quite plain, Polly? I do not think we have very far to look for the one who telephoned you to-night."

He could just see her in the darkness, a little white, shadowy form, as she stood slightly away from him now. One of her hands was pressed in an agitated way to her face and eyes; the other still held tightly to the throat of her dressing gown.

"Oh, yes, it's plain, guardy," she whispered miserably. "It's —it's too plain. Poor, poor Mr. Marlin! What are we to do? It would hurt Dora terribly if she knew her father had done this. I —I can't tell her."

"Of course, you can't," said Captain Francis Newcombe gravely. "Your position is even more delicate than mine was the other night. I do not see that you can do anything-except to say nothing about it to any one for the present."

"Yes," she agreed numbly.

She began to move toward the door.

"It's not likely to happen again," said Captain Francis Newcombe reassuringly; "and, anyway, you can make sure it won't by just leaving the receiver off the hook. Do that, Polly." And then, solicitously: "But you're not frightened any more now, are you, Polly? A mystery explained loses its terror, doesn't it? And, besides, the main thing was to know that your mother was all right."

"My mother —"

He thought he heard her catch her breath in a quick, sudden half sob.

"It's all right, Polly," he said hastily. "Don't think of that part of it any more. Everything's all right."

"Yes; I —I know." Her voice was very low. "It's —all right. I —good-night, guardy."

She had opened the door.

"I'll see you to your room," he said.

"No," she answered; "I'm not frightened any more. Good-good-night, guardy."

"Good-night, Polly," he said.

The door closed.

Captain Francis Newcombe stood in the darkness. And for a moment he did not move-but the mask was gone now, and the laughter that came low from his lips was a mirthless sound, and the working face was black with fury. And then he turned, and with a bound was back in the bedroom, and snatching at his clothes began to dress.

There was still an hour to daybreak.

Book III:
The Penalty

I

The White Shirt Sleeve

An hour to daybreak! Passion, unchecked and unrestrained, was stamped on Captain Francis Newcombe's face as he dressed now with savage, ferocious haste. He swore and snarled, making low venomous sounds in the fury that possessed him. There was no longer room for the fear that last night, here in his rooms, had gnawed at his soul itself-the fear of the *unknown*; there was no longer room for fear in any sense, whether born of the intangible, or whether it knew its source in man, or God, or devil-there was only *murder*, that alone, in his heart.

The blows were coming nearer and nearer home. Too near! And his efforts to strike one in return had resulted in little to boast about so far! Disaster, ruin, that dangling gibbet chain, were inevitable if this went on. He had been *too* cautious perhaps! Well, that was ended now! He swore again-bitter, sacrilegious in his rage. The luck had been running against him. Even an old fool had tricked him-even a maniac, a cracked-brained idiot, and one almost in his dotage besides, had tricked him! Last night after he had read that infernal message at the hut he had made no effort to uncover the madman's horde-he had lain there waiting. Hours of waiting, patient waiting-listening-his revolver in his hand-the one chance that the unknown might not have gone away, might have lingered, hidden in the foliage, to gloat —*and die*. He had waited in vain. To-night he had gone back to the hut only to find after hours of search that the old madman's money, wherever else it might be, was not there. And then he had returned here-and again the unknown had struck swiftly, viciously, cunningly.

When, where, how would the next blow fall? —unless he could now strike the quicker, and strike surely! How much farther was it to the abyss of exposure? To-night he had stood perilously close to its edge, hadn't he? If he had not been able to pull the wool over Polly's eyes with the specious explanation that it was old Marlin who had telephoned, he would —

He stood suddenly motionless, tense, with his coat half on, his working lips drawn for the moment tight together. Had it been, after all, merely a *specious* explanation? Was he so sure that it *wasn't* old Marlin, after all, who had telephoned? The old madman was cunning; and, granting that fact as a premise, his act last night in pretending to go to his money in the hut must have been prompted by suspicion of some sort. The money had never been in that hut. The bit of flooring that was loose was flush with the ground beneath, and the ground had never been disturbed-and this was true of everywhere else in the hut. The old maniac, then, was suspicious that he was being followed by somebody, and had set a false trail. Of whom would he be suspicious? The question answered itself. The newcomers on the island, of course. And, being suspicious of them, he would want to drive them away. To frighten Polly into the belief that her mother was dead might very easily appeal to an insane brain, and even to one that wasn't, as a very clever and effective means of accomplishing this end surreptitiously. Polly might very logically be expected in her grief to wish to bring her visit here to an end, even if she did not, indeed, insist on returning to England at once-and the result would be that all who had come here, Locke, Runnells and himself, would naturally leave with her. Why not? The madman was certainly cunning enough; he could have telephoned-and the motive was there.

No! With an angry, self-contemptuous snarl, Captain Francis Newcombe jerked on his coat. Was he trying to qualify for an insane asylum himself? The old maniac *could* have done this to-night, otherwise the explanation made to Polly would have been merely an absurdity; but old Marlin had not been on the liner and could not have fired that shot through the cabin window-nor could the old man have known, as instanced by that voice in the woods, that he, Newcombe, was Shadow Varne-or known anything of the murder of Sir Harris Greaves. The man who had telephoned to-night —making the fourth mysterious blow that had been struck-was the man who had showed his hand on those three former occasions. This was so blatantly obvious that to have allowed his brain to shoot off at a tangent so idiotic but increased his anger now.

He sneered at himself as he finished dressing. There was only one man on the island who could be made to fit into each and every one of the four niches. Runnells! Runnells *had* been on board ship, even though at the time Runnells had apparently been asleep; Runnells was in a position to know, and to know what now appeared to be certainly *too much*, about Shadow Varne; and Runnells, though the man could *prove* nothing, was, more than any one else, in a position to entertain suspicions in reference to the murder of the baronet who meddled so gratuitously with the affairs of others.

Captain Francis Newcombe slipped a flashlight and a revolver into his pocket, and made for the door of his room. Quite so! All this was nothing new-no new angle-he had mulled this over a hundred times before. But up to now he had held his hand-and for two very good reasons. In the first place, he had not been able to bring himself to believe that it was Runnells, for he could not see where Runnells would profit by any such game; and, secondly, as he had already argued with himself, should it not prove to be Runnells, he almost inevitably disclosed his own hand and his real purpose in coming here to Manwa Island, and it would in that case make a partner of Runnells-and partners shared in the profits! But the time for hesitation on any such score as that was gone now; not only because the ice he was treading on, already thin, had nearly broken through to-night, and the promise of imminent and final disaster was forcing his hand, but because, in respect of Runnells, the absence of apparent motive-Runnells would be made to explain that! —counted for nothing now in view of the fact that he, Newcombe, had more to go on to-night than he had had before. Not only was Runnells one who fitted into the role of the "unknown" on each of the four occasions, but Runnells, as though to clear the matter of all doubt, knew what surely no one else on the island could possibly know-that Mrs. Wickes *actually* was dead. He, Newcombe, had himself to blame for that, and it appeared now that he had trusted Runnells too far; but somebody had had to bury the old hag. Not Captain Francis Newcombe! To have left her in the status of a pauper for the authorities, or the Mission Boards, or any of that ilk to have taken care of, and in view of the fact that it must have been known amongst her neighbours that she had for a long time received money from somewhere, talk, comment, investigation, official this and official that would have been invited. It might have amounted to nothing-but if a rock that is held in one's hand is not thrown into the calm waters of a pool the placid surface is not disturbed! He had delegated Runnells to interview the undertaker and arrange for the quiet and unostentatious disposal of Mrs. Wickes' mortal remains. Runnells, for the time being, did very well as a nephew of the deceased, who, though in neither close nor loving touch with his somewhat questionable relation, at least recognised the family tie to the extent of paying for her very modest and unpretentious obsequies.

Captain Francis Newcombe crept quietly along the hall now. Runnells' room, thanks to the hospitable thoughtfulness of Miss Marlin, in order that the "man" might be nearer at hand and therefore the better able to serve his "master," was not in the servants' quarters, but was at the extreme end of the hall here just at the head of the stairs. Captain Francis Newcombe's hand felt along the wall to guide him in the darkness. He had no desire to stumble over anything and arouse anybody; Locke, or Dora Marlin, for instance-and he had not forgotten that Polly was probably lying wide awake. The only one to be aroused was Runnells-and that very quietly. Runnells was a professional criminal, not a particularly clever one, but possessed, where a question of self-preservation was concerned, of a certain low cunning born of his hazardous career, a cunning that was not to be ignored. Cornered here in his room, for instance, Runnells, though quite well aware that he, Captain Francis Newcombe, would have no more hesitation about putting an end to him than an end to an obnoxious fly, would be equally well aware that here in the house he was possessed of a defence that rendered him invulnerable because no threat could be put into execution in silence, and that a cry, a shout, and, if necessary, to those who came to his succour, a confession of his own past misdeeds in order to prove his alliance with, and implicate his "master" in criminal intrigue, would protect him-for the moment-utterly.

But he, Captain Francis Newcombe, had no intention of making any such unpardonable misplay as that! Runnells would never look down the barrel of a revolver with a confidence born of the fact that the trigger dared not be pulled; Runnells would never feel a grip upon his throat and still be able to defy the clutching fingers because he knew they feared the cry, the gasp, the *noise* of strangulation. It would not be in Runnells' room that the man would lay bare his soul through fear to-night! Runnells would be played as a fish is played!

Captain Francis Newcombe was halfway along the hall now. His mind, despite the fury that from smouldering rage had broken into flaming heat, was logical, measured, precise. That telephone message could have come from nowhere else but from the boathouse. That was self-evident. If Runnells, then, was at the bottom of this, the question now was whether Runnells had got back to his room yet or not? And, if he were back, how long he had been back? —the man must be allowed to undress and get into bed. To discover Runnells fully dressed at this hour was to force the issue then and there in Runnells' room; for Runnells, caught like that, while he might be voluble with explanations, would of necessity at the same time be thrown instantly upon his guard, and would not be fool enough to be enticed into any trap, no matter how apparently genuine the pretence of accepting his explanations might be made to appear.

Captain Francis Newcombe was at the door now listening. Runnells *would* have had time by now to have got to bed; certainly there was no sound from within, and — He drew back from the door suddenly, but as silently as a shadow. There was no sound from within, but some one was creeping, though with every attempt at silence, up the staircase. Captain Francis Newcombe retreated still a little farther back along the hall, and, with body hugged now close against the wall, waited in the darkness. He could see nothing-not even across the hall; and, therefore, he was quite secure from being observed himself, but his hand, in his pocket now, was closed over the butt of his revolver.

The sounds were very faint, but they were equally unmistakable-now the muffled, protesting creak of a stair tread; now that sound, like no other sound so much as the padded footfall of an animal, as weight was cautiously placed on the carpeted stairs. The footsteps came nearer and nearer to the upper landing, slow, laborious in their caution and stealth. And then another sound-equally faint and equally unmistakable-the opening and closing of the door at the head of the stairs.

Captain Francis Newcombe relaxed. His lips twisted into a smile of malignant satisfaction. Runnells!

So it *was* Runnells who had indulged in that little telephone conversation; Runnells, the pitiful, foolhardy moth-and the flame! Runnells, instead of being already in bed, was just getting back. So much the better-it would tax Runnells' ingenuity a little beyond its limitations to explain this unseemly hour! It made it perhaps just a little easier to handle and *break* the man.

Captain Francis Newcombe moved silently back again to the door of Runnells' room, and again listened at the panels. The sound of movement from within was distinctly audible. Runnells was preparing to go to bed.

The minutes passed-five-ten of them. It was quiet inside the room now. And then Captain Francis Newcombe knocked softly with his knuckles on the door-two raps in quick succession, then a single one followed by two more.

There was a sound almost on the instant as of the sudden creaking of the bed, and then the hurry of feet across the floor to the door. Then silence again. Captain Francis Newcombe smiled thinly to himself. Runnells was caution itself. He repeated the knocks precisely as before.

The door opened. Runnells showed as a white, vague figure in his night clothes.

"What's up?" whispered Runnells anxiously.

"I'm afraid we've been spotted," said Captain Francis Newcombe tersely.

"Spotted!" Runnells echoed the word with a gulp. "Who by?"

"Some swine from the Yard, I suppose," replied Captain Francis Newcombe as tersely as before. "Do you remember Detective-Sergeant Mullins?"

"Him?" gasped Runnells. "My Gawd, he ain't followed us here, has he? Strike me pink! My Gawd! I said all along it was damned queer him showing up at the rooms that night. Are you sure?"

"Not yet-and I never will be if you stand there gawking," said Captain Francis Newcombe sharply. "Go and get your clothes on-and hurry up about it! It'll soon be daylight. Every minute counts. Meet me down on the verandah."

He did not wait for Runnells' reply. It was not necessary. Runnells had swallowed bait, hook and line. Captain Francis Newcombe indulged in a low, savage chuckle, as, descending the stairs, he unlocked the front door and stepped quietly out on the verandah. He had not lunged in the dark, nor was it chance that had prompted him to endow his bogey with the personality of Detective-Sergeant Mullins-he had not forgotten Runnells' white face on the occasion when the man from Scotland Yard had sent in his card!

And now as he waited on the verandah, the low, savage chuckle came again. The boathouse would serve admirably-since Runnells seemed to have a penchant for it! It was far enough away to obviate the possibility of any sound carrying to the house; and, inside, it possessed light. He wanted light when he handled Runnells! Quite apart from the fact that darkness in itself afforded too many chances for a lucky escape, he could not *read* Runnells in the darkness. Also, affording him a malicious delight, there was exquisite irony in the thought that the setting for what was to come should be the one that Runnells had himself chosen to-night —for quite another purpose than that it should be the scene of his own undoing!

The front door opened and Runnells emerged.

"What's the game?" Runnells asked hoarsely. "D'ye know where he is?"

It was quite unnecessary to be anything but frank with Runnells as to their destination. Runnells, safe in the belief that *he* had been mistaken for one Detective-Sergeant Mullins and that his "master" was wide of the mark and astray, would also enjoy the *irony* to be found in a trip to the boathouse. It would be a pity to deprive Runnells of anything like that! Captain Francis Newcombe nodded curtly, as, motioning the other to follow, he led the way across the lawn.

"Yes; I think so," he said. "I've reason to believe he's been using the boathouse to hide and live in."

"Strike me pink!" mumbled Runnells. "That's what I always said to myself after that night: I says, 'look out for that bird' —and I was bloody well right."

"I fancy you were," agreed Captain Francis Newcombe coolly, "though I didn't think so at the time. But hurry up! There's no time to lose if we want to trap him."

They had entered the wooded path leading to the shore, and, curiously enough, Runnells was now in front-and in the darkness, as it swung at his side, Captain Francis Newcombe's hand held a revolver.

"How'd he get here?" Runnells jerked back over his shoulder. "How'd you twig it? And when did he come?"

"About the same time we did, I imagine," replied Captain Francis Newcombe shortly. "Don't talk so loud-or any more at all, for that matter. The wind has died down a bit, and we might be heard. Make straight for one of those little bridges at the boathouse-the one on this side-the nearer one. Understand? And look out for yourself-the man's no fool, I'll say that for him."

"Right!" said Runnells in a muffled voice, as they came out of the woods and the boathouse loomed up, shadowy and indistinct, some fifty yards away.

There was laughter in Captain Francis Newcombe's soul now, a mirth parented out of savagery and vindictiveness, a laugh at the blind fool treading so warily and cautiously and silently across the sandy beach here in order that he should not be denied the shambles! The laugh seemed to demand physical, audible expression. He choked it back. In a moment or so more he could laugh to his heart's content. The boathouse was only a few yards away now. He rubbed close against Runnells' side, as though to preserve touch with the other in the darkness. Runnells' revolver was in the right-hand coat pocket, and —

Both men had halted simultaneously. Close to the boathouse now and in its lee, the sound of the breaking waves was somewhat deadened, but from under the overhang of the verandah there had come another sound, as though a vicious *slapping* were being given the comparatively smooth water under the boathouse, and then a sudden floundering and splashing, and then the *slapping* again.

Runnells' hand went to his side pocket-but as it came out again with his revolver Captain Francis Newcombe's hand closed upon it like a vise, and with a quick twist and wrench secured the weapon.

"What-what did you do that for?" Runnells stammered in a low, startled way. "Didn't you hear that in under the boathouse? There's some one there. Maybe it's *him*."

Captain Francis Newcombe laughed now-aloud.

"So you think there's some one in under there, do you, Runnells?" he drawled.

"Yes," said Runnells, and drew away a little. "You heard it just the same as I did, but-but I don't understand what you —"

"You will in a minute!" Captain Francis Newcombe's voice was still a drawl. "But meanwhile we'll see whether you're right or not. You don't mind going first, do you, Runnells?" His revolver muzzle was suddenly pressed against the small of Runnells' back. "I've known you to be a bit tricky at times. Go on!"

Something like a whimper came from Runnells. He stood irresolute.

"Go on! In under there! We'll see this 'some one' of yours first of all!" Captain Francis Newcombe's voice snapped now. "Move!"

A push from the revolver muzzle sent Runnells forward.

"What-what are you doing this to me for?" the man burst out in a shaken voice again.

Captain Francis Newcombe made no answer. He too had heard the sounds in under here, but if Runnells were up to some more of his games it would avail Runnells very little now. Runnells' body, if there were by any chance some one ahead here in the darkness, made a most excellent and effective shield. It was inky black in here, and now underfoot, as they went forward, in place of the pure sand there were rocks and a slightly muddy bottom.

His left hand deposited the surplus revolver in his pocket, and in exchange drew out his flashlight. He thrust the flashlight out beyond Runnells' side in front of them both, and switched it on.

A cry broke on the instant from Runnells' lips —a cry of terror.

"Look! Look!" Runnells cried. "Let me go! Let me get out of here! This is a horrible, slimy, ghastly hole! Let me go-let me go! It's —it's a dead man!"

Captain Francis Newcombe's jaws had clamped. Into the focus of the round white ray had come the big concrete pier that supported the building in the centre, slime-draped, green and oozy now with the tide still low; and, nearer in again, a black ribbon of water, strangely like silk in its rippling under the light, for the sea wall way out beyond had lulled it here into the quiet almost of a pond, lapped at the shore, lapped and lapped, as though striving with hideous patience to creep yet another inch onward, and yet another, and always another, that it might reach a huddled thing that lay still several yards away.

A huddled thing!

Captain Francis Newcombe pushed Runnells ruthlessly forward until they both stood over it. And now the flashlight's ray played upon it-upon a twisted, crumpled form, a dead thing, a man whose clothes in places were in ribbons as though the very body had been mangled, a man in a white shirt sleeve where the sleeve of the coat had been torn away at the armpit, a man around whose neck and across whose face were long, horribly regular lines of round, lurid marks, near purple now against the bloodless skin.

And Runnells with a scream shrank back and covered his face with his hands.

"My Gawd!" he screamed out in terror. "It's Paul!" he screamed. "It's Paul Cremarre!"

II

The Bronze Key

Paul Cremarre!

And the man was not a pleasant sight! The slime, the water and the mud! The Stygian blackness that seemed to mock and jeer at the puny ray of the flashlight! The *lap-lap-lap* of the wavelets that echoed back in hollow, ghostly whispers from the flooring of the boathouse above! And Runnells, grovelling, drawing in his breath with loud sucking sounds. Noises of sea and air-indefinable-all discordant-like imps in jubilee! It was a ghouls' hole!

But Captain Francis Newcombe smiled-with a thin parting of the lips. He knew a sudden elation, a stupendous uplift. He found joy in each of those abominable marks on the face of the Thing that lay at the end of his flashlight's ray. They were not pretty-but they were all too few!

"Got your wind up, has it, Runnells?" he sneered-and thereafter for a moment, though he never let Runnells entirely out of the light's focus, gave his fuller attention to Paul Cremarre.

The man was dead, wasn't he? It was a matter that could not be left in doubt-even where doubt seemed to be dispelled at a glance. He bent down over the other. An instant's examination satisfied him. The man was dead. His eyes roved over the body, and held suddenly on one of the man's hands. Rather peculiar, that! The hand was tightly clenched. One did not ordinarily die with one hand clenched and the other open! He forced the hand open. Something fell to the ground. He picked it up. It was a large bronze key about three inches in length. Cupping it in his hand so that Runnells might not inadvertently see it, he stared at it speculatively for a moment, then dropped it into his pocket.

This was interesting, decidedly interesting-and suggestive! His flashlight became more inquisitive in respect of the immediate surroundings. Those footprints, for instance, in the half mud and sand, deep, irregular, which, leading up from the edge of the water some four or five yards away, ended where Paul Cremarre now lay-and another series of footprints, a little to the right, quite regular, which, though they also started from the water's edge, lost themselves in the direction of the beach in front of the boathouse.

Captain Francis Newcombe worked swiftly now. He searched through the dead man's pockets, transferring the contents, without stopping to examine them, to his own pockets-and then abruptly and without ceremony swung upon Runnells.

"We'll finish this up in the boathouse!" he snapped.

Runnells' reply was inarticulate.

Captain Francis Newcombe, with his revolver again at the small of Runnells' back, drove the man before him-out from under the verandah, up one of the ramp-like bridges and into the little lounge room of the boathouse. Here, he switched on the light-and with a sudden, savage grip around Runnells' throat, flung the man sprawling into one of the big easy chairs.

"Now, my man," he said, "we'll have our little settlement, since Paul has already had his! I congratulate you —*both*! And perhaps you may have a very early opportunity of letting him know that I did not overlook him in my felicitations. Very neat-very clever of you two to play the game like this! I must confess that I did not think of Paul Cremarre in connection with what has been going on. I fancy that the very fact of you being here-the three divided, as it were-must have helped to act as a sort of mental blanket upon me in that respect. And even you I was forced to eliminate until to-night because I could not arrive at any logical reason that would explain your motive-for if I left the island here you would leave too. The combination, however, would be very effective! Paul Cremarre would be left behind with a free hand, eh?" Captain Francis Newcombe's voice rasped suddenly. "Now, then, you cur, what happened under the boathouse here to-night? What killed Paul?"

Runnells' face was a pasty white. He shrank back into the farthest recesses of the chair, and licked nervously at his lips. He tried twice to speak-ineffectually. His eyes seemed fascinated, not by the revolver that Captain Francis Newcombe had transferred to his left hand, but by

Captain Francis Newcombe's right hand that came creeping now with menacing, half-curled fingers toward his throat.

"Answer me-and answer quick!" snarled Captain Francis Newcombe.

"I—I don't know." Runnells forced a shaken whisper. "So help me, Gawd, I don't! I don't know who killed him."

"I didn't say *who*; I said *what*!" Captain Francis Newcombe's hand crept still closer to Runnells' throat. "Don't try any of that kind of game-you're not brainy enough! It wasn't anything *human* that killed Paul Cremarre."

"No," mumbled Runnells, "no; it wasn't anything human. Oh, my Gawd, the *look* of it! It-it made me sick. Those-those round red things on his face-and the eyes-the eyes —I —I ain't afraid of a dead man, but-but I was afraid in there."

"Runnells," said Captain Francis Newcombe evenly, "at bottom you are a stinking coward, a spineless thing-you always were. But you've never really known fear —*not yet*! I'm going to teach you what *fear* is!"

"No!" Runnells screamed out, and pawed at the other's hand that was now tight around his throat. "I'm telling the truth. I swear to Gawd I am! I don't know what happened. I didn't know Paul was here. I never saw him since we left London."

"Don't lie!" Captain Francis Newcombe coolly and viciously twisted at the flesh in which his fingers were enmeshed. "I'm going to have the whole story now-or else you'll follow Paul Cremarre. You've seen enough in the last three years to know that I never make an idle threat. It will be quite simple. You will disappear. I, myself, will be the most solicitous of all about your disappearance. It would never be attributed to me. Is it quite plain, Runnells? You deserve it, anyway! Perhaps it's a waste of time to do anything but get rid of you now before daylight. I'd rather *like* to do it, Runnells. It's rather bad policy to give a man a chance to stab you a second time in the back."

The man was almost in a state of collapse. Captain Francis Newcombe loosened his hold, and, standing back a little and toying with caressing fingers at his revolver's mechanism, surveyed the other with eyes that, in meditation now, were utterly callous.

"I —I know you'd do it." Runnells, gasping for his breath, blurted out his words wildly. "I know it wouldn't do me any good to lie-but I ain't lying. Can't you believe me? I wasn't in it at all. I never knew Paul was on the island until just now."

"Go on!" encouraged Captain Francis Newcombe ironically. "So it wasn't you who telephoned Polly from the boathouse here a little while ago?"

Runnells' eyes widened.

"Me? No!" he cried out vehemently. "I haven't been near here."

Captain Francis Newcombe frowned. He knew Runnells and Runnells' calibre intimately and well. The man's surprise was genuine. Another angle! It was possible, of course, that Paul Cremarre had been playing a lone hand; but against that was Runnells' own actions to-night. Well, as it stood now, it was a very simple matter to put Runnells' sincerity, or insincerity, to the proof.

"No, of course not!" he observed caustically. "I didn't expect you to admit it. Why don't you tell me you spent the evening playing solitaire, then went to bed and slept like a child until I rapped on your door?"

Runnells lifted miserable, hunted eyes to Captain Francis Newcombe's face.

"Because I'm only telling you the truth," he said, with frantic insistence in his voice. "And that wouldn't be the truth. I'll tell you everything-everything. You can see for yourself it's Gawd's fact. I wasn't asleep when you knocked. I had been out of my room, but I hadn't been out of the house; and I hadn't been in bed more than ten minutes when I heard you at the door."

"You rather surprise me, Runnells," said Captain Francis Newcombe coolly. "Not at what you say, for I was standing in the hall when you entered your room-but that for once you are guilty of an honest statement. Go on! What were you doing around the house?"

Runnells gulped, nervously massaging his pinched throat.

"I got to go back to before we left London, if I'm going to make a clean breast of it," he said, searching Captain Francis Newcombe's face anxiously. "I—I knew then about the money out here. There was a letter under your pillow the day you got back from Cloverley's, and when I propped you up in bed for your lunch I—I took it, and read it while I was feeding you your—" His words were blotted out in a sudden cry of fear. He was staring into a revolver muzzle thrust close to his face, and behind the revolver were a pair of eyes that burned like living coals. "For Gawd's sake," he shrieked out, "captain—*don't!*"

Captain Francis Newcombe dropped the revolver to his side again.

"You are quite right, Runnells," he said whimsically. "It would be inexcusable to stem any tide of veracity flowing from you. Well?"

"I *got* to make you believe I'm telling the truth," choked Runnells, "and-and I know now I have. I didn't say anything to Paul about it—I was keeping it to myself. And Paul didn't say anything to me. I didn't know he knew about it, and I don't know now how he found out-but I suppose he must have somehow, for I suppose that's what brought him here. As for me, what I read in that letter didn't make any difference after all, because the minute I got here I knew what everybody else knew-that the dippy old bird had got half a million dollars hidden away somewhere." He hesitated a moment, drawing the back of his hand several times to and fro across his lips. "Well, that's what I was doing to-night, and that's what I was doing last night. I was searching the house trying to find out where he'd hidden the money. But I didn't find it."

"No," said Captain Francis Newcombe grimly; "I'm quite sure you didn't. But if you had, Runnells-what then?"

"I—I'm not sure." Runnells licked at his lips again. "I know what you mean. It-it would have depended on you. You told me before we left London that on account of the girl being your ward we weren't to do anything slippery in America, and if I'd made sure of that and was sure you wouldn't come in on the job, then I'd have copped the swag and got away with it if I could; but if you would have come in, then I'd have told you where it was."

"Anything more?" inquired Captain Francis Newcombe laconically.

Runnells shook his head.

"I've told you straight the whole thing," he said numbly.

It was a moment before Captain Francis Newcombe spoke again.

"Even on your own say-so," he said deliberately at last, "you were prepared to double-cross me. Once I let a man toss a coin to see whether I shot him or not-for less than that. But you are not even entitled to that much chance-except for the fact that perhaps after to-night you'll be less likely to stick your filthy hands into my affairs. But even that is not what is outweighing my inclination to have done with you here and now. The fact is that, though I regret to admit it, you are, for the moment at least, more valuable alive."

Runnells straightened up a little in his chair. He swept his hand over a wet brow.

"I'll play fair after this," he said hoarsely. "I take my oath to Gawd, I will!"

"Or turn at the first chance like the dog who has been whipped by his master," observed Captain Francis Newcombe indifferently. "Very good, Runnells! I never prolong discussions. The matter is ended-unless you are unfortunate enough to cause the subject to be reopened at some future date! It is near daylight-and before daylight Paul Cremarre, what is left of him, must be disposed of. If the man is found here, the victim of a violent death, it means an inquest, the influx of authorities, the possible discovery of Cremarre's identity-and ours!"

"We could tie something heavy on him," said Runnells thickly, "and drop him in the water."

"We could-but we won't," said Captain Francis Newcombe curtly. "One never feels at ease with bodies disposed of in that fashion-they have been known to come to the surface. It might be the easiest way, but it's not the *safest*. I think you've heard me say before, Runnells, that chance is the playground of fools. Besides, our close and intimate friendship with Paul demands a little more reverent and circumspect consideration at our hands-what? Paul shall have a decent burial. We'll dig a hole for him back there among the trees." He thrust his hand suddenly into his pocket, brought out his flashlight, and tossed it into Runnells' lap. "Go up to the house and get a spade, a couple of them if you can. There ought to be plenty somewhere in the out-houses at the back. And hurry!"

"Yes-right!" Runnells stammered, as he rose to his feet and stood hesitant as though trying to say something more.

"I said hurry-damn you!" snarled Captain Francis Newcombe.

"Yes-right!" said Runnells mechanically again-and stumbled, half running, across the room and out of the door.

Captain Francis Newcombe flung himself into the chair Runnells had vacated. His mind was on Paul Cremarre now. What was it that had caused the man's death? As Runnells had said, it was a sickening sight. Well, no matter! The mode or cause of death was an incident, wasn't it? Paul Cremarre found here on the island, whether dead or alive, was what mattered-it meant that the menace, that hellish nightmare of the "unknown," that had been hanging over him, Shadow Varne, was gone now-that the way was clear ahead —a fortune here-America once more an "open sesame" —riches, luxury, all he had builded for, his again to take at his leisure without fear now of any interference from any source. And yet he seemed to hate the man the more because he was dead. Cremarre had done what no other man had ever done to Shadow Varne-those black hours-last night-the night before.

His hands clenched fiercely. He knew a sudden, unbridled rush of anger directed against the agency, be it what it might, that had caused Paul Cremarre's death-that had forever removed the man beyond his reach, and had *robbed* him of a right that alone was his to settle with the man. He had owed the other a debt that he could never now repay-the sort of debt that Shadow Varne, until now, had never failed to pay. It was all clear enough now. Paul Cremarre, if not from the moment he had read Polly's letter that morning in London, had finally at any rate yielded to the temptation that the opportunity of securing so great a sum of money had dangled before his eyes. Cremarre, like Runnells, had very possibly, and perhaps not unwarrantably, been sceptical about his, Captain Francis Newcombe's, statement that the money here was to be held inviolable; but whether he had or not made very little difference in the last analysis, for, either way, it would be obvious to Paul Cremarre that he would get none of the money unless he got it through his own secret endeavours, since, even if he, Captain Francis Newcombe, were after it for himself, Cremarre would realise that he was not to share in the spoils.

It was quite plain! It was Paul Cremarre who had fired that shot through the cabin window in the storm on the liner that night in order to possess for himself a free hand on the island here. The man, in disguise of course, had sailed on the same ship-because he would not have dared to have left London before he, Newcombe, left, for fear of arousing suspicions, since he was known to be acquainted with the contents of the letter; and he would not have dared risk a later vessel for fear of arriving too late and only to find the money gone should he, Newcombe, prove to be after it for himself. It was Paul Cremarre here on the island who had on those three occasions, ending with to-night, sought through the medium of fear, no, more than that, through an appeal to the impulse for self-preservation, to drive him, Newcombe, away-and leave Paul Cremarre in sole possession of the field. And it was quite plain now, too, why the man had not, here on the island, attempted murder again as he had done on the liner. It was not that the chances of discovery were less on board the ship; but that here a murder would cause an invasion of the island by police and detectives which would automatically hamper Cremarre in his efforts to find the money, if, indeed, it would not force him to leave the island entirely in order to make his own escape.

Captain Francis Newcombe's hand was groping tentatively in his pocket now. It was not at all unnatural that the thought of Paul Cremarre had not entered his head. To begin with, he had trusted the hound; and, again, he had sailed immediately on the *first* ship after leaving the man in London. But now! Yes, that was where the crux of the whole thing lay-the time spent on that yachting trip of Locke's down the coast. Paul Cremarre had probably been on the island for several days before the *Talofa* arrived, and —

His hand came out of his pocket. In its palm lay the bronze key. He stared at it thoughtfully. No, Paul Cremarre had not succeeded in getting the madman's money prior to to-night, for in that case old Marlin would have discovered his loss and raised a wild fuss; and, besides, if successful, Cremarre would have left the island without loss of time. Nor had Cremarre been *quite* successful to-night, for the money was not on his person; but he had been-what? Captain Francis Newcombe stared for another long minute at the bronze key, then jumping suddenly up from the chair, he crossed over to the table and began to divest his pockets of the articles he had taken from Paul Cremarre. He tumbled them out on the table: A roll of bills; a passport-made out under an assumed name-to one André Belisle; a few papers such as railroad folders, a small map of the Florida Keys, some descriptive matter pertaining thereto, and among these a little book.

Captain Francis Newcombe snatched up the book-and suddenly he began to laugh, a strange laugh, hoarse with elation, a laugh that even found expression in the quick, triumphant glitter in his eyes. Several times in the short period during which he had been here on the island he had seen this little book, and more than once he had endeavoured unostentatiously to obtain a closer look at it, but without success. It was the old madman's little book-the little buff-coloured, paper-covered little book that the old fool, he had noticed, would frequently pull out of his pocket and consult for no reason apparently other than that it had become a habit with him. It was a common book, a very common book-an innocent book. Its title was on the cover. It was a book of tide tables.

And again and again now Captain Francis Newcombe laughed. The bronze key and the book of tide tables! The pieces of the puzzle aligned themselves of their own accord into a complete whole. An hour later every night! The old madman went out an hour later every night. *So did the tide*! Those footprints there under the boathouse-not Paul Cremarre's, the other ones! The succession of nights during which the old maniac went out until the hour just before daybreak was reached-and then the period of inaction. At *low* water, like to-night, eh? Yes, yes! He did not go out when the tide was low too early in the evening or too late in the morning; in the former case for fear of being seen, in the latter because it would be full daylight before the tide would creep in to wash away the tell-tale footprints. Paul Cremarre's presence there-his footmarks leading *away* from the water to the spot where he had collapsed and died! Cremarre with a bronze key in his hand, and the old maniac's book of tide tables-Cremarre had made an attempt to get the money *after* the old man had been there, and something, God knew what, had done him down instead. It must have been subsequent to the old man's visit, for Marlin was now in his room-he, Captain Francis Newcombe, had listened at the fool's door when he had returned long after three o'clock from that trip to the old hut in the woods-and three o'clock was past the hour of low water, and old Marlin had appeared to be quietly asleep, which under no circumstances would he have been had he been conscious of the loss of his key and book. There were a dozen theories that would logically reconstruct the scene-but none of them mattered. It was the existing fact that mattered. Cremarre, hidden himself, might, and very probably had, watched the old maniac at work; afterwards, whether the old man had lost the key and book from the pocket of his dressing gown as it flapped around him and Cremarre had found them, or Paul Cremarre, than whom there was no craftier thief in Christendom, had succeeded in purloining them, again mattered not a whit. What mattered was that there was only one place now where the old maniac's secret depository could be-only one. And he, Captain Francis Newcombe, now knew where that one place was.

And yet again he laughed-loud in his evil joy, vauntingly in his triumph. It was his now! There was no longer anything to mar his plans. Nemesis was dead! No haunting thing to strike any more out of the darkness and drive him back, with bared teeth, against the wall, to make of him little better than a cornered rat. Why shouldn't he laugh now-at man, or devil, or Heaven, or hell! He was *master* —as Shadow Varne had always been master. He tossed the bronze key up in the air and caught it again with deft, yet savage grasp. The hiding place was found. There was only a keyhole to look for now. A keyhole ... a keyhole.... Mad mirth caught up the words and flung them in jocular song hither and thither within his brain. A keyhole ... a keyhole....

"You'd raise your cursed voice to bawl at Shadow Varne, would you, Paul Cremarre?" he cried. "Well, damn you-thanks!"

Just the turning of a key in a lock! But the water was too high now-the tide was coming in. A key wasn't any good to-night —the place wasn't locked only by a key, it was time-locked by the tide. He snatched up the little book and consulted it hurriedly. It would be low tide to-morrow morning at a quarter past three. Well, to-morrow morning, then, since he couldn't have a look at the place to-night. He could well afford the time now! And meanwhile with the key gone, the old maniac couldn't do anything-except raise an infernal row, and become even a little more maniacal, if that were possible. Too bad! But then, the poor old man probably wouldn't *live* very long anyhow! And then, besides, quite apart from the tide to-night, there was Runnells, who —

He swept the articles from the table suddenly back into his pockets. Where was Runnells? What the devil was keeping the man? He should have been back by now!

Captain Francis Newcombe switched off the light, and, walking quickly from the room now, closed the door behind him. And now he frowned in impatient irritation as he made his way along the verandah of the boathouse and down to the shore. Confound Runnells, anyway! Where was he? It was already beginning to show colour in the east, and the darkness was giving way to a grey, shadowy half-light. In another quarter of an hour the dawn would have broken. There was no time to spare!

He stood for a moment staring toward the fringe of trees that hid the path to the house. There was still no sign of Runnells. With a quick, muttered execration at the man's tardiness, he turned abruptly and began to make his way in under the boathouse. At the spot where Paul Cremarre's body lay the slope of the shore was very gentle, and the incoming tide would therefore cover the ground the more rapidly. He had forgotten that. Paul Cremarre had only been four or five yards away from what was then the water's edge when he had left him, and unless he wanted to find the body floating around now, he had better —

He halted short in his tracks, but close to the water now. His heart had stopped. What was that? Involuntarily now he staggered back a pace. It wasn't light enough to see distinctly; it was only light enough to see shadowy things, things that suddenly moved in the gloom before him, things that, from the water, waved sinuously in the air-like slimy, monstrous, snake-like tentacles-that reached out and crept and wriggled upon the shore itself. The place was alive with them, swarming with them. They *were* tentacles! They were feeling out, feeling out everywhere, and-God, were they feeling out for him! He sprang sharply backward as a light breath of air seemed to have fanned his cheek. He heard a faint *pat* upon the earth as of something soft striking there; he saw a slithering thing, like a reptile in shape and movement, swaying this way and that as though in search of something upon the spot where he had stood.

He felt his face blanch. He drew back still farther. A dark blotch lay near the water's edge-that was Paul Cremarre's body. And now one of those sinuous, creeping tentacles, a grey, viscous, clutching arm, fell athwart the body-and the body seemed to move-slowly-jerkily as though it struggled itself to escape from some foul and loathsome touch-toward the water.

Captain Francis Newcombe gazed now, a fascination of horror seizing upon him. Two curious spots showed out there in the water. Not lights-they weren't lights-but they were in a sense luminous. They seemed to *stare*, full of insatiable lust, gibbous, protuberant from out of the midst of that waving, feeling, slithering forest of tentacled arms.

He swept his hand across his eyes. Was he mad? Was this some ugly fantasy that he was dreaming-and that in his sleep was making his blood run cold? Look! *Look!* Those two luminous spots were coming nearer and nearer-eyes, baleful, hungry-eyes, that's what they were! They were coming closer to the shore-to the body of Paul Cremarre. A dripping tentacle, waving in the air, swayed forward, and dropped and curled and fastened around the body-that was the second one there.

It was *too* light now! The sight was horror-but the fascination of horror held him motionless. There was no head to the thing, just a monstrous, formless continuation of abhorrent *bulk* from which were thrust out those huge, repulsive tentacles-from which was thrust out another now to fasten itself, for purchase, upon one of the small, outer concrete piers that rose from the deeper water beyond.

And again the body of Paul Cremarre moved. And there was a sound. The gurgling of water.

It had a beak like a parrot's beak, and the mandibles opened now-wide apart-to uncover a cavernous mouth. And the eyes and the tentacles of the thing began to retreat from the shore.

The gurgle of water again.

A white shirt sleeve showed for an instant-and was gone.

A splashing. A commotion. A swirl. An eddy.

Then in the shadowy light a placid surface, the looming central pier of the boathouse, the little piers, the roof above-the commonplace.

A voice spoke at his side-Runnells':

"Where's Paul Cremarre?"

Captain Francis Newcombe's handkerchief, with apparent nonchalance, went to his face. It wiped away beads of sweat.

"I don't know what you'd call the thing," he said casually. "The scientists seem to refer to the species under a variety of names-you may take your choice, Runnells, between poulpe, devil fish and octopus. It's a bit of an unpleasant specimen whatever name you choose. It's gone now-and so has Paul Cremarre."

"An octopus!" Runnells stared through the dim light toward the water. "You mean it-it got Paul?"

"Yes," said Captain Francis Newcombe. He returned the handkerchief to his pocket.

"Gawd!" said Runnells in a shaky whisper. "An octopus! I know what that is. The thing's got suckers that would tear the flesh off you. That's where those marks on Paul's face must have come from. He must have had a fight with it before we found him."

"Yes," said Captain Francis Newcombe, "he undoubtedly did. It's rather obvious now that he had just managed in a dying effort to break loose and reach the shore. And the brute was crafty enough to know, I fancy, and waited for the tide to come farther in to bag its prey. Anyway, you won't need those spades you've got there now-and incidentally, Runnells, where the devil have you been all this time?"

Runnells was swabbing at his brow.

"It-it knocked me flat, that did," he said with a sudden, wild rush of words; "but it ain't any worse than what's happened up there. Hell's broke loose-just hell-that's what! The old bird's gone and done it. Shot himself, he has."

Captain Francis Newcombe's hand reached out and closed in a quick, tight grip on the other's shoulder.

"Come out of here!" he said abruptly. He led Runnells out beyond the overhang of the verandah, and in the better light stared into the man's face. "Now, then, what's this you say? Old Marlin's shot himself?"

"By accident," said Runnells, nodding his head excitedly; "leastways, that's what I suppose you'd call it."

"Dead?" demanded Captain Francis Newcombe.

Runnells laughed nervously.

"You're bloody well right he's dead!" he said gruffly. "Dead as a herring! That's what the row's all about."

"Tell your story!" ordered Captain Francis Newcombe shortly.

"Well, when I went up there from here," said Runnells, "I saw the house all lit up, and the blacks all running around, and the whole place humming. And they spotted me, some of the servants did, and all began talking at once about the old bird having shot himself, and they seemed to take it for granted that I knew too —d'ye twig? —that I'd been in the house, of course, and had got up and dressed, having heard the shots. The only play I had was to keep my mouth shut and let 'em think so-and listen to them. It seems, as near as they knew, that his nibs had been asleep, and suddenly wakes up and goes blind off his top, and runs upstairs with a revolver, and goes to Locke's room, and opens the door and begins shooting, and all the time he's screaming out at the top of his lungs, 'you're one of them, you're one of them; but I'll kill you before you open it!' Locke must have had his nerve with him. Anyway, he jumped out of bed and tried to get the revolver away from the old fool. By this time the whole house was up, and some of the black servants took a hand by trying to collar his nibs, but Marlin breaks away from them somehow, and runs for the stairs like a mad bull. He must have tripped going down, or knocked his arm, or something, anyway his revolver goes off and when they got to him he was at the bottom of the stairs with a hole in his head." Runnells paused for a moment, but, eliciting no comment, went on again: "Well, while I was getting all this information that I was supposed to know, Locke comes out on the verandah and spots me. 'I've just been to your room, Runnells,' he says. 'Do you know where Captain Newcombe is?' And I says, 'No, sir, I don't; leastways,' I says, 'I've been too excited to notice.' Then he says I'd better try and find you, and that gave me the first chance to get away and cop these spades. I sneaked around through the woods at the back of the house with them."

Captain Francis Newcombe lighted a cigarette.

"Sneak back with them, then, the same way," he said calmly.

"Right!" said Runnells.

"*Now!*" said Captain Francis Newcombe. "And you haven't been able to find me."

"Right!" said Runnells again, and started off at a run.

Captain Francis Newcombe began to walk leisurely across the beach toward the path leading to the house. He puffed leisurely and with immense content at his cigarette. In the light of certain knowledge possessed by himself alone, the whole thing was as clear as daylight. The old maniac had wakened up, and in some way had discovered for the first time that his key and book were gone-that had set him off. It was rather rough on Locke to have been selected as the thief! But there was no accounting for what a lunatic would do!

He was chuckling to himself now. An explanation of his absence from the house at this hour? It was too simple! Polly would substantiate it. Polly's scruples about keeping silent were now useless-to him! He had thought the old madman must have telephoned from the boathouse. He had got up and dressed, and gone down to see-and, of course, had seen nothing!

He flicked his cigarette away. And now he laughed-laughed with the same evil joy, the same savage triumph, but magnified a hundredfold now, with which he had laughed a little while ago in the boathouse back there. Only the laughter was silent now-it was his soul that rocked with mirth. The gods were very good! The black of the night had brought a dawn of incomparable radiance! That was poetic! Ha, ha! Well, why not poetry? He was in exquisite humour. It was like wine in his head-that, too, was poetry, wasn't it? —somebody had said it was-or something like it. Nor God, nor man, nor the devil could stay him now! He had only to be circumspect in the house of death-and help himself. Almost poetry again! Excellent! The old fool dead! Even the trouble and annoyance of staging an accident was now removed. The old fool dead-with his secret. They would hunt a long time-and it would forever be a secret.

Except to Shadow Varne!

III

The Warp and the Woof

Howard Locke stood leaning with his shoulder against one of the verandah pillars. Behind him, in the house, he was conscious of a sort of hushed commotion. Out on the lawn in front of him little groups of negroes stood staring at the house with strained, uplifted faces, or moved across his line of vision in frightened, pathetically humorous efforts to keep an unobtrusive silence-walking on tiptoes in their bare feet on the velvet lawn. Queer how the black faces were mellowed into softer colours in the early morning light!

Mr. Marlin was dead. Locke's eyes half closed; his lips drew together, compressed in a hard line. Strange! In one sense, he seemed still dazed with the events of the last hour; in another sense, his mind was brutally clear. He was dazed because even yet it seemed impossible to grasp the fact that so sorrowful, and dire, and unrecallable a tragedy was an actual, immutable, existent truth. It was not that Mr. Marlin in a sudden paroxysm of demented frenzy should have done what he had-even to the extent that the old man's attack should have been directed against his, Locke's, person. He could quite understand that. In the aquarium, only a few hours before, the old man had used identically the same words that he had shouted as he had burst in the bedroom door and had begun firing wildly: "You are one of them! ...You are one of them!" And then, apart from what had transpired in the aquarium, there had been the shock of the attack on the path almost immediately afterward. The old man had not lost his money, but he had gone back to the house-he, Locke, had seen that too-and, instead of sleeping, these things had probably preyed and preyed upon his mind until he had lost the little reason that had been left to him and a homicidal mania had developed. All that was quite easily understood. As Polly had said, the specialist had predicted it if the old man became over-excited —and Miss Marlin had feared it. It was not this phase, so logically explainable, of what had happened that affected him still in that dazed, numbed way; it was the fact, so much harder to understand, that quick and sudden, in the passing of a moment, old Mr. Marlin was gone.

He straightened up a little, easing the position of his shoulder against the pillar. On the other hand, from an entirely different aspect, that of the *consequences* as applied to his own course of action, his mind had been clear, irrevocable, settled in its purpose almost from the instant that-first to reach the old madman's side-he had found Mr. Marlin dead. It was the end! He was waiting now for Captain Francis Newcombe to return-from wherever the man had taken himself to.

The sight of the awed, grief-stricken figures on the lawn stirred him suddenly with keen emotion. The girls were upstairs in Dora Marlin's room together and — He wrenched his mind away from the course toward which it was trending. For the moment it would do neither them nor himself any good; for the moment he was waiting for-Captain Francis Newcombe.

A queer smile came and twisted at his lips. Was it defeat-or victory?

The smile passed. His face became grave again. There was Captain Francis Newcombe now-at the far edge of the lawn.

The man was strolling leisurely toward the house, then, suddenly pausing for an instant, he as suddenly broke into a run, elbowing his way unceremoniously through the groups of negroes, and, reaching the steps, covered them in a bound to the verandah.

"I say!" he burst out breathlessly as he halted before Locke. "Whatever is the matter? This hour in the morning and every light on in the house-and all those negroes out there?"

"I've been waiting for you," said Locke quietly. "Come in here." He led the way to the French window by which he had found entry into the house a few hours before, and passed through into the room beyond.

Captain Francis Newcombe followed.

"I say!" he repeated, closing the glass door with a push behind him. "What's up, old man?"

"Mr. Marlin is dead," said Locke briefly.

"Dead!" Captain Francis Newcombe stared incredulously. "Why, he wasn't ill-at least not in that way. I don't understand."

It was a small room, a sort of adjunct to the library which led off from it toward the rear of the house. Howard Locke's fingers were aimlessly turning the leaves of a book which lay on the table in the centre of the room, and beside which he was standing now.

"A belief that he was being followed, that some one was trying to take his money away from him, turned him from a harmless lunatic into a dangerous madman," Locke said slowly. "He seemed to believe that I was, to use his own words, 'one of them,' and he tried to shoot me in my room. The household was aroused. The servants came. We tried to subdue him. But he broke away from us then, and in running down the stairs fell, I think, and his revolver went off in his hand, killing him instantly."

"Good God!" said Captain Francis Newcombe heavily. "That's awful! And that poor girl-Miss Marlin!"

"Yes," said Howard Locke, his fingers still playing with the leaves of the book.

Captain Francis Newcombe appeared to be greatly agitated. He took out his cigarette case, opened and shut it several times, and finally restored it to his pocket with its contents untouched.

"It's ghastly!" he ejaculated; and then in a slower, more meditative tone: "But with the shock of it over, I can't say I'm particularly surprised. He struck me as acting in a more than usually peculiar manner all day yesterday, and especially last night, or, rather, this morning-as a matter of fact, it was on account of Mr. Marlin himself that I was out of the house when it happened. He telephoned Polly about four o'clock this morning and nearly frightened her to death. She came to my room in a pitiful state of distress. He told her her mother was dead. God knows why-except that it shows how mad he was. From Polly's description of the conversation during which she had distinctly heard the sound of waves and the slam of a door in the wind, I decided that he must have telephoned from somewhere outside. The only place I could think of was the boathouse. If the man was as bad as that, I was afraid something might happen to him, so I dressed and went out. It is obviously unnecessary to say that I did not find him. Polly and I both decided, on Miss Marlin's account, to say nothing about it, but I can see nothing to be gained now, in view of what has happened, by keeping silent."

"No; there could be nothing gained by it now," agreed Locke a little monotonously. "As you imply, it is only cumulative evidence of the man's state of mind just prior to his death."

"Exactly!" nodded Captain Francis Newcombe gravely. "But, after all, that is apart from the immediate present. I suppose you have already seen to what you could here in the house, but there still must be many things to do."

Howard Locke closed the book, and stepped a little away from the table, a little nearer the other.

"There are," he said with quiet deliberation. "But there is one thing in particular for you to do. The mail came over from the mainland very late last night. It naturally hasn't been touched this morning and is still in there" —he motioned toward the door leading from the rear of the room —"on the library table. There is a letter there for you, a very urgent one, demanding your instant return to London."

Captain Francis Newcombe's eyes narrowed almost imperceptibly-but his voice was a drawl:

"I don't think I quite understand. May I ask how you happen to know the contents of the letter?"

"I am speaking in a purely suggestive sense," Locke answered, his voice hardening a little. "There is no letter for you that I know of. I am suggesting a plausible explanation which you can make to Miss Marlin —*and Miss Wickes* —for leaving this place at once."

Captain Francis Newcombe stiffened, but his voice still retained its drawl.

"I am tempted to believe that insanity is infectious," he said; "either that, or perhaps my own intelligence is sadly astray this morning. I have neither the desire nor the intention to leave here, and especially at a time such as this when I might possibly be of even a little assistance to those who have been so hospitable to me, and so I do not require any excuse, however plausible or ingenious, for going away."

Locke's eyes rested appraisingly for a long moment on the other's cool, composed, suave face. Well, was it any cooler, any more self-possessed than his own? What of passion that was boiling within did not show on the surface!

"Nevertheless," he said steadily, "that is the excuse you will give. One of the motor boats is going over to the mainland in a little while, and you are going on her. I have already had your baggage-and Runnells' —put on board."

"You —*what*?" The red was suddenly in Captain Francis Newcombe's face. He took a quick step forward, his hands clenched. "My baggage sent out of the house-by your orders!" he said hoarsely. "You've gone a bit too far now, my man, and you'll explain yourself-and explain yourself damned quick! Out with it! What's the meaning of this?"

Locke had not moved. His eyes had not left the other's face. There was something strangely *tempting* about that face; it induced an almost uncontrollable impulse to *mark* it, to batter it, to wreck it with a rain of blows that would not cease until physical exhaustion intervened and one could strike no more. And yet his hands hung idly at his sides.

"Yes" —Locke's voice was not raised —"I will tell you the meaning of it. You are going for two reasons. The first is because you are morally responsible for Mr. Marlin's death; and the second is because you are —*what you are* —and as such, from the moment you say good-bye to her here, you are going out of Polly's life forever."

Captain Francis Newcombe came still a step nearer.

Locke's eyes had not left the other's face. He read a cold, ugly glitter in the gaze that held on his; he saw the curious whitening of the other's lips-and a knotted fist suddenly drawn back to strike. And with a lightning movement Locke caught the other's wrist and flung the blow aside.

"Don't do that!" he said in a dead tone. "God knows, it's hard enough to keep my hands off you as it is; but what is between you and me is not measured, or in any way altered by a brawl-and besides I cannot brawl here in this house where Mr. Marlin lies dead, and where there is already distress enough."

For a moment Captain Francis Newcombe did not speak; then abruptly he began to laugh, and, stepping over to a chair at the end of the table, flung himself nonchalantly into it.

"Upon my soul, Locke," he said coolly, "what I said at first in jest, I believe now must be true. I believe you've gone completely off your head. I'd like to hear why you think I am morally responsible for Mr. Marlin's death; and, particularly, I'd like to know what —"

"I want to get this over," said Locke, with a set face. "You are clever. If it appeals to a certain sense of morbid vanity in you, that they say all criminals possess, I grant at once that you are as clever a scoundrel, and as miserable and inhuman and unscrupulous a one, as ever blasphemed the image in which God made him."

Captain Francis Newcombe strained upward from the chair, his lips working-but Locke stood over him now and pushed him back.

"Don't get up!" he said with savage curtness. "You are going to hear more than that before I am through. I said you were clever-but your cleverness will do you no good here. This is the end, Newcombe. You took a child out of the slums of London-bought her in some unholy fashion, I imagine, from a woman named Mrs. Wickes; you sent the child out of England to America, and educated her in a school, especially selected I also imagine, where she would be brought into intimate contact with, and form her friendships amongst, the daughters of wealthy Americans of high social position. Why? In the light of what has happened, the answer is plain enough: That you might use her introduction into these homes as an entrée for yourself to further your own criminal purposes."

Locke paused.

A cold sneer had gathered on Captain Francis Newcombe's lips.

"You employed the word 'imagine' on both counts," he said. "I congratulate you."

"Quite so!" said Locke icily. "I may even employ it again. I am not imagining, however, when I say that you received a letter from Polly telling you that Mr. Marlin had half a million dollars in cash here on this island, and —"

"Did Polly tell you that?" demanded Captain Francis Newcombe sharply.

"Innocently-yes," Locke answered. "And in her letter she also told you 'all about everything here,' to use her own words, which could not help but embrace the fact that Mr. Marlin was not right in his mind-yet, strangely enough, in the smoking room of the liner, you will perhaps remember, you had had no idea of any such thing, and even expressed anxiety for the safety of your ward."

Captain Francis Newcombe was painstakingly polishing the finger nails of one hand on the palm of the other now.

"One might possibly conceive a man to be eccentric and attribute his idiosyncrasies to that cause-without thought of classifying him as a raving lunatic," he observed in a bored voice.

Locke shrugged his shoulders.

"Perhaps there is a better explanation of your *mistake*," he said evenly. "You did not, at that time, have the slightest idea that I, too, would be one of the party on this island."

Captain Francis Newcombe looked up from his finger nails.

"Did you?" he inquired softly.

"Yes," said Locke curtly.

"Ah!" Captain Francis Newcombe, with eyes half closed now, studied Locke's face for a full minute before he spoke again. "I am becoming rather curious as to just who you are, Locke," he murmured finally.

"You ought to know," Locke responded grimly. "I imagine it was you who went through my papers that night in my cabin."

"That is the third time," suggested Captain Francis Newcombe, "that you have said 'imagine.'"

"Yes." Locke smiled without humour. "I happen to *know*, however, that from the moment of your arrival here Mr. Marlin became more and more obsessed with the belief that he was being watched and followed. I know from his own statement that he rather cunningly laid a false trail-to an old hut in the woods behind the house, wasn't it, Newcombe? And it is rather conclusive evidence, I should say, that the man who followed that trail was the man who was watching Mr. Marlin. I saw you coming from that direction at three o'clock this morning. You were unsuccessful, of course; but you are none the less, as I said before, morally responsible for Mr. Marlin's death."

Captain Francis Newcombe leaned back in his chair, and laughed softly, insolently, contemptuously.

"As I understand the indictment," he said coolly, "it is to the effect that I left London for the purpose of coming here and stealing some money that I knew a madman had hidden. The evidence against me is from beginning to end purely circumstantial, and most of it is admittedly imaginative. The one 'damning' fact adduced is that I was seen coming from somewhere at three o'clock this morning. This is a bit thick, Locke-coming from you!" His voice was beginning to lose its suavity. "You don't *imagine*, do you, that any such 'case' as that would hold water for an instant in any court of law?"

"No," said Locke quietly; "I know it wouldn't. I quite agree with you there."

Captain Francis Newcombe's face for an instant held a look of puzzlement, as though he had not heard aright-then it stiffened into ugly menace.

"I think you need a lesson!" He spoke from between set lips. "This is no longer merely ridiculous, or absurd, or cracked-brained. It is monstrous!"

"Again I agree with you." Locke's voice was low now, rasping his words. "It is so monstrous that, strong as the circumstantial evidence against you is, I would not have been able to credit it had I not had a basis for belief that permitted of no denial. I know you for exactly what you are.

I know that you are a criminal, that you are one by profession, that you have no other profession, that you are without conscience, inhuman, ruthless, a fiend who would do honour to hell itself."

"By God!" Captain Francis Newcombe with livid face surged up from the chair to his feet.

But Locke's face, too, was white now with passion, as with a suddenly outflung hand he thrust the other away.

"I am not through yet," he said. "Denial, any attitude of pretended righteous indignation, or any other attitude that may suggest itself to you as the best mask to adopt, is hardly worth your while when attempted with one who once very narrowly escaped being one of your victims-with a man who once, because you feared he possessed the information that you know now he does possess, you tried to murder with cold-blooded deliberation."

"You?" Captain Francis Newcombe, with head thrust forward, his eyes narrowed, searched every lineament of Locke's face.

"Look well!" Locke spoke with scarcely any movement of the lips, in a cold, dead way, without inflexion in his voice. "Look well! It will do you little good. You never saw my face before. Shall I tell you where I first saw *yours*? It was in a thicket one night, a night during the great German offensive. There were four men there. Three of them sat together with their backs against the trees; the other lay face down on the ground a little distance away. A stray shell burst nearby. One of the three, a Frenchman, called it a straggler. 'Like us,' you said. I am the fourth straggler."

Captain Francis Newcombe drew slightly back. He made no other movement. He said nothing. His eyes remained riveted on Locke's face.

"I was almost done in that night," said Locke. "I'd had two days and two nights of it. I did not hear all you said-what particular place it was, for instance, that had been robbed. I heard of the share that each of you had played in the affair. I saw your faces. I heard the Frenchman, a self-admitted crook, hail you as a greater than himself-yes, as a greater even than any criminal in all France. I heard you check him with your name on his lips. I heard him call your attention to my presence there. I heard you say you had not forgotten-and in a flare of light I saw you with your rifle across your knees, its muzzle only a few feet away from my head. Then in the ensuing darkness I was lucky enough to be able to wriggle silently back a few yards in among the trees-and a second later I saw the flash of your rifle shot."

Locke stopped. His lips were dry. He touched them with the tip of his tongue.

The two men stood eying each other. Neither moved.

Locke spoke again:

"As I crawled out of that thicket I swore that I would pay you for that shot if it took all my life to bring you to account. I did not know your name, I did not know where you came from or where you lived; but I knew your face-and I was sure, as we are sometimes strangely sure of the future, that some time, in some place, you and I would meet again. But it was four years before we did; and in those four years, during which I have travelled a great deal on my father's business, no man's face, in a crowd, or merely in passing on the street, whether here or abroad, but that I searched in the hope that it might be yours. And then I saw you-in London-just a few days before we sailed. I followed you to your apartment, and I saw the other two-Runnells, and the Frenchman, whose name I discovered was Paul Cremarre. I secured an introduction to you at your club, and I learned from you that you were sailing within a day or so on a certain ship. I told you I was sailing on the same ship. Within an hour after I had left you at the club, I did two things: I booked passage on that ship; and I engaged a man who was recommended to me as one of the best private detectives in England. With the knowledge that you were a criminal, it was only a question of a short time then before the detective would unearth your record, or that you would be caught in some new venture; and meanwhile, leaving him to work up your 'history,' I crossed with you, and suggested the yachting trip as I did not intend to let you out of my sight again until you were trapped. And I think, but for the fact that you have been told now, that would have been accomplished even more quickly than I had expected. At one of the stops that I purposely made on the way down the coast on the *Talofa,* I received a letter from the detective mailed in London the day after we sailed. He said that developments had been such that he was working in conjunction with Scotland Yard, and that he expected to be able to send me a very *satisfactory* report within a day or so."

Captain Francis Newcombe took his cigarette case from his pocket for the second time-but now he calmly lighted a cigarette.

"And so," he said smoothly, "just at the moment when, after four long years, you are about to reap the fruits of your labour, you tell me to go. Where? Into the trap-waiting for me over there on the mainland?"

"No," said Locke bitterly. "Where you will; you and Runnells-and Paul Cremarre. We'll have no more trouble from any of you here."

Captain Francis Newcombe paused suddenly in the act of lifting his cigarette to his lips.

"This Paul Cremarre you speak of," he said, "what makes you think he is here?"

"Because I expected him to be here," said Locke shortly. "He was one of the three of you. He could not very well form part of your retinue as Runnells did. He would have to come separately. I know he is here because I saw a man wearing a mask last night. I have reason to know it was not you; and since I superintended the packing of Runnells' baggage and have also seen Runnells himself, I know-for reasons that need not be explained-that it was not Runnells."

"I see," said Captain Francis Newcombe. "So it must have been this Paul Cremarre-since the three would be here together. I regret that I was not fortunate enough to have the advantage of your viewpoint, even though you honour me with the credit of having arranged all these little details. And so, at the moment of your supreme success we are to go-we three. May I ask why this change of heart?"

Howard Locke reached into his pocket and took out a faded envelope that was torn at one end.

"These," he said, his voice rasping hoarsely again, "are Polly's papers-her birth certificate, the marriage certificate of her parents-the proof of perhaps the most contemptible and scoundrelly crime you have ever committed; I say 'perhaps' because there may be lower depths of beastliness and inhumanity of which only a mind such as yours could conceive. You know where these papers were found. Besides using Polly as your cat's-paw and your tool, making her innocence serve your vile ends, you robbed her of her claim to even honest parentage!" His face had grown white to the lips, his voice was almost out of control. "And yet it is Polly —*Polly Gray* —who is saving you now! I have no change of heart. I never, even on that night in the thicket, wanted to square my account with you as I do now. But for Polly's sake I cannot do it. I love her more than I hate you. I want to save her from the sorrow and distress she would suffer if she knew the truth of what has happened here; and above all I want to save her from the misery and shame of having her name publicly connected with yours were you brought as a common criminal to stand in the dock. And so you are going-where I do not know. Not London, or anywhere else, as Captain Francis Newcombe any more-for you would no longer dare do that with the police at last hot on the investigation of your career. But you are going out of her life never to contaminate it again. And this is the bargain that I make with you-that she shall never hear from you again. I compound no felony with you. I have no power to hold you, even were I an officer of the law, without specific evidence of a specific crime. That such evidence will inevitably be forthcoming is certain, but for the moment there is no warrant for your arrest. You will make the excuse for your departure as I have suggested-and later on a brief notice of the death of Captain Francis Newcombe in some distant place will account for your continued silence, and remove you out of her life."

Captain Francis Newcombe blew a smoke ring in the air and watched it meditatively.

"Excellent!" he murmured. "And if I refuse? To save Polly, you would have to call your bloodhounds off."

"It is too late for that," said Locke sternly. "And even if it were not, it would be better that Polly should suffer even the shame of publicity than that you should remain in any way in touch with her life."

"I see!" murmured Captain Francis Newcombe again. "But with exposure as inevitable as you say it is, it is too bad that Polly should-er-nevertheless suffer her share of this shameful publicity whether I go or not."

"You fence well," said Locke with a grim smile. "Scotland Yard sooner or later *will* know, but they will not make public what they know until they have laid hands upon their man. It is *your* freedom that is at stake. I told you I did not think you would venture to return to London."

"Locke," said Captain Francis Newcombe softly, "permit me to return the compliment-but also with reservations. You are clever-but having overlooked one little detail, as so often happens even to the cleverest of us all, your scheme as regards keeping Polly in ignorance of my unworthiness falls to the ground. That envelope you hold in your hand —I was wondering-it simply occurred to me-how Polly was to be informed that-er-her name is —I think you said-Gray."

"I had not overlooked it," Locke answered evenly. "Polly's parentage is a matter that precedes your entry into her life by many years; it is a matter that is logically within the knowledge of this Mrs. Wickes. I shall cable London to-day. There will be means of securing Mrs. Wickes' confession on this point. These papers will come from her."

"Ah, yes!" said Captain Francis Newcombe gently. "Quite so! Perhaps, after all, *I* am the one who overlooked detail. But if by any chance this Mrs. Wickes could not be found-what then?"

Locke studied the other's face. It was impassive; no, not quite that-there was something that lurked around the corners of the man's mouth-like a hint of mockery.

"In that case," he said steadily, "I should have done my best to save her from the knowledge of what you are, for I should have to tell her; but meanwhile you will have gone from here, and, as I have already said, she will be saved the brutal notoriety that would attach to her wherever she went, and until she died mar her life, if Captain Francis Newcombe's 'case' were blazoned abroad from the criminal courts of England-and that, in the last analysis, is what really matters." He thrust the envelope abruptly back into his pocket, and as abruptly took out his watch and looked at it. "I do not want to detain the boat. You know where to find Paul Cremarre. Get him, and take him with you. Your baggage has been searched-so has Runnells'. I do not for a moment think you found that which specifically brought you to this house. I doubt, indeed, now that Mr. Marlin is dead, if it ever will be found by anybody. But in so far as you are concerned, assurance will be made doubly sure-the three of you will be subjected to a *personal* search before you are landed on the other side." He snapped his watch back into his pocket. "Shall I find out if Miss Marlin is able to see you?"

Captain Francis Newcombe examined the glowing tip of his cigarette with every appearance of nonchalance-but the brain of the man was seething in a fury of action. He was beaten-in so far as the existence, the entity of a character known as Captain Francis Newcombe was concerned-he was beaten.... This cursed, meddling fool had beaten him.... Damn that shot that he had missed in the darkness.... He could not draw his revolver and fire another and kill this man-not *now*.... To do that here would be suicide.... And, besides, there was still half a million dollars.... Quite a sop! ...Mrs. Wickes didn't count one way or the other-but Paul Cremarre-that was awkward.... The island must be left in quiet and repose in so far as anything pertaining to the attempted robbery was concerned-an incident that with his departure was closed.... Paul Cremarre must be accounted for.... Well, the *truth* was probably the safest, since denial would only result in a search for a *third* man that Locke knew had been here.... That Locke should think that Paul Cremarre had come here as part of the prearranged plan was probably all the better.... It left no lingering doubts....

He looked up-his eyes cold and steady on Locke.

"I regret, I shall *always* regret, that I missed that shot," he said deliberately; "but for whatever satisfaction it will bring you, I admit now that you have beaten me. I agree to your terms. I will go; so will Runnells-but I can't take Paul Cremarre. Paul Cremarre is dead. He died this morning. A rather horrible death. I found him on the shore a little way from the water's edge, his clothes in ribbons-in fact, one of his coat sleeves was completely torn away and —"

"The man I was looking for had a white shirt sleeve," said Locke quietly.

"Well, your search is ended then, if that will give you any further satisfaction," said Captain Francis Newcombe gruffly. "His white shirt sleeve was the least of it. His face and throat were covered with round, purplish blotches, and the man was absolutely mangled. He had the appearance of having been *crushed* —as they say a python crushes a victim in its folds. And, damn it, that's not far from what happened! How he had first come into contact with the monster I don't know, but he had been in a fight with a gigantic octopus, and had evidently just managed to crawl ashore out of the thing's reach temporarily, and had died there." Captain Francis Newcombe laughed unpleasantly. "The reason I know this is because I saw the creature-the tide was higher, of course, when I found the body-come back and carry off its prey. You will pardon me, perhaps, if I do not describe it in detail. It-er-wasn't nice."

Locke stared at the other for a moment.

"That's a rather strange story," he said slowly. "But I can't see where it would do you any good to lie now."

Captain Francis Newcombe helped himself to another cigarette, lighted it, and suddenly flung a mocking laugh at Locke.

"No," he said, "I'm afraid that's the trouble-it wouldn't do me any good to lie now. And so I might as well tell you, too, that there's no use sending that cable to London about Mrs. Wickes, either. Mrs. Wickes is also dead. For reasons best known to myself, I did not choose to tell Polly about the woman's death, so I fear now that, lacking that estimable old hag's co-operation in the resurrection of those papers, you will have to resort to telling Polly, after all, a little something about her cherished guardian. However, Locke, on the main count, that of notoriety, if it depends upon Scotland Yard ever getting their man, I think I can give you my personal guarantee that she will never be —"

He stopped, and whirled sharply around.

One half of the French window was swaying inward.

With a low cry, Locke sprang past the other.

"Polly!" he cried.

She was clutching at the edge of the door, her form drooping lower and lower as though her support were evading her and she could not keep pace with its escape, her face a deathly white, her eyes half closed.

Locke caught her as she fell, gathered her in his arms and carried her to a couch. She had fainted. As he looked hurriedly around for some means of reviving her, Captain Francis Newcombe spoke at his elbow.

"Permit me," said Captain Francis Newcombe. He was proffering the water in a flower vase from which he had thrown out the flowers.

Mechanically Locke took it, and began to sprinkle the girl's face.

"Too bad!" said Captain Francis Newcombe pleasantly. "Er-hardly necessary, I fancy, for me to explain my sudden departure for England to her-what? I'll say *au revoir*, Locke-merely *au revoir*. We may meet again. Who knows-in another four years! And I'll leave you to make my adieus to Miss Marlin."

Locke made no reply.

The door closed. Captain Francis Newcombe was gone.

Polly stirred now on the couch. Her eyes opened, rested for an instant on Locke's, then circled the room in a strange, quick, fascinated way, as though fearful of what she might see yet still impelled to look.

"He-he's gone?" she whispered.

"Yes," Locke answered softly. "Don't try to talk, Polly."

She shook her head. A smile came, bravely forced.

"I —I saw him from upstairs-on the lawn coming toward the house," she said. "After a little while when he did not come in, I went down to find him. I did not see him anywhere, and-and I walked along the verandah, and I heard your voices in here-heard something you were saying. I —I was close to the door then-and-somehow I —I couldn't move-and —I wanted to cry out-and I couldn't. And-and I heard-all. And then I felt myself swaying against the window, and somehow it gave way and-and —"

She turned her face away and buried it in her hands.

Something subconscious in Locke's mind seemed to be at work. He was staring at the French window. It had given way. It hadn't any socket for the bolt at top or bottom. Strange it should have been that window! He brushed his hand across his eyes.

"Polly," he said tenderly, and, kneeling, drew her to him until her head lay upon his shoulder.

And then her tears came.

And neither spoke.

But her hand had crept into his and held it tightly, like that of a tired and weary child who had lost its way-and found it again.

IV

The Time-lock of the Sea

Low tide at three-fifteen! Captain Francis Newcombe, in the stern of a small motor boat, drew his flashlight from his pocket and consulted his watch. Five minutes after two. He nodded his head in satisfaction. Just right! And the night was just right-just cloudy enough to make of the moonlight an ally rather than a foe. It disclosed the island there looming up ahead now perhaps a mile away; it would not disclose so diminutive a thing as this little motor boat out here on the water creeping in toward the shore.

The boat was barely large enough to accommodate the baggage, piled forward, and still leave room for Runnells and himself. Also the boat leaked abominably; also the engine, not only decrepit but in bad repair, was troublesome and spiteful. Captain Francis Newcombe shrugged his shoulders. The engine was Runnells' look-out; that was why, as a matter of fact, Runnells was here at all. As for the rest, what did it matter? The boat had been bought for the proverbial song over there on the mainland, and it was good enough to serve its present purpose.

Again he changed his position, but his eyes narrowed now as they fixed on Runnells' back. Runnells sat amidships where he could both nurse the engine and manipulate the little steering wheel at his side. Runnells was a necessary evil. He, Newcombe, did not know how to run the engine. Therefore he had been obliged to bring Runnells along, and therefore Runnells would participate after all in the old fool's half million —*temporarily*. Afterwards-well there were so many things that might happen when Runnells had lost his present usefulness!

Runnells spoke now abruptly.

"It's pretty hard to make out anything ashore," he said; "but if we've hit it right, we ought to be just about heading for a little above the boathouse. Can you pick up anything?"

"Nothing but the outline of the island against the sky," Captain Francis Newcombe answered. "We're too far out yet."

Runnells' sequence of thought was obviously irrelevant and disconnected.

"The blinking swine!" he muttered savagely. "Stripped to the pelt and searched, I was-and you, too! And kicked ashore like a dog! Gawd, it's too bad they ain't going to know they'll have had the trick turned on 'em after all! I'd give a good bit of my share to see Locke's face if he knew. He wouldn't think himself such a wily bird maybe!"

"You're a bit of a fool, Runnells," said Captain Francis Newcombe shortly.

His train of thought had been interrupted. Runnells had suggested another-Locke. Captain Francis Newcombe's hands clenched suddenly, fiercely in the darkness. *Locke*! Some day, somewhere-but not now; not until the days and months, yes even years, if necessary, were past and gone, and Locke had forgotten Captain Francis Newcombe, and Scotland Yard had forgotten-he would meet Locke again. And when that time came there would be no ammunition *wasted* as there had been in that damned thicket that night! Locke! The fool doubtless thought that he had been completely master of the situation and of Captain Francis Newcombe-even to the extent of *obliterating* Captain Francis Newcombe. Well, perhaps he had! It was quite true that the clubs of London, and, yes, for instance, the charming old Earl of Cloverley, would know Captain Francis Newcombe no more-but *Shadow Varne* still lived, and Shadow Varne with half a million dollars, even in a new environment, wherever it might be, did not present so drear and uninviting a prospect. Ha, ha! Locke! Locke could wait-that was a *pleasure* the future held in store! What counted now, the only thing that counted, was getting the money actually into his possession-that, and the assurance that the trail was smothered and lost behind him. Well, the former was only a matter of, say, an hour or so at the most now; and the latter left nothing to be desired, did it?

He smiled with cool, ironic complacency. Locke, having in mind Scotland Yard, would expect him to disappear as effectually and as rapidly as possible. Locke ought not to be disappointed! He *had* disappeared; he and Runnells-and, equally important, their luggage. One was sometimes too easily traced by luggage-especially with that infernally efficient checking system they employed on the railroads here in America! It had been rather simple. When Runnells and the luggage and himself had all been dumped with equal lack of ceremony on a wharf over there on the mainland, he had had some of the negroes that were loitering around carry the luggage into a sort of storage shed that was on the dock, and, merely saying that he would send for his things, he and Runnells had unostentatiously allowed themselves to be swallowed up by the city. And then they had separated. The rest had been a matter of detail-detail in which Runnells, with the experience of years, was particularly efficient. A purchase here, a purchase there-quite innocent purchases in themselves-and later on a man, *not two men*, but one man, a man who did not at all look like Runnells, seeing the chance of picking up a bargain in a second-hand motor boat somewhere along the waterfront, had bought it and gone away with it. Later on again, but not until after nightfall, not until nine o'clock in fact, he, Captain Francis Newcombe, had "sent" for the luggage-by the very simple expedient of forcing an entry into the shed and loading it into the motor boat that Runnells had brought alongside the dock. Thereafter, Runnells, the luggage and himself had disappeared. Surely Locke ought to be quite satisfied-he, Captain Francis Newcombe, was doing his best to guarantee Polly against any unseemly publicity in connection with Scotland Yard! And he would continue to do so! With any kind of luck, he would be away from the island here again long before daylight; then, say, a few nights' cruising along the coast, laying up by day, and then, as circumstances dictated, by railroad, or whatever means were safest, a final —

With a smothered oath, Captain Francis Newcombe snatched at the gunwale of the boat for support, as he was thrown suddenly forward from his seat. The boat seemed to stagger and recoil as from some vicious blow that had been dealt it, and then, as he recovered his balance, it surged forward again with an ugly, rending, tearing sound along the bottom planks, rocking violently-then an even keel again-and silence.

Runnells had stopped the engine.

"My Gawd," Runnells cried out wildly, "we've gone and done it!"

Captain Francis Newcombe was on his feet peering through the darkness to where Runnells, who after stopping the engine had sprung forward from his seat, was now groping around beneath the pile of luggage.

"A reef, eh?" said Captain Francis Newcombe coolly. "Well, we got over it. We're in deep water again. Carry on!"

Runnells' voice came back full of fear.

"We're done, we are," he mumbled. "I stopped the engine the minute she hit, but she had too much way on her-that's what carried her over. She's bashed a hole in her the size of your head. She won't float five minutes."

"Start her ahead again, then!" Captain Francis Newcombe's voice snapped now.

"It won't do any good," Runnells answered, as he stumbled back to his former place. "She won't anywhere near make the shore-it's half a mile at least."

"Quite so!" said Captain Francis Newcombe. "But, in that case, we won't have so far to swim!"

The engine started up again.

"It ain't as though we didn't know there was reefs" —Runnells was stuttering his words — "only we'd figured with our light draft we wouldn't any more than scrape one anyhow, and it wouldn't do us any harm. But she's rotten, that's what she is-plain rotten and putty! And we must have hit a sharp ledge of rock. Gawd, we've a foot of water in us now!"

"Yes," said Captain Francis Newcombe calmly. "Well, don't blubber about it! We'll get ashore-and we'll get away again. There's half a dozen skiffs and things of that sort stowed away in the boathouse that are never used now. One of them will never be missed, and we can at least get far enough away from the island by daybreak not to be seen, and eventually we'll make the other side even if it is a bit of a row."

"Row!" ejaculated Runnells.

"Yes," said Captain Francis Newcombe curtly. "Why not-since we *have* to? We can't steal a motor boat whose loss would be discovered, can we?"

"My Gawd!" said Runnells.

The water was sloshing around Captain Francis Newcombe's feet; the boat had already grown noticeably sluggish in its movement. He cast an appraising eye toward the land. It was almost impossible to judge the distance. Runnells had said half a mile a few minutes ago. Call it a quarter of a mile now. But Runnells was quite right in one respect; it was certain now that the boat would scuttle before the shore was reached.

"How far can you swim, Runnells?" he demanded abruptly.

"It ain't that," choked Runnells, "I can swim all right; it's —"

"It was just a matter of whether your body would be washed up on the shore, which would be equally as bad as though the boat stranded there for the edification of our friend Locke," drawled Captain Francis Newcombe. "But since you can swim that far, and since the boat's got to sink, let her sink here in deep water where she won't keep anybody awake at night wondering about her-or us. Stop the engine again!"

"But the luggage," said Runnels, "I —"

"It will sink out of sight quite readily, but run a rope through the handles and lash the stuff to the boat so it won't drift ashore-yes, and anything else that's loose!" said Captain Francis Newcombe tersely. "I can't swim a quarter of a mile with portmanteaus! Stop the engine!"

"Strike me pink!" said Runnells faintly, as he obeyed and again stumbled forward to the luggage.

Captain Francis Newcombe sat down and began to unlace his boots. The water was nearly level with the bottom of the seat.

"Hurry up, Runnells!" he called.

"It's all right," said Runnells after a moment.

"Take your boots off then, and sling them around your neck," ordered Captain Francis Newcombe.

"Yes," said Runnells.

Captain Francis Newcombe stood up and divested himself of a light raincoat he had been wearing. From the skirt of the garment he ripped off a generous portion, and, taking out his revolver and flashlight, wrapped them around and around with the waterproof cloth. The coat itself he thrust into an already water-filled locker under the seat where it could not float away.

"Ready, Runnells?" he inquired.

"Yes," said Runnells.

"Come on, then," said Captain Francis Newcombe.

The gunwale was awash as he struck out. A dozen strokes away, as he looked back, the boat had disappeared. He cursed sullenly under his breath-then laughed defiantly. It would take more than that to beat Shadow Varne.

Runnells swam steadily at his side.

Presently they stepped out on the shore.

Captain Francis Newcombe stared up and down the beach, as he seated himself on the sand and began to pull on his boots.

"We're a bit off our bearings, Runnells," he said. "I couldn't see any sign of the boathouse even when I was swimming in. And I can't see it now. Which way do you think it is?"

Runnells was also struggling with his wet boots.

"We're too far up," he answered. "I thought I had it about right, but I figured that if I didn't quite hit it, it would be safer to be on this side than the other so we wouldn't have to pass either the wharf or the house in getting to it."

"Good!" commented Captain Francis Newcombe. "We'll walk back that way, then."

They started on along the beach. For perhaps half a mile they walked in silence, and then, rounding a little point, the boathouse came into view a short distance ahead. A moment later they passed in under the overhang of the verandah.

And then Runnells snarled suddenly.

Captain Francis Newcombe was unwrapping his flashlight. The faint, stray rays of moonlight that managed to penetrate the place did little more than accomplish the creation of innumerable black shadows of grotesque shapes.

"What's the matter?" he demanded.

"The damned place in under here gives me the creeps after last night," Runnells growled.

"It's not exactly pleasant," admitted Captain Francis Newcombe casually.

"You're bloody well right, it ain't!" agreed Runnells fervently. And then sharply, as the ray from the flashlight in Captain Francis Newcombe's hand streamed out: "That's where *he* lay last night, only the water's farther out now. It's blasted queer the thing never tackled the old madman in all this time."

"On the contrary," said Captain Francis Newcombe, "it would rather indicate that the brute was a transient visitor."

"Then I hope to Gawd," mumbled Runnells, "that it didn't like the quarters well enough to stick them for another night."

"I agree with you," laughed Captain Francis Newcombe coolly; "but, as it happens, it's low tide now and the water is out beyond where we are going-which may offer an alternative solution to old Marlin's escape. However, Runnells, that's not what we are looking for-we're looking for a keyhole."

He led the way forward, his flashlight playing on the big central concrete pier, some eight feet square, in front of him. He was chuckling quietly to himself. It being established that the old maniac's hiding place was here under the boathouse, a hiding place that was opened by a key, and that, except at low tide, was inaccessible, the precise location of that hiding place became obvious even to a child. The row of little piers that supported the structure at the sides and front were all individually too small to be *hollow* —and there was absolutely nothing else here except the big centre support.

With Runnells beside him now, he began to examine this centre pier under the ray of his flashlight. He walked once completely around it, making a quick, preliminary examination. The pier was some six or seven feet in height, and the concrete construction was reinforced with massive iron bands placed both horizontally and transversely between two and three feet apart, the small squares thus formed giving a sort of checkerboard effect to the mass. The lower portion was green with sea-slime. There was no apparent evidence of any opening.

But Captain Francis Newcombe had not expected that there would be.

"Look for a little hole, Runnells," he said. "Anything, for instance, that might appear to be no more than a *fault* in the concrete. And look particularly above high water mark. The opening is below because the old man could only get in at low tide; but the keyhole is more likely to be above out of the reach of the water because it must be watertight inside."

"Yes," said Runnells.

They made a second circuit of the pier, but carefully now, searching minutely over every inch of surface. It took a long time —a very long time —a quarter of an hour —a half hour-more.

And still there was no sign of either keyhole or opening.

"Strike me pink!" grumbled Runnells. "It looks like it was sticking to us to-night! This is what I calls rotten luck!"

"And I was thinking that it was excellent-even beyond expectations, Runnells," said Captain Francis Newcombe smoothly. "The old man has done his work so well that it is certain no one would *stumble* on it. Therefore, when we get away, we do so with the absolute knowledge that an *empty* hiding place will never be discovered. You follow that, don't you, Runnells? No one except you and I will know that the money was ever found-or taken."

"Yes," said Runnells gruffly; "but we ain't got it yet. And we must have been at it a good hour already-and the tide's coming back in now."

"Quite so!" said Captain Francis Newcombe evenly. "But if we don't get it to-night, there is to-morrow night-and the night after that again. There are always the woods, and your ability as a thief guarantees us plenty to eat. Meanwhile, we'll stick to this side here fronting the sea-it's the logical place-one couldn't be seen even from under the verandah back there. Go over every bit of the iron work now."

Another quarter of an hour passed in silence-save for the lap of the water that, with the tide on the turn now, had crept up almost to the base of the pier. The flashlight moved slowly up and down and to right and left as the two men crouched there, bent forward, their fingers, augmenting the sense of sight, feeling over the surface of the cement and iron that here was barnacle-coated, and there covered with festoons of the green slime.

"It's no good!" said Runnells pessimistically at last. "Let's try around on another side, and get out of the water —I'm standing in it now."

"It's here-and nowhere else," said Captain Francis Newcombe doggedly. "And, furthermore, I'm certain it's one of these squares inside the intersecting pieces of iron. It would be just big enough to allow a man to crawl in and out-and not too big or too heavy for one man to handle alone. It can't be anything else. Whatever's here the old man made himself-no one helped him, understand, Runnells? His secret wouldn't be worth anything in that case. Go on-hunt!"

But Runnells, instead, had suddenly straightened up.

"I thought I heard something out there like-like a low splashing," he said tensely.

Captain Francis Newcombe paid no heed. He was laughing, low, jubilantly, triumphantly.

"I've got it, Runnells!" he cried. "Here's a bit of the iron down here that moves to one side-just a little piece. Look! And the keyhole underneath! I was wrong about the keyhole being above high water-it isn't, or anywhere near it-but we'll see how the contrivance works." He thrust his hand into his pocket, brought out the bronze key, fitted it quickly into the keyhole, and turned it. A faint *click* answered him. "Push, Runnells, on that square just above the water-it's bound to swing inward-these iron strips hide the joints."

But he did not wait for Runnells to obey his injunction. He snatched the key out of the lock again, and even as he saw the piece of iron swing back into place covering the keyhole, he was pushing against the concrete slab himself. It swung back and inward from its upper edge with a sort of oscillating movement. His flashlight bored into the opening. Clever! The old maniac had had the cunning of —a maniac! It was quite clear. Old Marlin had cut away the square and fitted it with a new block-yes, he could see! —the interior would, of course, have been flooded at high water while the old madman was preparing the new block, but that made no difference-the place would always empty itself at low tide again because the flooring, or base, in there was on the same level as the lower edge of the opening-and it would be when it was empty of water, naturally, that the new block would be fitted into place-and thereafter it would remain empty.

He was crawling through the opening now-the weight of the swinging block causing it to press against his shoulders, but giving way easily before his advance. There was just room to squeeze through. Very ingenious! The walls were a good foot to a foot and a half thick. The lock-bar worked through the side of the pier wall into the *middle* of the edge of the movable block so no water could get in that way; and the block when closed fitted in a series of gas-kets against the inside of the iron bands that reinforced the outside of the pier, which latter, overlapping the edges of the block, hid any indication of an entrance from view. It must have taken the old fool weeks! Again Captain Francis Newcombe laughed. His head and shoulders were through now, and, with his flashlight's ray flooding the interior, he could see that —

A cry, sudden, wild, terror-stricken, from Runnells reached him.

"Quick!" Runnells cried frantically. "For the love of Gawd make room for me-the *thing's* here! Quick! Quick! Let me get in!"

The *thing*! In a flash Captain Francis Newcombe wriggled the rest of his body through the opening, and, holding back the movable block, sent his flashlight's ray streaming out through the opening. It lighted up Runnells' face, contorted with fear, ashen to the lips, as the man came plunging along; and out beyond, it played on a waving, sinuous tentacle, another and another, groping, snatching, feeling-and from out of the midst of these a revolting pair of eyes, and a beak, horny, monstrous, in shape like a parrot's beak.

With a gasp Runnells came through, sprawling on the floor.

The movable block swung back into place with a little *click*.

Captain Francis Newcombe shrugged his shoulders.

"A bit of a close shave, Runnells," he said. "I fancy you're right-last night was enough to his liking to bring the brute back again. Rather a bore, too! Unless he moves off again, he's got us penned up until low water."

"That'll be twelve hours," whimpered Runnells; "and it'll be daylight then-and another twelve before we could get out when it's dark."

Captain Francis Newcombe shrugged his shoulders again. His flashlight was playing around him. The hollow space here inside the pier was perhaps six feet square, and solid concrete, top, bottom and sides. This fact he absorbed subconsciously, as he reached quickly out now to a little shelf that had been built out from one side of the wall. There was a half burned candle here and some matches, and, lying beside these, a package wrapped in oiled-silk. He struck a match, lighted the candle, switched off his flashlight, thrust it into his pocket, and snatched up the package. An instant more and he had unwrapped it.

And unholy laughter came, and the soul of the man rocked with it. It rose and fell, hollow and muffled in the little space where there was scarcely room for the two men to move without jostling one another. *The money!* He had won! It was his! Locke-Paul Cremarre-Scotland Yard-ha, ha! Well, they had pitted themselves against Shadow Varne-and Shadow Varne had never yet failed to get what he went after, in spite of man, or God, or devil-and he had not failed now-and he never would fail!

He was tossing the bundles of bank notes from hand to hand with boastful glee.

"This'll buck you up a bit, Runnells!" he laughed. "You'll be well paid for waiting even if it has to be until to-morrow night-eh, what?"

Runnells, on his feet now, a sudden red of avarice burning in his cheeks, grabbed at one of the bundles, and began to fondle the notes with eager fingers.

"Gawd!" he croaked hoarsely. "Thousand-dollar notes! Strike me pink! Gawd!"

Captain Francis Newcombe was still laughing, but his eyes had narrowed now as, watching Runnells, there came a sudden thought. Would he *need* Runnells any more? There wasn't any motor boat to run-but it was a long way in a rowboat for one man over to the mainland. *Here* in the old maniac's hiding place-ideal-and a bit of irony in it too-delicious irony! Well, it did not require *instant* decision. Meanwhile it seemed to be strangely oppressive in here in the confined space.

"It's stuffy in here, Runnells," he said. "Pull that door, or block, or whatever you like to call it, back a crack and freshen the place up."

The "door" was fitted with a light brass handle, similar to a handle used on a bureau drawer. Runnells stooped, still clutching a bundle of bank notes in one hand, and gave the handle a careless pull. The block did not move. He gave the handle a vicious tug then, but still with the same result. He dropped the bundle of bank notes, and used both hands. The block did not yield.

"I can't move the damned thing," he snarled. "It seems to be locked."

Captain Francis Newcombe's voice was suddenly cold and hard.

"Try again!" he said. "Here, I'll help you! Take your coat off and run the sleeve, the two of them if you can, through the handle so we can both get hold."

Runnells obeyed.

Both men pulled.

The handle broke away from its fastenings. The block did not move.

"It's locked, I tell you," panted Runnells. "Haven't you got the key?"

"Yes," said Captain Francis Newcombe quietly; "but there's no hidden keyhole here. It's locked from the outside —a spring lock. I remember now hearing it click. The old man would set it so that he could get out, of course, every time he entered. We didn't."

"Gawd!" said Runnells thickly. "What're we going to do?"

Captain Francis Newcombe's eyes studied the four walls and roof. He spoke more to himself than Runnells.

"Say, six by six by six," he said. "Roughly, two hundred cubic feet. Watertight-hermetically sealed-no air except what's in here now. One hundred cubic feet per man-short work-very short."

"What do you mean?" whispered Runnells with whitening face-and coughed.

"I mean that brute out there, if it still is out there, counts for nothing now," said Captain Francis Newcombe steadily. "We could at least *fight* that-we can't fight suffocation. I'd say a very few minutes, Runnells, before we're groggy if we can't get air —I don't know how long the rest of it will take."

Runnells screamed. His face grey, beads of sweat suddenly spurting from his forehead, he flung himself against the cement "door," clawing with his finger nails, where no finger nails could grip, around the edges of the block. And then in maniacal frenzy he attacked the wall with his pocketknife.

The blades broke.

Captain Francis Newcombe, with a queer, set smile, drew his revolver, and, holding the muzzle close to the wall, fired. The bullet made little impression. With the muzzle now held over the same spot he fired again.

And now he choked and coughed a little.

The acrid fumes helped to vitiate the air.

"You're making it worse-my Gawd, you're making it worse!" shrieked Runnells. "I can't breathe that stuff into me."

"I prefer to be doing something, even if it's pretty well a foregone conclusion that it's useless-than sit on the floor and *wait*," Captain Francis Newcombe answered. "A bullet probably hasn't the ghost of a chance of going through-but if a bullet won't, nothing that we have got to work with will."

The lighted candle on the shelf began to flicker.

Captain Francis Newcombe fired again-once more-and yet still another shot.

Runnells moaned and staggered. He went to the floor, his fists beating at the wall until they bled.

Captain Francis Newcombe watched the candle.

The minutes passed.

The light grew dim.

Captain Francis Newcombe sat down on the floor.

A strange coughing, a mingling of choking sounds.

The candle flickered and went out.

Captain Francis Newcombe spoke. There was something debonair in his voice in spite of its laboured utterance:

"The house divided, Runnells. Do you remember that night in the thicket?"

There was no answer.

Again Captain Francis Newcombe spoke:

"I've saved two shots. Will you have one, Runnells? Suffocation's a rotten way to go out."

"*No!*" Runnells screamed. "No, no-my Gawd-no!"

Captain Francis Newcombe's laugh was choked and gasping.

"You always were a stinking coward, Runnells," he said. "Well, suit yourself."

The tongue flame of a revolver lanced through the blackness.

Runnells screamed and screamed again. Sprawling on the floor, his hand fell upon the package of bank notes he had dropped there. He tore at them now in his raving, tore them to pieces, tore and tore and tore-and screamed.

But presently there was no sound in the old madman's hiding place.

The tides are tongueless. They came and went, and kept their secret. In England, Scotland Yard sought diligently for the murderer of Sir Harris Greaves; and on a little island of the Florida

Keys long search was made for a great sum of money that an old madman in his demented folly had hidden-but neither the one nor the other was ever found.

THE END